My Girl

An Erotic Horror Novel

Audrey Rush

My Girl: An Erotic Horror Novel by Audrey Rush

Independently Published

Cover Photography from DepositPhotos.com

Cover Design by Kai

Amazon ISBN: 9798873005048
Barnes & Noble ISBN: 9798855690262

for the horror readers who like lust mixed with disgust

Author's Note

This content notification contains spoilers.

This is a *horror* novel. It contains child abuse, corrupt law enforcement, and graphic violence. Furthermore, it also contains disturbing sexual content, including but *not* limited to incest, rape, urophilia, and extreme degradation. A detailed list of content can be found on the author's website.

Reader discretion is advised.

My Girl

Prologue

Crave

three years earlier

The girl slides across the back seat of the car, her stockings swishing against the leather. She never leaves her legs exposed, always covering herself up with sheer stockings: the picture of purity. A man in a button-up shirt—her latest boyfriend—stumbles in after her and immediately grabs her breasts. She smacks his arm playfully, then tucks her red hair behind her ear.

Another night of being good. Another blue-balled boyfriend she'll dump.

It's boring how predictable she is.

"You have to wait," she says.

"I've been waiting all night," he whines.

"Where to?" I ask loudly.

"Just keep this thing going," the boyfriend murmurs, shoving me a twenty. I pull into the stop-and-go traffic on Las Vegas Boulevard. Alcohol seeps from their pores, stinking up the air, mixing with her jasmine perfume. Skin and fabric shuffle. A giggle erupts.

"Oh my god!" she squeals.

"Come on," the boyfriend slurs. "He's not watching, babe."

"Oh—"

I glance in the rearview mirror. Lips against lips, their eyes closed in lust. My eyes flick to the road, then back to the show reflected in the mirror: she straddles him, her back to me.

The good girl riding her newest boyfriend in the backseat. Unexpected. *Interesting.*

Raven Sinclair, nicknamed Rae, has always *seemed* coy. Shy. Inexperienced. Breaking it off with each boyfriend before they get too handsy. This man must be different. *Worthy* of her physical affection.

What's changed in her?

The answer is insignificant though. After years of seeing her up and down the Strip, watching her has begun to bore me. I picked her up for the first time because I want to use the knife tonight. When you get bored of something, it no longer has a purpose. You discard it. After all, good girls deserve to die too.

I keep a safe distance from the car in front of us, then twist my head to see the couple. The girl's dress bunches around her hips, revealing the tears in her stockings. I can't see his cock, but I know it's inside of her. Did she make him use a condom? That would mean she came prepared.

The scent of arousal—his sweat, her juices—mixes with the aroma of stale beer and jasmine. My dick throbs. I settle back in my seat, keeping one hand on the wheel as I run the other over my bulge, savoring the sensation. The hunger grows inside of me.

I didn't think she'd make me hard. This started as pure curiosity. Now, I don't know what it is.

They change positions, a slight moan coming from her lips. At the stoplight, I watch as best as I can in the rearview mirror.

She rests her ass on the edge of the seat. He groans as he thrusts harder into her. He falls into the back seat, resting his head on the padding.

She pulls his wallet out of his back pocket.

My jaw loosens. I'm *intrigued.*

She opens it.

Removes a handful of bills.

Shoves it back in his pocket.

At that moment, the girl's eyes find mine in the rearview

mirror. She winks at me, then turns her attention back to the boyfriend, pressing her hips forward as if she truly wants this.

She's not such a good girl after all.

A car honks. I drive forward, focusing on the road just long enough to get us on an empty street. I drive slowly, keeping my eyes on the mirror, watching the show unfold as much as I can.

She steals his watch too, hiding it before he can come, and she moans every few seconds. Once she's done getting what she wants, she renews with vigor.

"Give it to me," she cries.

The boyfriend tosses his head back and comes inside of her.

The two of them scoot back to their separate seats, laughing to each other and talking in low voices.

It shouldn't surprise me that she fucked him in the back seat of my taxi.

But it does.

She plays the good girl. Always has. And yet, it's an act. A disguise she puts on for the world.

I should've known that, or suspected it at least. I simply thought she was too pure to put out. This theft can't be financial. I've been working on the Strip for decades, and I know for a fact that the girl's mother is in upper management at a luxury resort nearby. She doesn't need the money.

These thoughts mull around in my mind, fascinating me. I head back to the girl's luxury resort, pull up to the cab stand, and park.

"Hey," Rae says. She leans on the front seats. "How'd you know where to take me?"

"You said the Opulence," I say.

"Oh." She laughs, the sound pleasing, yet stiff. "I forgot."

"Were you a little distracted, babe?" the boyfriend teases.

She didn't say anything. I know where she lives.

She gets out and gives the new boyfriend—or her conquest—a kiss on the cheek.

"Call me," he says.

She smiles. "I told you. I have to study for exams. Then we'll talk."

She slams the door closed. Before the conquest can get out of the car and follow her inside, I start driving.

"Take me to the Wynn," he sighs. His eyelids are heavy now that the girl is gone. He looks out the window at the bright lights. He has no idea that his watch is gone or that his wallet is lighter.

"Where are you from?" I ask.

"Cali," he says.

"Nice place."

I drive, taking the long way so that the conquest thinks we're going to his hotel. By the time he falls asleep, we're on the freeway, heading into the desert.

In an hour, we're surrounded by dirt, sand, and cacti. The gravel crunches under the tires, stirring him awake.

"Where are we?" he asks.

I park the car.

Turn off the lights.

Take the knife from the glove box.

Remove the hacksaw from under my seat.

Step out of the car.

Flick open the knife. The click echoes in the desert.

"The fuck, man?" he asks.

I yank him out of the backseat. He crashes into the dirt. I shove the knife into his stomach, and he shrieks, his fists flying.

I pull out the knife and stab his neck. The blade comes out, blood squirting into the air. Then it dribbles down his neck. I can smell her perfume on him. Floral. Synthetic. My dick gets hard.

He gurgles, and I work hastily, unbuttoning and unzipping his pants. I don't want him to die before I finish my task. I hold his damp dick and cut off what I can with the hacksaw. The blood and flesh ooze out. I squeeze his length. He sputters, panting, a scream finally ripping from his chest as the hacksaw reaches those sensitive balls. His eyes roll back as he faints.

I hold up his dick against the dark sky. The violence is beautiful. It's a shame she didn't get to see it up close and personal.

I sniff his dick. It smells like latex and ammonia. Semen. The faintest hint of pussy—sour and sweet, like a slice of pineapple burning on an open fire—surrounds me.

I want more.

I search the backseat of the taxi. The condom lies on the leather. I stuff it into my mouth. Past the rubber, I taste *her*.

Raven Sinclair. The deviant little thief with a good girl disguise. I know that now.

I jerk off, my palm under me as I hump the backseat of the car, my head deep in the cushion, sniffing the fabric for hints of her floral perfume. In my mind, I see her dyed, cherry-red hair. Her tanned skin. Her brown eyes rolling back in pleasure, but it's not because we're fucking. It's because we're both holding a knife.

We clutch it together. Thrust it into a body. The blood pools on the ground. And the girl smiles at me.

I come, my jizz splattering against the leather.

I stand and wipe my hands on my pants. Everything is silent, even that nagging inner voice. Come to think of it, that voice hasn't spoken up since I picked up Rae.

"Good one, little girl," I say out loud. "You think you're smart, don't you?"

Perhaps she is.

I had planned to finally kill the girl, but she survived another night. Behind closed doors—even the car doors of a taxi cab—Rae is a different person. We both are. We look like normal, innocent people. I murder. She steals—a petty little thief—but she's capable of so much more.

And that makes her interesting.

I rub my hands together. Watching her from the confines of my taxi isn't enough anymore, and neither is the idea of killing her.

I need her to find her way to my hometown. It'll be easier to manipulate her there.

First, she needs to be fired. She works for her mother at Opulence, but if she's been stealing from her hookups, it's likely she's already moved onto bigger hits. Plenty of billionaires and celebrities stay at the Opulence. Soon, I'll drop a hint or two to one of them, and her reputation will spread across the city. Blocked from employment, she'll have no choice; she'll have to leave Las Vegas. Then I'll fake internet ads, claiming that my town has better rent. Perhaps I'll even find a way to get her mother to tell Rae the truth about her connection to the place.

A curious, economic girl like her won't be able to resist exploring that connection. And right now, I'm curious too. How far can I pull her away from the good girl exterior? How bad can she become? Can I manipulate her into hurting others for pleasure? Deep down, is she a killer like me?

We'll find out.

Chapter 1

Rae

present

I narrow my eyes. Across the mall's cracked parking lot and up a dirt driveway, a dilapidated two-story house stares down like a guard watching over the gates of hell. The two windows on the top floor are reminiscent of boxy, judging eyes. The blue, peeling paint is like layers of tattooed skin. The gray front door resembles rotting flesh. Desert surrounds the outside perimeter of the mall's parking lot, *except* for that one house, almost like the house was never meant to be there. It's a scar that will never truly go away.

The Galloway House.

The house was constructed in the seventies and nicknamed after the first residents that lived there, a family of four that died by murder-suicide. I'd be willing to bet their deaths helped my father get a deal on the house…before he died inside of it too.

I start my car's engine and drive through town, back to my new apartment. There are sections of Pahrump that remind me of Anywhere, USA. Places that seem like they would be a good place to raise a family. Places that blend in, full of the same commercial buildings, the same chain restaurants, the same brick schools, and the same good old Americans that roll around, pretending as if nothing can go wrong. Some parts of Pahrump show their true colors: the old casinos, the signs pointing to the bunny ranches, the slot machines inside of the grocery stores.

All of it is mundane.

My apartment's carpet matches the walls—a bile yellow—and the countertops are black and scratched. A bed. A dresser. A fold-up table and a matching chair. Surveillance cameras are nestled into each corner of the living room, kitchen, and bedroom, which, so far, is my only personal touch to the space. It's not like the penthouse back in Vegas, but it's still mine.

I check the surveillance camera footage on my laptop. There's nothing interesting. Still, I keep the cameras rolling. A person could steal the most important thing from you, and unless you're ready, you'd never know it.

My last hookup—a firearms CEO who was very protective of his family's heirloom pocket pistol—was ready for me. I was caught on camera and fired for attempting to steal the pistol from him. And that night, my mother told me the truth.

You're just like him, my mother had said.

Who? I asked.

One minute, I think I know who you are, and the next, it's like you're a complete stranger, she rasped. *This isn't a joke, Raven. The world isn't yours to take. Your choices have consequences; don't you get that? You stole from a real person.*

I've stolen from a lot of people, I snarked. *You know that. He's not special.*

Jesus Christ, Raven, she had shouted. *You're just like Michael.*

Who the fuck is Michael? I asked.

She stared at me for a moment, her jaw quivering. *Your father,* she whispered.

"'My choices have consequences.'" I laugh out loud. "What choices?"

It's not like I chose to have a blank space for my father's name on my birth certificate. It's not like I chose to get videotaped without my knowledge, nor did I choose to get fired from the Opulence, nor did I choose for that infamous night to be the night where my mother finally told me my father's name. And I sure as fuck didn't choose to be the illegitimate child of a cheating husband who murdered his wife.

I huff, then open up the internet browser on my laptop, and quickly search for my father's name: *Michael Hall.* Links to different articles sprout up over the screen. I've clicked them all now, and most of them are sourced back to the original newspaper articles. There's no new information.

Frustration swirls inside of me, mixing between my temples. I grit my teeth, then scrutinize each link, thinking of my mother.

You're just like Michael, she had said. As if I was born a bad person, like him.

Knowing exactly how much my mother turned a blind eye to the rules I broke proves that there's more to my father's story. Even now, keeping quiet about our biological connection, is proof of that. She's hiding something.

I roll my eyes. You can fuck someone. Suck their dick. Let them go down on you. You can get them drunk and steal their watches. Their white gold cufflinks. Even their heirloom pistol, as long as you look like a good daughter. But if you get caught, you're suddenly the devil's spawn.

Since that night, I've been determined to prove my mother wrong. To show her, and the entire fucking world, that my father was murdered. He didn't kill himself. He didn't even kill his wife. Yeah, he may have been a cheating dirt bag, but he wasn't *that* bad.

I'm not that bad either.

I click on another article—the main one I've been obsessing over—and enlarge the photo of Michael Hall, the same blurry image that's on every website. Trees in the background. A man with light brown hair and soft blue eyes. There's a kindness to his gaze that is the opposite of how my mother described him.

I've got dyed red hair and brown eyes. I used to have dark brown hair, but with enough bleach, you can change even the darkest hair to apple red. My mother, on the other hand, is platinum blond—she started dying it once the grays came in—and she has light blue eyes like my father. Eyes I didn't get.

In my case, brown eyes are very rare, but they are still a possibility. *Lucky me.* Two blue-eyed beauties making one messed-up, brown-eyed child. More proof that I'm the ugly duckling. The devil's spawn with sin in her eyes.

Husband kills wife, then himself, the article subtitle reads. *Another murder-suicide at the Galloway House.*

"Michael Hall," I read aloud. Then I absentmindedly add my own name to his surname: "Raven Hall." It could have worked.

I reread the article for the hundredth time. My eyes scan quickly, and I hyper-focus on sets of words.

wife cheats—

murder in a fit of rage—

drugs in his system—

gunshot wound to the temple—

killed himself.

I shake my head. Even if I wasn't closely connected to the late suspect, I would still think the circumstances of the crime were off. Why would a man have drugs in his system if he was going to kill his wife *then* himself? Wouldn't the drugs have made it difficult to kill her? Wouldn't he have drugged himself as a way *to* commit suicide? Why would he use a gun too?

His wife was cheating; in the autopsy, among deep lacerations noted inside of her vaginal canal, there was also trace evidence of condom usage. But I'm proof that Michael Hall was cheating too. He fucked my mother while he was married, so why would infidelity make him kill his wife? And why didn't the police investigate the wife's lover? Was it more convenient for them to conclude that it was a murder-suicide and be done with it? Maybe the police are more involved than it seems.

Either way, none of it makes sense.

Or...maybe it does, and I don't want to accept the truth that my father is nothing more than a hypocritical misogynist that killed his own wife. Maybe I don't want to accept that the first person I might be able to relate to is objectively horrible.

I slam my laptop close, then scroll through my phone's gallery. I open a picture of the Galloway House. The peeling, blue paint. The slumped overhang. The dull gray door. The tattered curtains in the windows. I squint as I zoom in on one of the second-story windows.

A shadow hovers behind the curtains, as if someone's there, watching me take the picture. I'm just imagining it though; it's probably an old coat rack or something.

Still, the house still draws me in, like the answers to my father's death are waiting inside of those walls.

My phone rings, and I jolt. The picture vanishes from view, replaced with my mother's name and profile picture. I deny the call, then dim the phone's screen.

The device rattles again. I glance at the text message preview: *The director says your job—*

I don't have to read it to know what it says. My mother thinks she can get my job back. I never wanted to work at the hotel, and I really *don't* want to work there now that I have a new goal.

The next text message preview: *Please come home. You can't—*

"Home," I snicker as I delete her text messages. I can read through her words. Asking me to come "home" is not about helping me; it's about her guilt. She feels bad that I was fired, and she definitely does not want me to find out the truth about my father.

I open up the picture of the Galloway House again. I imagine a male voice—my dead father's voice—calling to me from the pixels on the screen. *Come find me, Rae.*

When I go inside, what will I find?

Chapter 2

Rae

The next day, I find myself leaning on the exterior of the mall, staring at the Galloway House. The employee door to the side opens. A middle-aged man with freshly dyed blonde hair and light blue eyes grins at me. The mall owner, Ned. He playfully bumps his broad shoulder into mine.

"Fancy seeing you here, beautiful," Ned teases, as if he hadn't just gone down on me in his office. "I didn't know you were out of the bathroom already."

"All clean now." I wink.

For a while, we stand in silence. Ned pulls out a vape pen, raspberry-flavored smoke wafting in the air, then offers it to me. I hold back a grimace—I hate raspberry—but I take a drag anyway, pretending to enjoy it.

The Galloway House's front porch overhang is slumped to the side, and the surrounding desert is littered with garbage and tumbleweeds. The only people who have stepped foot inside of it in years are probably squatters or teenagers looking for ghosts.

I gesture to the house. "Have you ever been in there?"

"The Galloway House?" Ned asks. He laughs, then shakes his head. "I own it technically. With the mall land, you know?"

My eyebrows lift in faux surprise. I did, in fact, know that he owned the house. It's exactly why I got a retail job at the mall. I wanted better access to the house, which meant I needed direct access to the mall owner himself. Older men like him are always easier to seduce.

"We were going to use it for an expansion," he adds. "Why do you ask?"

I shrug my shoulders. Ned doesn't need to know that my father died in that house.

"Curious, I guess," I say. "Why haven't you bulldozed it yet?"

"The architect got superstitious. And by the time—"

"Superstitious?"

He exhales slowly. "People died in there."

Not murdered. Not committed suicide. *Died.*

He motions to the house. "The architect said there were still bad vibes there. I mean, I can see why she said that. It looks like it would collapse if you sneezed on it."

Ned offers me the vape pen again. This time I shake my head. I tap my lip, focusing on those words. It's not like I'm upset that my father is dead. I never knew him, and after twenty-five years, I'm doing fine without him. Still, it's strange to know that he once lived *and* died there.

The house glares down at us, looming from across the parking lot. I don't know much about the family of four that died there first, but I do know that my father died exactly like the first owner of the house: a gunshot wound to the head. There's something odd about that, but maybe it's a simple coincidence.

"It's not haunted, right?" I knock into Ned's shoulder. "Don't tell me you're scared."

"I let the dead rest." He puts the vape pen back in his pocket. "It's funny, though. This death bus tour used to come from Vegas. They'd use the Galloway House as one of their murder stops."

"And you allowed it?"

"We charged, of course, and we didn't let them go inside. The tour guide told the story, then they took pictures in front of it, like it was funny to see a place where six people were either murdered or killed themselves."

My shoulders stiffen, annoyance leaking through. It's always so easy for everyone to accept the "facts" of the case and not question anything. Especially someone good, like Ned.

"Maybe those people wanted to see the house because it *wasn't* murder-suicide," I say. "Maybe the police are hiding something."

Ned's jaw twitches. He studies me, his blue eyes suddenly cold.

"My brother works for the sheriff," he says. "The law enforcement out here does their best, Raven. They're here to protect us."

Not Rae. Not "beautiful." *Raven.*

"People have the right to know what happened," I say.

"And I have a duty to do what's right," he says. "And that includes always respecting law enforcement."

For the first time, I think I finally see the real Ned, the man that actually cares enough about something to let his sunny attitude fall to the wayside. A man who wants to keep people safe, even if that means arguing with me.

I shudder and bring myself back to the present.

"I'll be honest," I say quietly. Ned straightens, his eyes bright and full of concern again. "I'm personally interested in the house. It's not that I want to go in there. It's just that—"

I think for a minute. If I tell Ned the truth, that my father is one of the supposed murder-suicide victims, it will explain why I can't let the past go. But then Ned may eventually realize that I'm using him to get closer to the property, that the only reason I'm at the mall in the first place, is for my father.

I almost feel bad for the lies I'm about to tell him, but no matter how many times he eats my pussy, my personal life is not his business.

"It's a project of mine," I say. "A podcast. Unsolved cases, you know? True crime. Super popular right now."

"The case *is* solved."

I laugh politely, then tuck hair behind my ears, playing it off like it's not a big deal. I fix my skirt and straighten my stockings. Ned's eyes follow my movements.

"I have a friend who knew the couple that died there," I say.

His eyes are glazed, fixed on my legs. "Ah, okay."

"You know, the Halls?" He nods. I continue: "You were around back then, right?"

"Yeah, but I was commuting to the university. I didn't spend a lot of time on the local news."

Just as I suspected: useless, I internally mock.

"But you've lived here your whole life, right?" I ask, trying another tactic.

"Yeah."

"Maybe you can help me find some locals to interview. People who were around here. Maybe even someone who knew Michael Hall personally."

"I'll have to introduce you to my niece."

"She was alive then?"

He shakes his head. "But she calls herself the Pahrump Crime Expert."

The corners of my lips raise in appreciation. "Honestly, I'll take all the help I can get."

"Are you going to let me take you out this time?" he asks suddenly.

Ned is in his forties, and yet even with his age, he's not used to having casual sex. Even though this is our fourth time hooking up, he still thinks we need to date. He's the kind of man my mother would like. An older man that can take care of me.

I've never been a girl you can take to family dinners though.

I force a smile. "Maybe next week," I say. I squeeze his shoulder, and he blushes. "I gotta go." I wink. "You already made me work overtime!"

He scratches the back of his neck sheepishly. "I'll see you tomorrow?"

"Of course."

Before I go inside, I turn over my shoulder. I picture a shadow behind the curtains in the Galloway House. The strange figure watching me. Waiting for me.

I shrug my shoulders, then go inside the mall.

Chapter 3

Crave

The girl finds her pattern. Work at the mall. Home to her apartment. Hooking up with her conquests. Back to work again. Fifteen minute breaks to gawk at the Galloway House, fascinated by the potential truths locked inside of those dried-out walls.

I study her from one of the second-floor windows. Rae leans against the mall, texting on her phone—probably swiping right on her next valuable hookup. The desert wind snakes through her hair, and the mall hovers behind her like the bars of a cage. Her chin tilts up, and in my mind, I can see her right in front of me: those dust-brown eyes peering at this house, searching so hard that she doesn't see me in the window looking down at her.

I don't see her either. I see myself.

The meat bag groans under my boot. I shift my weight. The mask clings to my face, soaking up my sweat. The leather is tight around my head with sheer material across my eyes and a zipper on my mouth. My leather-gloved fingers drum the fabric of my mask as I contemplate this situation.

Rae is standing here. In my hometown. So close, I could run out of this house, tackle her, and shove her head into the pavement if I wanted.

"I lorve—" the meat bag garbles, facing the other body in the room: the soon-to-be corpse that looks entirely too similar to the meat bag. The bodies always spew nonsense at this point in the game. Sometimes, it's entertaining.

But right now, I'm distracted. I knew Rae was moving to Pahrump. I knew she'd find the house. I didn't think she'd start working at the goddamn mall. I wanted her close, just not *that* fucking close. Not yet anyway.

"I love you," the meat bag chokes out. I kneel down on top of its legs, just outside of view from the window. I brace the hips, preparing to insert myself. Blood and mucus crust the asshole, and the fuzzy hair surrounding it matted down with secretions. The body whimpers. It's not about the gender or the physical pleasure of the act. It's about knowing that I'm in control, and the meat bag's body is mine to use. Just like I'll use Rae one day.

The window's shaggy, floral-printed curtains obscure my view. I imagine Rae is still there, staring at the house.

One day, she's going to use and kill a body too. Just like this.

The body cries, and I thrust my dick inside. The warm cavity surrounds me, the friction enveloping me in the body's pain.

I angle my head toward the window again.

"I love you," the meat bag cries with each jolt of pain from my cock. "I swear, I've always loved you—"

The look-alike's eyes water. "I love you too!"

I sneer, my cock growing numb. They're predictable. The groans, the tears, the desperate promises they make in an effort to save their lives.

Rae isn't predictable. Not yet.

"If you love her so much, then fuck her," I say.

It twists over its shoulder. "But she's my— my—"

"Your sister?" I smirk. Does the meat bag really care about social rules right now? It wails, and I jerk into it harder. I lean down, my dick still inserted into the meat bag. "It wouldn't be the first time though, right?" I ask. "You've fucked her before, haven't you?"

"Yes," he cries. "I love her so much."

I turn to the female look-alike. "Crawl to your brother then," I bark.

Tears drip down her face. She ambles forward like a dog, then spreads herself for her brother. He licks her up, hungry for her, even with my dick in his bloody asshole.

It's easy. Anything for survival. For love.

But love doesn't exist in these walls.

And just like that, my cock is softer than a pillow. The meat bag's words echo in my mind: *I swear I've always loved you.* They crawl over my skin like ants, causing heat to flicker in my veins. It's not about the incest; I don't give a fuck who fucks who. It's something about the past tense in this scenario—*loved,* not love—that stops me. It should amuse me, knowing that the meat bag and its look-alike have basically already accepted their place at the bottom of the food chain, resorting to fucking for the last time.

I don't find any amusement right now.

My dick flops out of the bloody rectum. Red-tinged mucus glistens on my skin, the fleshy juices coating my piercings: the four metal bars on the bottom of my shaft, the horseshoe metal in my tip, and the curved barbell right above my balls. I yank the zipper on the back of my mask and rip off the leather. Stale air sends a shock wave across my skin, refreshing me.

The bodies scramble, a tangle of limbs and adrenaline, thinking they have seconds to escape just because I removed my dick.

I grab the baton off of the ground, swinging the weight into my palm. It's too easy. Too predictable. Too much of the same goddamned thing. I can switch from a straight couple to an incestuous fuck fest, and *every* human being turns into a sopping mess of final confessions before they take their last breaths.

One last word. One last regret. One last love. As if that's all that matters.

Love isn't real. Possession is.

I slam the baton against the back of their heads in quick succession. It's easy. So fucking easy.

They fall silent.

The bodies lie limp, like male cicadas after mating. The blunt force trauma is obvious, but once I dump the corpses off in the desert, no one will give a shit. I hook my fingers into their mouths and drag them across the floor until they're piled up in the center of the room. The media will think they disappeared on a hiking trip. Perhaps dehydration or starvation will be their supposed downfall. And if I could figure out their forbidden love by following them for a few short weeks, then their parents definitely knew. To them, their two adult children may be starting over in a foreign country. A place where they aren't brother and sister. A place where they're simply in love.

I step behind the curtains. The mall's employee smoking area is empty now. I imagine Rae in the boutique inside, folding another pile of designer shirts, checking her phone, flirting with the next man she'll steal from.

The corpses should make me feel powerful, but it's meaningless. Rae is the only one who can make me feel something these days.

I zip up my pants.

The logic is there, written in our connection. I should have killed her that first night she was in my taxi, and yet, I continue to keep her alive. She's had a good life so far. What will she do when I truly enter it?

You are obsessed, my mother's voice rings in my mind.

"It's an experiment," I clarify.

Rae isn't a person; she's an object. It's more interesting to think of her as a thing with autonomy, a female version of myself. And honestly, I don't care what she does with her free time. Who she fucks. What she steals. It's a game to her, a way to use her sex appeal.

And she's a game to me too.

She'll use her cunt to overpower you, my mother's nauseating voice says inside of me. *If you really wanted to control her, you should have put cameras in her apartment already. If you had a single brain cell left, you would have done that by now.*

My mother is dead, but my inner thoughts have since taken on her voice like she's part of me.

"You fucking bitch," I mutter. "She won't overpower me."

I stomp to the two bodies, imagining my dumb mother bent over the pile. I pull out my knife. I shove the blade into one of the corpse's neck, slicing to the spine. A mix of adrenaline and desire courses through me. I promised myself that I wouldn't put any cameras in Rae's new apartment. It's enough to be in the same town. I trust my instincts to know her well enough. I can control her from this distance.

But maybe I should install hidden cameras. I did it for the firearms CEO. The same strategy could help me now.

I stab the knife into the corpses again and again, the rhythm thumping through me, my dick twitching in anticipation. Then I pull out my cock again, squeezing it until blood reddens the pierced tip. The bodies blur until I don't see them anymore. I see Rae.

Rae against the wall.

Rae pulling at her torn stockings.

Rae with her tongue down her conquest's throat.

Rae winking at me.

My dick strains. "Raven Sinclair," I say. "I see you. The real you."

On the outside, she's normal. A generic girl with a smile so plastic, she seems defenseless. A person capable of fitting in.

I blend in too.

CHAPTER 4

RAE

THE CRESCENT MOON HANGS OVER THE PARKING LOT, AN EYELESS mouth grinning down at the mall. Even though there's no one around at one a.m., I still park my car under a tree in the far corner of the lot. There may be after-hours security, and I don't want to draw attention right now.

I clutch my purse to my chest and trudge toward the Galloway House. It stretches into the night sky, a giant growing in strength.

The asphalt turns to dirt. Eventually, I'm right in front of the house.

I picture my father hanging his wife from the rafters, blood dripping down her legs.

I imagine my father holding the pistol to his own head.

Did he think about his choice to kill her? Or did he surrender to a fit of rage, like they say he did? Maybe the fury took hold of him, possessing him so completely that his mind went blank, and when he saw what he had done, he couldn't deal with the grief. Is that why he killed himself?

Or does it have to do with me?

No... Michael Hall never knew I existed. And besides, the whole crime is too convenient. The rumor was that there weren't enough resources to give it a thorough investigation, but I still think the cops were too quick to call it "solved." And if they didn't investigate back then, I may as well try to now.

My footsteps crunch on the desert sand. I raise my eyes, taking in the height of the Galloway House, sucking in the scent of metal and brittle wood. I meditate on my mother's words: *Your choices have consequences.*

Every part of our lives is a result, a consequence. I'm proof of that.

I turn on my phone's flashlight, then start recording a video. I open the front door. The hinges open smoothly. I furrow my brow. Given the state of the house, I would've thought that entering would've taken more effort.

I keep the camera aimed in front of me.

Inside, the house opens to an entryway. To the right, stairs lead up to the second floor. And to the left of the front door, the living room contains an old floral couch with a chunk of the back cushion ripped out. There's a clear hallway from the front door to the kitchen in the back, with a section of concave wall, as if the house tried to decompose, but the desert heat wouldn't let it.

I inch toward the back of the house. Yellow laminate with white designs stretch across the kitchen, slightly more modern than I expected; perhaps the laminate is an upgrade from when my father and his wife lived in the house. A broken window sits above the sink. I twist the faucet handle. It stays dry.

But there is a back door.

I focus the phone's lens on the back door, open it, then let it slam shut behind me.

My eyes catch on a boulder. The gray stone is about waist high with a brown, almost black stain on top of it. The executioner's block.

I don't know much about the first family—the Galloways—who lived here, but I know that they *also* tragically died in a murder-suicide. Images of the mother fill my mind—bent over the boulder, the father with a hatchet in his hand, her decapitated head rolling over the desert sand.

I zoom in on the camera app, focusing on the brown-black

stain on the stone. It's probably not blood, but there's something exciting about knowing that it *could* be the only evidence left of the Galloway mother, an evilness still lingering in this place...

Chills run down my back. Something is here. A presence watching me.

I swing around, using the phone's light to see.

The peeling paint. The boulder. The back door.

I'm alone.

I pause the recording and turn off the light, scowling at myself for being so nervous. It's just an old house and me. There's nothing to worry about.

Still, Ned's reference to the architect's warning surfaces in my brain. She was right; there *are* bad vibes around this place, an urge that sinks into your skin and festers inside, burrowing down until there's no way to dig it out.

I should leave.

But not yet.

I slip back inside and take a deep breath. It's not like it's any safer inside of the house, but at least I'm not exposed.

A door to the side of the kitchen catches my eye. Scratched blond-colored wood, as if someone struggled to move something through the doorway.

I open it.

Stairs lead down to a pitch-black basement.

A man's sniffle—almost like a broken horn—echoes through the air.

My heart races. There's *someone* down there.

But I have the advantage: they don't know I'm here.

It's probably someone sleeping. Someone without a home. Someone who needs shelter. Nothing to worry about.

But I can't let it go. I *have* to see. The ghosts of the past—of *my* past—are calling me, dragging me down to the depths of the house. I hit the record button on my phone, though I leave the flashlight off this time; I don't want the person to see me. I cross my fingers that with enough editing, I can get a decent image.

My feet descend those stairs at a snail's pace.

Consequences, my mother's voice repeats. *Your choices have consequences.*

The stairs creak. I stiffen in place.

"Is someone there?" a man croaks. "Please! Help us!"

Help with *what?*

Outside, the faint chirp of desert insects dissipates, replaced by a panting breath. A person filled with fear. And the languid, easy breathing of another that I can just make out.

What are they doing down there?

The rhythmic beat of skin against skin begins. A moan. A heavy object slung into another. More skin beating together like a tarp flapping in the wind.

Are they having sex?

I squint my eyes. I can't see anything. My eyes haven't adjusted yet. The more I listen, the more positive I am that it has to be people having sex, or at the very least, a man masturbating.

Why did he ask for help though?

I should leave. This has nothing to do with my father and everything to do with the fact that an abandoned house is being used by random people. Those people may be dangerous.

But sex leads to distraction, and having footage gives you power.

I crouch down, squinting, trying to get my eyes to adjust.

Finally, I see it.

The outline of three people. A man tied to a support beam. A woman on her hands and knees, and a man fucking her from behind, his profile distorted, almost like he has a mask clinging to his face.

A tingling sensation starts in my chest, then spreads to my limbs. I flex my fingers, then carefully creep down a few more steps into the darkness. The masked man is covered in black fabric. The material seems almost glued to him, making him more like a toy action figure than a human being. An open zipper frames his mouth. The metal elements of the zipper gleam like fangs.

His masked face turns in my direction. I freeze in the shadows of the stairs, not daring to breathe until he turns back to the woman before him.

He rips a knife from his back pocket and stabs the woman's side. She grunts before going limp, and the man tied in front of her wails, each sob squawking out of him like an angry bird.

My jaw drops. Each sense heightens, everything at its peak. My mouth is chalky. My pulse races in my temples. I clench and unclench my free hand, as if I can summon a knife to protect myself. What should I do?

I'm a witness to another murder in this house.

This masked man could kill me too.

If I had a weapon, I could kill *him*.

I should call for help.

I should do something.

I should run.

I need to leave.

I can't leave. I should—

"Please. Just..." the bound man begs. "Just kill me."

The phone keeps recording in the darkness. My body tightens like it's bracing for a tornado to sweep me away. I'm stuck.

Terror runs cold in my chest.

I don't *want* to move.

I can't.

"Beg me," the masked man says, his voice low and rough.

"P-p-please," the man sobs. "Kill me. Please."

The masked man runs a gloved hand over his groin, then he stabs the man's stomach, pulling the knife down, his intestines slopping to the ground like spilled chili.

I hold my breath. I'm transfixed by the masked man. The dark clothes. The thump of his heavy combat boots. Even the mask which must have sheer material covering his eyes.

The masked man faces me. Even though I can't see his eyes, I know he's watching me. It's like he knows I've been here this entire time. Like he killed these people just to show me he could. To warn me that I'm next.

I blink rapidly, but it doesn't feel real. Things like this don't happen. But choices always have consequences. Sometimes, there are twisted results. Like choosing to be in an abandoned house after midnight, then watching a masked man murder two people.

And he's about to take your life too, my brain screams.

I race back up the stairs and shove my phone into my purse. The masked man takes four giant steps, his boots smashing into the floor. I reach the hallway, but he shoves me back, pinning me to the wall.

The bloody knife presses into my neck, my skin electric at the pinch of the blade. The wallpaper is slick and sticky on my cheek. My fingers are numb. The pressure of his body keeps me in place.

Consequences. Like getting killed when you could have kept your distance and *lived.*

"Tell me," the masked man says, his deep, gravelly voice seeping into my ears. "Did you think I didn't know you were there?"

Tears fill my eyes. It's not sorrow or anger or terror, or even pain, but an overwhelming sensation that I can't control. I don't know how to comprehend this. It doesn't feel real.

It can't be.

He leans his elbow against my shoulder blades, keeping me in place. Then he wraps his arm around my waist. His body is so warm it's like being steeped inside of a hot spring.

"I bet you thought you'd get away with it." He breathes against my neck. "You didn't think I'd see you. Waving your phone like it's some kind of shield. A phone can't protect you from murder, little girl."

"No," I whisper. "No—"

He chuckles, then flings me around violently. Holding my neck with one hand, the other hand plants the knife against my stomach, ready to disembowel me like the man in the basement.

My heart swells against my rib cage. *Do something!* my brain demands.

I shout: "I called the police!"

Everything falls silent. The cicadas and desert insects hold their breaths. The wind is stale. I can't hear a thing.

He chuckles again, and my world shatters.

"You didn't," he murmurs. "You were too busy watching me. Face it: you get off on violence, you sick little freak."

A boiling sensation buzzes inside of me, widening my blood vessels, my cheeks hot with an emotion I can't quite place. I can't see his expression, but when I look up at those black mesh screens covering his eyes, I can tell he's staring down at me.

"I don't," I whisper. "I don't. I swear I—"

He lowers the knife, pressing it into my inner thigh until I'm forced to widen my stance to avoid the pain. Then his other gloved hand slips into my skirt and stockings.

His leather fingertips slide along my slit, my pussy parting easily for him. My face broils. A gasp escapes my throat.

He lifts his finger, his glove glistening in the dim light. He rubs the arousal on my face, streaking me with my own wetness. My body throbs.

"You're sopping wet," he says. "Greedy little freak."

A chill runs through me.

Why is my body doing this?

I clench my jaw. I'm *not* turned on by this. This is nature's reaction to stress. A primal coping mechanism. Don't think. Just do. Give the predator sex. This is normal. This is—

This is—

I don't know what the fuck *this is,* but arousal like this is insane. He's a murderer. And I'm just—

He lets go of my neck. The lack of pressure deflates me, my body smaller than before.

Am I disappointed that he's not touching me anymore?

The masked man towers over me. A pillar. A grand beast. A god waiting to see what his subject does. What I do next.

I can't move.

What the fuck is wrong with me?

"I'll be watching you, little girl," he says.

Watching you, my brain repeats.

Suddenly, I'm back in my body, present in my own skin, aware that I'm in an abandoned house with my legs spread, my underwear and skirt disheveled, with two corpses in the basement, and a masked murderer standing in front of me.

I run.

I run so fast that my sides cramp. And once I'm in my car, I drive. I drive so recklessly that I pass my new apartment. I don't care. I don't stop. I can't. If I do, that murderer will be right behind me with those meshed eyes, and I don't know what I'll do.

Twenty minutes pass.

Eventually, my heart rate slows. I pull over on the side of the highway and get out of the car. In the distance, Las Vegas glows like a giant sun coming over the horizon, and in the other direction, Pahrump is fuzzy, but there. My new home is waiting for me to return.

The masked man is there, waiting for me too.

I suck in the night air, grounding myself. The shadows of cacti. Sand and small rocks under my feet. Rocky hills. The glow of city lights. Millions of stars.

I'm alone.

I lean against my car, then open my phone. It's still recording. I end the recording, then click to the dial pad.

I should call the cops.

Two people died, and I saw it happen. I didn't see the murderer's face, but the police will be able to do something with the video on my phone. I could even try to edit it before I give it to them.

What if the police can hear the murderer say that I'm wet?

I bite my lip, then look back at the dim lights of Pahrump. My arousal doesn't matter. What matters is putting a murderer behind bars so that it doesn't happen again. It's the right thing to do.

I open the video file of the house, scrubbing through the footage until the lens focuses on the dark basement stairs. I turn up the volume.

It's static.

Would the cops want something like this? Or would they laugh in my face?

Should I go back and get pictures of the bodies?

"I'm going to call the cops," I say out loud.

But I can't make my fingers move.

It's another choice. Another choice where I'm letting my

mother and society's righteousness dictate what I'm supposed to do when there's a desire inside of me that wants more.

I play with the limited editing software until the footage turns into scraggly figures, like shadows shimmering on a bank of water. That's all the murderer is right now: a shadow.

What can I get out of this footage? Because right now, I've got nothing.

CHAPTER 5

RAE

THE NEXT MORNING, I STARE AT MY PHONE'S SCREEN AGAIN. THE police department's phone number is already punched in, the green digits glowing. All I have to do is press the *Call* button.

I should report the murders I saw in the Galloway House. I should also accept that there's no mystery or hidden meaning behind my father's death: he was a murderer, just like the masked killer. End of story.

I don't do anything.

I've never trusted cops. Growing up in Las Vegas, I've seen corruption firsthand. Give a man money or power, and he'll switch sides, doing exactly what the boss wants him to do, even if it means selling his soul. Even my mother, who *always* does the right thing, used her position as Director of Operations to save my ass multiple times. I was stealing things from the cheaper guests long before I moved up to the higher paying clients, and my mother always blamed the housekeepers. That way she didn't have to deal with the fallout, and I got to keep doing what I loved most. It was easier for both of us.

I drive to the mall and suck down a peppermint mocha flavored coffee, my brain wandering over the Michael Hall murder-suicide details. It's not like proving his innocence will give me peace.

But it will prove my mother wrong.

He must have been good enough for you to fuck him, I had said to my mother. Her jaw dropped, her hand clutching a tube of toothpaste like it was a life preserver. Power swelled inside of me then. She hates it when I curse, and I knew that little f-bomb would get her attention, especially since she was helping me pack for my move to Pahrump. *Did you see the violence with your own eyes, Mother? Did you see my father murder his cheating wife?*

The police aren't going to lie about something like that, she had said, raising her voice. *He was a bad man, Rae. There's a reason I kept him from you.*

It was one of the few times she yelled at me. Energy had rumbled inside of me, knowing that I had finally stirred a reaction in her.

Even now, my chest vibrates, needing more of that.

I guide my car to my usual parking spot, but something in the back of the mall's parking lot catches my eye. Something different. Near the Galloway House.

A chain-link fence.

What the fuck?

I drive closer, then park at the edge of the parking lot, as close to the house as possible. A mall cop—dark hair, average height, broad shoulders—paces around the perimeter, muttering to himself. A padlock is clutched in his hand. A stun gun hangs on his belt next to dangling handcuffs.

Can a mall cop even arrest someone?

I scoff. He's the type of man that wants to *act* like he has that power when he can't actually do anything. He'd probably try to arrest a trespasser of the house. It's sad, really.

And irritating.

I get out of my car, heading toward the open gate before the mall cop can lock it up.

"Ma'am," he barks, his southern accent alarming. "You can't go in there."

"Oh," I say. I press my legs together, drawing his attention to my sheer stockings, teasing out of my short skirt. He sneers, and I tuck my hair behind my ear, pretending to be shy. "I was just going to check on it. The mall owner, Ned"—I say, dropping his name in hopes that it'll make the mall cop give me some slack—"he left his jacket in there."

"That so?" the mall cop says, his dark eyes fixed on me like he can read through my lies. Like he knows exactly where I was last night.

My face grows hot.

He doesn't know anything, I tell myself. *You can figure him out.*

He straightens his shoulders, an act of dominance to show off his physique, when in reality, he's only a few inches taller than me. He *is* more muscular than I am though; his chest is visibly toned, and a middle-aged man like him has to get credit for that. His age shows; white hair feathers his temples, and the rest of his black hair is arched into a widow's peak, like a sad, wannabe Dracula. The strong stench of cheap cologne creates a fog around him. A clean-shaven face. His uniform is stiff too, freshly ironed, like he takes his job in mall security very seriously. He probably likes to call himself "Officer" too.

A chill runs down my spine. I don't trust anyone in positions of authority, even mall cops.

"I'm just doing a favor for Ned," I say.

"I follow the rules, ma'am," the mall cop says, his words blunt. "No one goes in there, besides Mr. Ned. If Mr. Ned left his jacket in there, then *I'll* retrieve it. It's not safe in there for a girl like you."

A girl like me?

I laugh hard. His brows furrow together, and my fists ball at my sides, a metaphorical knife twisting inside of me.

He wants to belittle me because I'm a woman? All it would take is a few minutes alone with him, and I'd have him literally eating out of the palm of my hand. What's *not* safe is for him to be underestimating me like that.

I smile, my straight teeth perfectly exposed, the practiced smile I gave in corporate meetings at the Opulence, the same one I use with my valuable hookups too. Even Ned.

"You're right," I say in my sweetest voice. "I'll make sure Ned knows you're watching over this place so carefully."

"Tell him I said hi."

I grit my teeth, then head back to my car. I start the engine, roll down the window, and wave.

"Have a good day, Officer!" I say, my insides mocking him with everything I've got. He nods curtly, then clicks the padlock shut over the gate's loop, already dismissing me, too self important to care about what I do now.

I smile through clenched teeth, in case he turns around. "Fucking asshole," I mutter. Then I park in my normal spot.

The shift at the boutique inches on. Mothers push their strollers by, and a few teenagers spill a trash can in the food court. The janitor is on break, so Ned makes the mall cop clean it up. Serves him right.

Ned strolls by the boutique. I race out to the walkway to meet him.

"Hey," I say. Ned swings around, his styled blonde hair perfectly coiffed above him like streams of sunlight. "What's up with the gate around the Galloway House?"

"There was some trouble last night," he says. "Noise complaints. Surveillance caught teenagers sneaking in. We didn't find anything though."

My fingers twitch at my sides. Teenagers sneaking in? The murder victims didn't look *that* young, but they were also in the dark. Is that who he means?

Did the surveillance cameras catch me too?

"Don't worry," Ned says. "It's a routine safety thing. Overly precautious, in my opinion. I told my dad we'd put up a fence years ago. Might as well now, right? Better late than never."

Noise complaints. Not murder.

Teenagers. Not me.

I stare at the heathered gray tile beneath us. If I go back to the Galloway House, I'll have to jump the fence now.

What do I think I'll find there anyway?

I should tell Ned what happened. It wasn't teenagers. It was me and three other adults. Two of which were murdered.

"What's wrong?" Ned asks. His hand grips my shoulder. "Are you okay, beautiful?"

I lift my shoulders. *Beautiful.* He always likes complimenting me. My mother loves men like that. She especially loves it when they're older. It's the daddy figure she always liked, the daddy I probably needed.

But when men like Ned call me "beautiful," it's a lie—sweet words to get someone to like you. It's what I do too.

I could tell Ned the truth, that there were no teenagers. Just me, two bodies, and a masked murderer.

Then the house would be a crime scene again, and I wouldn't be able to go back by myself.

"I'm fine." I wink. "You can cheer me up later though."

He grins. "You going to let me eat your cake?"

"Hope you're hungry."

"You know I'm starving."

Once my shift ends, Ned goes down on me in his office, and I quickly fake an orgasm. Then I drive to my apartment, my mind running in a million different directions. I have to decide what to do about the Galloway House. *Now.*

I can do the right thing and tell the police I was there last night. I can help them find the culprit…

Or I can do something else. Something that will help *me.*

My father's death—his real cause of death—wells inside of me, boiling over the edges of my sense of self. I need to know. I need to find out the truth, with or without anyone's help, to prove to my mother that I'm not *that* bad. And until I uncover the real story, I can't let the Galloway House go.

Those mesh-screened eyes fill my head.

Don't killers come back to their crime scenes?

What if that masked man was around when my father died?

What if *he* is my father's true murderer?

I laugh. I can't tell the police that, especially not without evidence. They would think I'm crazy.

I close my fist around my phone, then hold it to my chest like it's a teddy bear comforting me.

I can use my footage against the murderer. Wield it as leverage. Get closer to him. Use him to find out more about my father.

The masked murderer is a man, and men are always more

inclined to listen to other men, especially at a place like a police department. He can steal the evidence for me.

I can blackmail him.

"That's crazy," I say out loud. "I can't blackmail a murderer."

I cock my head to the side, letting the idea spread its fingers around my brain.

A sense of invincibility curls inside of me. That masked man could have killed me. He *should* have killed me.

But I'm still here.

"What are you even talking about?" I say. "It's not like you're too hot to kill. He was horny. You were there. He *meant* to kill you, but he got preoccupied with cleaning up dead bodies."

The words come out, but the logic doesn't process in my head.

If that masked man is willing to murder, then he'll be willing to steal evidence from a government building. If anything, a criminal like him would likely enjoy the challenge. And at the very least, with this footage, I'll have power over him. Someone *I* can mold.

A lethargic warmth crawls over me, my body throbbing in its heat. It's settled, then. I know what I'm going to do. I'm going to need more surveillance equipment to take with me—a camera or something to keep in my purse—because I'll need to gather more evidence against the masked man. I'll also need the key to the padlock on the new gate.

Most of all, I need a solid way to protect myself.

I go to a local electronics store and buy a tiny camera—the size of a grommet—that fits into my purse strap. Then when I'm back at the apartment, I dial Ned. He answers on the first ring.

"Hey, beautiful," he says.

"Hey, I've got a favor to ask." I adjust the phone. "Can you help me get a gun?"

His jaw audibly drops. "A *gun?*"

"Yeah, it's just—" I pause. I don't want him to get worried, but I also *need* a gun if I'm going to blackmail a murderer. I could get one myself, but having Ned get one seems better. I'll convince him to put it under his name, and he'll be on *my* side in case anything bad happens.

"I need to protect myself, you know?" I say. It's honest enough. "And I'm not really sure what the protocol is to get one in Nevada."

"Tell me who it is," he growls.

Ned, the good man, is always trying to protect others. Protecting me probably means keeping me locked in his tower so that no one could get near me, *and* so that Ned wouldn't have to hurt my enemies. He would never kill an ant. It's sweet, in a vomit-inducing way.

"I live alone, you know?" I say. "I just want to protect myself. You never know what can happen."

He sighs. "You're right about that."

In the corner of the kitchen, a camera records the phone call; I installed it so that I'll always be ready to prove my innocence. In the past, a surveillance camera like that proved my guilt. One day, it may help me.

"Well," Ned says, clearing his throat. "It's late, but I've got a friend who owns a shop. I can pick you up in an hour. We'll get you something."

Chapter 6

Crave

I use the bolt cutters on the padlock. It's annoying, but at least they're doing something.

You should have destroyed it when you still had the chance, my mother's voice says. *Stupid, stupid boy.*

"And where would that leave my legacy?" I ask.

I toss the bolt cutters into the dirt, then whip open the gate. My boots pound into the floor with the same determination as an adopted son ready to shake some goddamn sense into his legal mother. I scan the first floor of the Galloway House through the mesh screens of my mask.

Gray and brown shadows cover the kitchen. My mother's voice rings in my mind again.

I told you to stay down there, she says.

I tried to leave. Tried to stay far away from this place. Tried to move on with my life. But this desert town always haunts me, begging me to stay.

And now, it's called Rae here too.

After unlocking the basement door, I flip a switch. A dim light illuminates in the back corner like the embers of a dying fire. A few objects come into view: a stool, a table, a ladder, and a shower stall in the corner. A red, sticky stain marks the floor. I'm lucky that no one goes down here.

The door upstairs creaks open. Right on time.

Ballet flats shuffle against the stairs. I stand tall, my boots giving me extra height, and with my shadow, I must look too tall to be real. I grin behind the mask, knowing that this kind of thing gets to a woman like Rae. She likes knowing I can squash her in a second, but no, I'd rather fuck her instead.

It's not about sex for me, though. It's about using her. Her body. Her mind. Her fucking soul.

Rae stops on the bottom step. Wavy red hair straddles her shoulders, her black eyeliner thicker than usual, a mask of her own that says, *Don't fuck with me.*

She's already fucking with you, my mother—that stupid inner voice—says. I ignore it.

Rae raises a small handgun. Aims it at me. Her shoulders are tight. Her arms quiver under the weight, not used to a real weapon. She thinks she's going to shoot me.

"The little girl got herself a gun?" I ask.

"Don't move," she warns in a voice that's impressively confident. A gun always does that to a person. She takes another step forward and joins me on the ground floor, her body filling with bravery. "I just want to talk."

I undo the metal zipper over my mouth, exposing my lips. She focuses for a second too long on my mouth, then shifts back up at my mesh eyes. The dirty little bitch.

She aims the gun at my chest, then at my stomach.

"You killed those people the other night," she says. Her chin curls up, her brown eyes locked on mine. "Why kill them here?"

"Why not?" I say.

Her eyes inspect every inch of me. My body is covered in leather, a second layer of animal skin. I imagine her in leather too, a bondage mask clinging to her face.

Rae hasn't killed anyone, but there's a lack of remorse in the things she does. The way she *takes.* The way she doesn't see humanity in others. The way she only sees herself.

That's what this is. She sees an opportunity in me, just like I see one in her.

I sniff deeply, sucking in her natural scent: pineapple and

vinegar. A sweetness in the tang. The floral stench of jasmine perfume tries to cover up her natural funk, but when you're aroused, you can't hide something that sour under a flower's perfume.

"You didn't answer the question," she says.

Smart girl. I can give her an answer.

"No one cares about this place," I say. "It's as simple as that."

"Nothing is ever that simple."

My lips twist. I hold back my laughter. She fidgets uncomfortably, the gun's aim sinking, then she raises it up again, the silence eating away at her.

"You broke the lock," she says. "I know the mall owner. I can make it so that no one knows we are here."

We.

Her eyes flicker back and forth across my mask, searching for answers. People don't like it when they can't see your emotions. I don't have many, but I like how the mask hides the few that I have. Anyone can buy a bondage mask at a leather shop. You can even order a customized one with zippers and mesh. All it takes is a down payment in cash.

"There was a husband and wife that were murdered here twenty-five years ago," Rae says. "You're going to steal the evidence from that case for me."

"Am I?"

"Or I will give the video of you murdering those people to the police."

I can't help it. My loud laughter ricochets against the walls. This little girl thinks she can control me?

"A round of applause for the brave little girl," I mock. Her eyes betray her, widening as she tries to figure out why someone like me—someone she knows is a killer—would find entertainment in this situation. I give her a clue: "A little girl using coercive measures to get a murderer to steal for her is absurd."

I step closer. She refocuses the gun's aim on my chest.

"What do you think you'll find exactly?" I ask. "It's not like that couple has anything to do with you."

The corners of her lips sink. "My father died here."

"Michael Hall," I say. Her lips quiver. "He committed suicide."

Her gaze lowers slightly, then comes back to me. "No," she says. "He was murdered."

I clap my gloved hands together triumphantly, and she jumps, almost tripping on the wooden step behind her. I meet her at the base of the stairs.

"Good for you, thinking on your own," I say in a low voice. I move closer, eating up her personal space until we're inches apart. "And you think a little girl like you is going to find this killer?"

"I know I will," she says. "Maybe it was *you.*"

I chuckle at that. She's good. I'll give her that.

"Do you know how long it's been since the murder-suicide happened?" I ask. A flash of disgust ripples across her face. I click my teeth. "If it is a murderer, they wouldn't stick around Pahrump now, would they?"

"Murderers like to revisit the places where they committed their crimes," she says. "It's in their blood."

"Textbook information. A well-versed murderer would know that. It's an easy clue. A way for the police to find him again."

"Not if he's good at covering his tracks."

I pore over her, licking my teeth. There's a haughtiness to her words, a confidence that annoys *and* intrigues me. A confidence that I want to strip away from her right now.

I rip the gun from her hand. She reaches for it. I immediately wrench the barrel under her chin, forcing her to look up at me. She strains her neck.

She could fight me. The fiery expression in her brown eyes knows this. Instead, her breathing quickens. The adrenaline fuels her. She may not know it, but she likes her own primal reaction. Being forced to endure. To stop thinking. Being made to do exactly what I want.

"Tell me," I murmur. "When you turn in the footage, are you going to tell the police how exciting it was to see those people die?"

Her thighs tense. The sour scent of her arousal mixes in the air, swirling around us, my head soaring higher.

"Blackmailing a murderer," I say. "What if I save us both the trouble and kill you right now?"

I lick my lips. A large gulp eases down her throat.

"If you kill me, Ned knows to give the video to the cops," she says.

Anger flutters inside of me. The owner of the mall. The technical owner of this house. *That* Ned. Another pathetic little freak hiding behind a good boy disguise.

If she told Ned anything about this, she wouldn't be here right now. Neither of us would.

I grab her jaw, force it open, and put the gun between her teeth. Her eyelids flutter, her pupils dilated. The little girl *likes* the oral stimulation.

I pull back the hammer.

"You think you can fuck with me, Rae?" I ask. Her eyes widen, wondering how I know her name. "I've always been ahead of you." I smirk. "I will *always* be ahead of you. Stronger than you. Better than you."

I grab her neck, keeping her in place, then I move the gun, putting it under her chin again. Her pupils flicker back and forth, shining with the faintest hint of light. She shivers. Her musk and fear tinges the air, and I drink it in. With one hand still fixed on her neck, I slide the gun back into her purse.

"I can smell your cunt," I snicker. "You like this, don't you? You depraved little slut. Being powerless. Being weak. You can't think when you're like this. You can't use your sexuality to control me. You're just a pathetic little girl. Better yet, an object. A toy that I'll use, get tired of, and eventually throw away."

She whimpers. "No—"

I shove her shoulders, slamming her down to her knees. I unzip my pants, bringing out my cock, heavy with desire, the metal jewelry shining in the light. Six goddamn piercings. A fucking weapon, a metal and skin cock, ready to tear her insides apart. To render her throat useless like the used-up cock whore she is.

Her jaw hangs open, and I shove myself inside. She blubbers in pain, but those brown eyes glaze over. I know her. I've watched her for years. She's used to giving others what they want, so she can get what *she* wants.

This isn't about giving though. It's about taking what I want. And I want more than to come. I want her to realize that *I'm* in control. I owned her long before she stepped foot into this house.

Her tongue darts across my pierced tip. She inches forward, grinding her pussy into the ground, and I snicker in amusement. I bring my boot forward, kicking the steel toe between her legs until it's resting under her folds.

"Look at you on your pedestal," I say. I brace the sides of her head, shoving her head down on my shaft until she's gagging on the metal. "Be a good little fuck hole and take me."

Her throat muscles squeeze. I keep her there. Her nose is smashed into the curly hairs above my cock. The bitch can't even use her nostrils right now.

"Relax, little girl," I say, dragging out each word. "Don't be afraid. It wouldn't be so bad to die like this, now would it? It's what you're good at after all."

A moan tumbles out of her, the noise vibrating against my dick. I pull back. She gasps for air, holding herself up with her fists on my thighs. I shove right back down, then angle her until she's pinned against the wall with my hips.

"Don't you want to make me come?" I ask. She holds her breath, her body loose, and her throat relaxes. She's trying hard, so fucking hard, to open herself up for me. "What would you do if your mother saw you like this?" I ask. "Should I record *you?* Show her what a pathetic little slut you really are?"

A sharp pain surges from my dick to my temples—her jaws snapping down, biting my shaft. The fucking chompers on this bitch. I toss my head back, slapping my hand into the wall, the sensation spreading through me like wildfire. She's still pinned underneath me, and I'm still fucking that tight little throat.

I love it when they bite.

I smack the side of her head, and she cries, her jaw easing its grip. I fist her hair, raising her until she's on her toes. I lick the salt from her throat, the teeth of the zipper scraping across her saliva-covered flesh.

"You're going to have to bite harder than that," I murmur.

Rae pants on the verge of hyperventilation. I reach a gloved hand inside of her skirt, her stockings, between her legs. Her thong tangles against my glove. My leather fingertips slide along her folds. She loosens, her eyes glazed.

She wants it. *Badly.*

I drag my finger down lower, teasing her puckered asshole. Her eyes stay on mine, unconsciously begging me to penetrate her there.

I remove my hand and step back.

This will destroy her. She won't be able to think until she can make me come. She wants that control over me.

And I refuse to give it to her.

"That's it?" she asks. "That's fucking it?"

"What?" I chuckle. "Are you sad you couldn't make me come like your other love sick boys? Like your precious *Ned?*"

"Fuck you," she snarls.

"You'd like that, wouldn't you?"

I keep our eyes locked as I lick her juices off of my glove. Tangy. Sweet. A spicy pineapple, ripe and waiting for my tongue.

Her thighs twitch, her lips open in hunger. It's going to be harder to seduce me than that.

I zip up my pants. Rae takes a long, slow inhale, leveling herself.

"What's your name?" she asks, her tone back to business.

"You can call me Crave."

"Crave," she whispers. "Crave and Rae," she says, louder this time, processing the information like it's a clue. Like there's meaning there.

A name is just a name. A couple of letters that produce a sound. A string of symbols which make it easier to communicate. She can use any name for me as long as she knows that I'll always be in control.

"Do we have a deal, then?" she asks.

I keep her locked under my stare. The lust is still there, but it's dampened by the authority in her stance, her determination to get what she wants. There's a hunger inside of her that surprises me.

A confidence someone like her shouldn't have. A power she doesn't know she has yet.

She startles herself out of the daze.

"There might be more evidence that the police overlooked. I'll find out where the police keep the evidence for the Hall murders, and then I'll tell you how to steal it," she says with a brusque voice. "Until then, search this place."

She walks up the stairs. Her ass bounces under her short skirt, her legs subtly trembling from the skull fucking. The scared little girl is trying to reassert her control again.

Rae thinks she's strong, thinks she's smarter, *better* than everyone else. And she thinks that the truth will prove her superiority.

I love seeing a woman like that suffer.

One day, she'll bend to my will, and I'll lose interest. That's when I'll kill her. When she accepts—truly fucking accepts, with her body, mind, and soul—that she's a killer, just like me, then that's when I'll end her.

It doesn't matter where you come from or how you're raised: sometimes violence is inside of you.

She disappears behind the basement door, and I rub my cock through my pants. An experiment like this takes time. When you savor a possession for as long as I have, you make every second count.

Chapter 7

Rae

With every breath, my senses heighten, as if something was awakened inside of me in the Galloway House. Still, I put on my normal face and walk through the employee hallway in the back of the mall. It's an act. I'm wearing a mask too—my normal mask. The one where I pretend to be a good person when I'm just as sick as any criminal.

Am I as sick as Crave?

No, I'm not. Even if I wear a symbolic mask, I'm *not* as bad as Crave. I didn't kill anyone. I just happen to have footage of Crave killing people, and I happen to have clear footage from last night. He's wearing a mask, but it's better than before. Soon, he'll do something horrific in front of me again, and I'll have something *real* over him.

I knock on Ned's office door. The door opens, and Ned's blue eyes widen, fluttering in approval as he scans me from head to toe.

"Hey, beautiful," he says. "You're early."

"Well, you did all of this for me," I say. "It would be rude if I were late to these interviews."

He laughs brightly. "You? Being rude? Impossible."

I let myself into his office, then plop down on the suede chair in front of his desk. An older picture of his family is framed on the wall. Ned and his brothers, back when they were teenagers, stand with their parents in front of their ranch-style house on the rich side of Pahrump. Everyone is smiling, their blue eyes brighter than the sky. You can almost smell the barbecue cooking in the background. A picture-perfect life.

Or so it seems anyway. Maybe they wear masks too.

A set of keys shine on Ned's desk, each of them labeled with colors and destinations, except for one: a gray key with a small brand name etched into the head.

With Crave using those bolt cutters last night, Ned must have replaced the padlock. This gray one has to be the new key.

"Mrs. Line will be here soon," he says. He grabs his phone and responds to a text. "She's the one who knew the Halls personally. And my niece—"

His walkie-talkie beeps.

Sir, there's a code blue in the food court, a gruff Southern voice crackled through the walkie. The mall cop. How lovely.

"Crap," Ned mutters, stuffing his phone in his pocket. "Let me take care of this. By then, Mrs. Line and Penny should be here."

"Take your time," I say.

The office door clicks shut. I run around the desk, quickly looping through the keys. I pull off the new key and get back into the seat.

The door opens, and Ned beams at me. A buzzing sensation burns inside of me. Ned doesn't know I just stole his key. He doesn't suspect a thing.

"Never a dull day at the mall," I say.

"You're telling me." He waves toward the door. "Mrs. Line is here. You're going to love her."

I join him, and we walk down the employee hallway.

In the food court, the different kitchens whir with activity. Utensils clink against pans. Hot oil pops. Grease hangs in the air. I study Ned. He's taller than me by a foot, and he's got width too, plenty of muscle for a middle-aged man.

Crave is taller than me too. I haven't seen him in direct light, but I can tell he's strong.

Could someone like Ned *be* Crave? Serial killers tend to have charming personas to the public eye. Is "Ned" the normal mask Crave puts on for the world to see?

I concentrate, sniffing past the grease and sugar of the food court. Ned smells fresh and slightly masculine, like he just rinsed off at the gym. Ned doesn't smell like Crave. Crave smells bitter, like charred leather and motor oil. But Crave could wash that scent off with some soap and water.

If Ned *is* Crave, then he'd have access to the house. The padlock could be an act, a way to pretend like he's preparing for potential danger. And using bolt cutters to cut open the lock could be a way to trick *me* into thinking Ned and Crave are separate people.

Perhaps there's a bigger reason *why* Ned doesn't want anyone in that house. He wants that space, that privacy, to kill his victims. It would make sense.

Could Ned actually kill someone?

A woman with wavy gray hair sits at a table still glimmering with cleaning fluids. Her skin is loose. The wrinkles around her eyes are warm. She spots Ned and lights up.

"You must be Ned's new girlfriend," she says.

"Oh, come on, Mrs. Line," Ned says. His cheeks redden. I laugh, but neither confirm nor deny the girlfriend title. I offer Mrs. Line my hand.

"I'm Rae Sinclair. I'm doing a podcast on the Hall murder-suicide." I sit across from her. "Ned tells me you lived here during that time?"

Ned pats me on the shoulder. "I'll see you ladies later."

Mrs. Line smiles at Ned's back as he walks away. Once he's out of earshot, she leans forward and grabs my hands.

"He's a bit older than you, but he'd make a very good husband," she says. "He'd always take care of you, just like my husband took care of me."

I force a smile. Ned is undeniably nice, and Mrs. Line is probably right about him. About *us.* I'm not interested in dating though, especially if there's a possibility that Ned is Crave.

"Mrs. Line," I ask, focusing back on our main purpose. "Is it okay if I record our conversation today?"

"Ned told me you would."

I take that as a yes and pull out my phone. A young woman with dirty blonde hair tucked into a low ponytail zooms over to our table, taking one of the empty seats.

"Hi," I say. "Can I help you?"

"Ned said you were investigating the murders in the Galloway House," she says. "I'm your best resource on it."

A flash of happiness blooms inside of me. Murder, *not* murder-suicide. The young woman narrows her eyes at me, as if ready to interview *me* instead of the other way around.

"You must be Penny, then," I say, extending my hand.

She shakes it firmly. "I know all of our local crime history. It's my passion." A nervous laugh chortles out of me. Penny wrinkles her nose. "My dad works for the sheriff. Sometimes he even spills confidential details."

"Ah," I say. Another piece of evidence that law enforcement cannot be trusted. "So criminal justice is in your blood?"

Mrs. Line chirps in: "Your father is a good man."

"Please don't tell my dad I'm here, Mrs. Line," Penny says quietly. "He doesn't want me to go into criminal justice. He wants me to let it go."

Those words ring close to home. My mother wants me to let go of the Hall case too.

"I was about to interview Mrs. Line," I say.

"Go ahead," Penny says.

The recording app blinks red, the duration numbers increasing at the bottom. I turn to Mrs. Line.

"Ned said you knew Michael Hall?" I ask.

"Good man," Mrs. Line says. "A very good man. He always helped me carry my groceries to my car."

My throat tightens. Penny chimes in with questions. I nod, pretending to believe every word Mrs. Line says. My mind goes blank. When I focus back on their words, Mrs. Line is lecturing us on the increased cost of groceries.

"So when it comes to Michael Hall"—I interrupt—"did you suspect that he was capable of murder?"

Mrs. Line crosses her arms over her chest, then sits up straight.

"Well, I suppose anyone is capable of murder. But no, sweetheart. I never suspected a good man like Michael would kill his wife." She shakes her head. "Sometimes, I still find it hard to believe."

I can agree with that.

Like a nervous tick, Mrs. Line goes back to discussing inflation as Penny fights her to stay on topic. My brain drifts again. Mrs. Line is in her eighties. Back then, she still would've been an older woman. How can a murderous man help an old lady to her car? How can someone like that blend in so well?

That's a stupid question though. Everyone blends in, even serial killers. It's just another mask.

"Do you think the police are correct that it was murder-suicide?" I ask.

Penny raises a brow at me. Mrs. Line pulls at her sweater's collar.

"Of course! You know, the sheriff is a good man," Mrs. Line says quickly, her attention focused on Penny. "In fact, he was on the force right around that time. A young deputy, of course, but he could help your radio show. Why don't you interview him?"

My mind flashes with different pictures from the old news articles, searching for the law enforcement in the background. It's odd to think that the current sheriff worked on the Michael Hall case back then, but it makes sense. He may have even helped cover up the truth.

Ned said his brother works for the sheriff. What if his brother is hiding Ned's involvement in the case?

A lightness flutters in my chest. Whether or not Ned is guilty, I can still ask his brother for help in the investigation.

"We'll be in touch," Penny says, shaking Mrs. Line's hand. I startle, not realizing the interview had already ended. I shake Mrs. Line's hand too, then turn to Penny.

"Can I talk to you for a few minutes?" I ask.

Penny looks down at her phone. "I've got to leave for college soon. Make it quick."

"How much do you know about the Hall murder-suicide?" I ask.

"You mean the *murders?*" she corrects. My chest swells in

excitement all over again. She gets it then; there was no mistaking her word choice earlier. "They say it was murder-suicide, but there was no definitive proof, especially with the type of drugs in Michael Hall's system. There was a gunshot wound to his head, and the gun had his fingerprints, but if he was *that* drugged, he wouldn't have been able to lift a gun, let alone shoot himself. He would have been paralyzed." Her head bobs with fervor. "Someone shot him. I'm certain of it."

My heart pangs. Penny's blue eyes—so much like Ned's—blaze with anger, as if she's tired of no one believing her. I can relate to that.

"You know they weren't the first people to die in that house," she adds.

Nor the last, I think. "What do you know about the other murders?"

"Everything."

"And do you think those murders are another fake murder-suicide?"

She shrugs. "I'm not so sure about that. The decapitation. The burned bodies. It seems too personal, you know? The father probably saved the easiest death for himself because his life's purpose was over by then."

"Didn't the father shoot himself too?"

She squints her eyes as she studies me. "Why are you so curious about them? Come to think of it, why are you so interested in any of the murders?"

I think about telling her the truth, that my mother knew Michael Hall, and that he's my father. She seems too smart though, like she'll latch onto me as another piece of evidence.

Right now, I want her to be on my side. I have to come up with a reason she'll accept without any doubts.

I lift my shoulders. "I have a friend who knew the Halls. I guess I wanted to investigate the Galloway House crimes because it's so local, you know? Everyone focuses on the Vegas mobster crimes. I want to work on something outside of the Strip."

"I completely understand that."

I smile automatically. She thinks she understands me; she

doesn't know it's a lie. I'm not interested in local crime or history like her, but if she's the local crime expert, then I need her help to figure out how my father died.

"We should meet up sometime," I say. "Talk about this stuff. I could interview you for the podcast, or maybe you could co-host with me."

She smiles. "I'd like that."

Chapter 8

Crave

More "investigating" for a fake podcast. More bullshit. More nights. More days. More time spent waiting for the perfect moment to fuck with her.

Rae's red hair flashes between the white slats in her window. My mind ticks, itching to see more. I keep settled in my truck, stationed in the far corner of her apartment parking lot. She never goes over here. Her car is near the building.

You're obsessed, my mother's voice hisses. *You're letting her control you.*

My facial muscles twitch. I force myself to relax, to not let that fake maternal voice get to me.

Rae exits her apartment, then patters down the stairs. Her sedan zooms off, and once her tires hit the main road, I head to the dumpster. I pop over, then grab a grease-stained pizza box. It's too early for pizza, but if someone sees me, they won't think twice about it. And once I get a key to her place, I won't need the cover.

A black rubber doormat, marked with dirt, sits in front of Rae's front door, the same one they give to all of the new residents. Rae hasn't put her own flair on the place; she blends in with the rest. It's not a bad thing in this situation.

I lift the rubber mat and grab the extra key. I put it in my pocket, then head back down the stairs and drop the empty pizza box in front of a random apartment.

Stupid little boy, that matronly voice screams inside of me. *Thinking you can do anything to her when you've been putting off killing her for years. She's smarter than you think.*

"Just like you thought you were smarter than me," I mutter.

That inner voice gets loud again, so I whistle, drowning out those thoughts. If it were just about killing Rae, we'd be done by now.

I'm not simply interested in Rae's blood; I'm interested in fucking with her mind.

At a chain one-stop shop, I use the automated key copy machine in the front entryway. Once that's done, I head to the electronics section and grab every home surveillance system they have. Because now that my mission is to properly get inside of her head, I need to have the ability to see her at all times.

Is that what you're telling yourself now? my mother's voice says. *You're pathetic.*

An edgy, restless sensation cycles through me. Years of rage coming to the surface of my skin.

A different voice enters: *Come on,* Rae whispers. *I deserve more than a camera.*

I spin around, different aisles melting together, chunks of metal and plastic swirling into nothingness.

A spark simmers inside of me.

The gardening section.

I stop right before the sliding doors to the outdoor patio, my vision scanning over the shelves.

Pesticides. Ant killer. Rodent traps. And poison.

The exterior is simple. A black bottle with a white skull on the front. *Keep out of reach of children,* the label reads. I snicker; the thought amuses me. They even use a cartoon caricature to illustrate the potential carnage. *May cause death.*

Death. Not murder.

Poison is too easy. I like knowing that *I* inflicted the damage, and poison doesn't do that. The chemicals do the work for you.

Would someone—a new killer, a woman—enjoy something subtle like poison?

"Is that what you need?" I ask out loud.

I wait for a moment, the squeaks of cart wheels and shuffling products filling my ears. I even close my eyes, waiting to hear Rae's voice.

Nothing happens.

Fuck it.

I stuff the poison bottle in my cart, then head to the cashier stands. Each camera box is a brick in my hands, a wall I'm building around her. A fortress meant to bury her in her own secrets. My ears pound with blood.

You want to save her, my mother says. *Don't you?*

"Rat problem?" the cashier asks, stirring me out of those thoughts. She continues to babble; I don't hear a word.

I remember holding a dead rat in the basement.

What is wrong with you? my mother had said. *What are you doing with that? Put it—*

I snapped it in half, its bones crunching in the darkness. She gasped.

Just waiting for you, I had said.

I pay in cash, then stop at a drive-thru for breakfast. I eat the egg sandwich in two bites, then gulp the coffee. It scalds my throat.

"Shit!" I yell. I shove the cardboard cup into the holder in my console and toss the top out the window. "Goddamn it."

Rae will have something in her fridge to fix it. I head back to her apartment.

Since she's at work, her bedroom window is dark, the blinds closed.

With my coffee, cameras, poison, and new key in hand, I head up the stairs and tuck her spare key back under her doormat. My new key glides into the lock easily.

Inside her apartment, garlic and butter linger in the air from last night's dinner. Her floral perfume faintly sifts through the food smells.

I set my bags on the counter, then open her fridge. A peppermint mocha creamer is in the back. I don't care for peppermint, but it's better than boiling hot coffee. I pour some into my cup, then take a sip.

A surge of adrenaline runs through me. Rae will never know that I was here, drinking her coffee creamer. Maybe I'll even eat her food.

My eyes are drawn to the corners of the room.

A camera is set up in each corner. In the kitchen. The living room. The bedroom. Even outside of the bathroom. She's been recording herself like she's sure someone is going to break in and hurt her, and she wants evidence to put them in jail. *Funny.*

It makes it a hell of a lot easier for me.

I open up her laptop. It doesn't take long to find the surveillance programs linked to the cameras. I erase the footage of me, then schedule the cameras to turn on again in an hour. I'll be out of her apartment by then.

After that, I copy her surveillance program login information so that I can have access from anywhere I want.

My dick bulges, and for a split second, I picture myself fucking her from behind, my piercings tearing through that sweet little hole, digging out a new cavern for me. I squeeze the head of my cock through my pants.

"Dirty little girl," I murmur, pulling myself out to stroke.

You are obsessed, my mother's voice chimes.

Irritation and numbness flow into my palm. My dick is in my hand, red from the friction, my fingers throbbing around the metal jewelry. I'm *not* obsessed—not like my inner voice seems to think—but I need to calm down. Rae is just a woman, and I've raped and killed more than my fair share of people. Even if she reminds me of myself, she's not *that* special. I'd get hard doing this to anyone.

It's not about *her.*

I click my tongue, then zip my pants and head to the kitchen to grab my coffee and the extra cameras. Jasmine dances in the air, and my mind wanders back to her.

Fake red hair. Tan skin. Plain brown eyes.

I hold the bottle of poison. I could leave it on the counter for her, a gift to let her know that I was here. I have no doubt that she'll know it's from me.

I open the creamer, and for a split second, I entertain the idea of pouring the poison into it. Flavored creamer is such a small indulgence, and the idea of killing her when she least expects it would be amusing. With these cameras, I'd get to see her die. It would almost be worth it to see her expression—fear, betrayal, then anger—as she realizes I poisoned her. Someone who was there even before she moved to Pahrump.

Instead, I close my eyes, thinking of her pussy's sour tang as she watched me kill those people, and I work the zipper of my jeans with one hand. An image of her tanned skin riddled with purple bruises fills my mind, and my hand grips my fleshy cock and the metal jewelry. I'm practically foaming at the mouth. When it comes to our sex, she'll never have the ability to fake it like she does with her conquests. Every scream will be pure agony, and every scream will belong to me.

My cock bursts, and I moan, the head of my cock resting on that open bottle. My cum drips into her creamer.

I sigh, then close the bottle and shove it back into the fridge. I put the sealed poison back into the plastic grocery bag with the unopened cameras. I head toward the door.

Rae doesn't need to know that I've got a key to her apartment yet. If I told her now, that would be too easy for her…and for me.

I need more than that.

Chapter 9

Rae

I stare at the Galloway House in the morning light. The chain-link fence stretches up, full of holes and metal. Keeping people out. Keeping someone inside. *Crave.*

I take a sip of my mint coffee. A lump—like curdled milk—catches on my tongue. I gag and accidentally swallow the lump before I can spit it out. I go back through the employee door and dump the rest of my coffee into the nearest trash can.

I pass Ned in the hallway.

"Hey," he says.

I poke his side teasingly. "Can I wait in your office?" I ask. "My shift doesn't start for a while."

He waves me back. "Go for it."

As soon as I'm in his office alone, I scan his desk. A pile of papers. A globe paperweight. No keys. My chest thuds with adrenaline. Where should I put Ned's key to the Galloway House's padlock?

I open up his desk drawer and stuff it inside. The office door opens, and I slam myself back into my seat and huff through my nostrils. Ned lifts his brows.

I'm not out of breath from doing something bad, I tell myself. *I'm just—*

"You okay, beautiful?" Ned asks.

"Sorry—I was just playing with myself," I blurt out. His cheeks turn red. "Sometimes it helps me feel better."

"You're right," he says. "We should make you feel better." His embarrassment melts away, turning into hunger. "The boutique will be fine. Don't worry about it."

"You're so nice," I whimper.

He kneels down between my legs.

Afterward, I call out of my shift and leave the mall, then head to the Pahrump Police Station. As the front desk secretary helps me set up an appointment with the sheriff, the urge to do something *more* flickers inside of me. It's a fast pulse, like my insides are vibrating, waiting for my next move.

A man with peppered gray hair struts through the office. A small group of younger men follow him. He moves past me, heading toward the exit.

"Sheriff?" I ask. The gray-haired man swings around. "Can I talk to you, sir?"

He dismisses the men and leans on the counter beside me. He ogles me up and down. I pretend not to notice.

"What can I do for you, young lady?" he asks.

I curl my fists at my sides. "Young lady" sounds so much like "little girl," and yet it feels *wrong* coming from him. Condescending. Like the sheriff thinks he's such a big man for helping a weak woman.

Crave made it clear that he thinks he's better than me, but for some reason, I don't find it irritating when he calls me "little girl." Instead, it arouses me. If a little girl can get a killer's attention, then what else can I do to him?

Instead of letting the sheriff's words get to me, I play into it, shrinking my shoulders meekly so the sheriff feels extra manly.

"I heard that you worked here during the Michael and Miranda Hall murders," I say. "I'm working on a college project. Could I ask you a few questions about it?"

His expression frosts over with vacancy, like I'm not in front of him anymore.

"You mean the murder-suicide," he says dryly.

Of course he would say that.

"What if it wasn't a murder-suicide?" I ask, dropping the shy girl act. "Why would Michael Hall drug *and* kill himself when—"

"I imagine that if you kill your wife, you may have a lot of guilt," the sheriff interrupts. "I imagine you'd want to numb that pain."

"True," I say quickly. "But what if he was drugged by someone else? What if it was a setup to make it *look* like a murder-suicide?"

He blinks. "Perhaps the overdose was taking too long."

He's got the excuses lined up already. Still, I'm determined.

"But the autopsy information said that there wasn't enough in his system to overdose. There was only enough to keep him immobile, as if someone wanted him to comply with their orders. As if *someone else* was there, controlling the situation."

My knees subtly shake, so full of pent-up irritation that I can barely contain myself. I clench my jaw. What if the sheriff knows who truly murdered my father? What if he's covering up for one of his men? What if the sheriff *is* my father's murderer?

"I'm not making this up, and you know it," I say.

The sheriff takes a deep breath, filling himself with patience.

"I know you worked on the case," I say, enunciating every word so he knows what I'm actually saying: *I know you're trying to cover up that none of your men know shit about what really happened.* "And I know you worked hard to get to your position as sheriff too."

He looks down his nose at me, emphasizing our height difference. I straighten, broadening my shoulders, meeting his icy gaze. I narrow my eyes too, warning him.

"You're not the first kid to come in here making accusations like that," he says.

Kid? "I never made any accusations—"

"Ma'am, it was ruled a murder-suicide. Michael Hall hung his wife, then he drugged and shot himself. There was a suicide note. There's not much else to determine about that." He clicks his tongue. "He was an insecure man."

I shake my head. It's too easy, and he must see that. "But what if the suicide note was a setup too?"

He forces a laugh, then turns toward the entrance. "You're from Vegas, aren't you?"

"Yes, but—"

"You're all about the hustle."

"What—"

"You want to make a quick buck by digging up whatever grief you can find."

My knuckles turn white. "I'm doing this for school—"

"Yeah, yeah," he scoffs. "You're doing it for an A. You care nothing about the Hall family." He steps toward the exit, and I follow after him. He frowns. "Don't go digging where you don't belong. The Halls need rest. I do too."

"I'll see you at the appointment then," I say.

He stops in his tracks.

"Appointment?" he says. He and the secretary exchange a silent look, and the secretary nods. "Right." He dips his chin at me. "See you then."

The building doors close behind him. I stand frozen in the lobby. What the hell just happened?

Did he just silently tell his secretary to cancel my appointment?

He *has* to be covering it up. That's the only way to explain everything that happened.

I dash over to the front desk. "I've still got an appointment, right?"

"Yes, ma'am," the secretary says.

"The sheriff didn't just tell you to cancel it?"

"Your appointment is still on the books." She gestures to the computer screen. I can't see anything though.

"He can still cancel it later," I say.

The phone rings, and the secretary holds up a hand, asking me to wait. I don't. There's no reason to stay right now.

This obsession I have with my father's maybe-murder is ridiculous. It's not like I can change the past. Even when I prove it to my mother—that I didn't come from a murderous father—it won't do anything besides give me the chance to say I told you so.

And you think a little girl like you is going to find this killer? Crave had asked.

My skin flushes with heat as the ghost of his hand tangles in my hair. He was brutal and unrelenting, and he never gave me a chance to think. To feel. To plan. For once, I *had* to let go.

I can't let Crave control me like that. I have to use *him* to my advantage. And fucking him like I actually want him won't help me blackmail him.

At the apartment, restless energy stirs inside of me, bouncing around like bolts of electricity.

I have to do something. I have to remind myself that *I* am in control.

I open a dating app and find a local with an average face.

Are you free? I text. *I want to fuck now.*

What's your address? he responds.

I switch on the surveillance cameras and double-check that the red recording lights are off. Even if I'm the one doing the stealing, you can never be too careful about what you catch on film. If this hookup tries to mess with me, I'll have proof. And with enough editing, I'll have proof of my innocence.

A knock pounds my door, and as soon as I open it, the hookup rushes inside, smacking his lips to mine. I close the door behind him and flip off the lights—it's the best way to disorient them—then I shove my tongue into his mouth. The taste of toothpaste and bubblegum swishes between my lips.

In the bedroom, I pull at his belt buckle. His cock bounces free, hard and ready for me.

"Fuck me," I demand.

He complies. They always do. They're so simple.

As his cock enters me, I grab his ass, his wallet thick in his back pocket. I don't need the money, but there's a thrill inside of me when I find something I can take. A picture. Car keys. A stack of cash. A card. It's like gaining physical strength. And even if he doesn't have cash, I can always use one of his debit cards to fill up my gas tank or get a few groceries. They never notice a charge like that.

I pull us down to the bed. The hookup moves me to the edge

of the mattress so he can fuck me better, and I imagine Crave sitting in the corner of the room. Watching me. Judging me. Stroking his cock as he watches the hookup stuff my pussy. Crave's dark and knowing eyes fixed on me, like he can peel back my skin and taste the layers underneath. He unsettles me, and yet, at the same time, he makes me feel so fucking alive.

I grab the hookup's hand, slapping both of our hands onto my tits. The crash of skin against skin dissipates. The hookup curls his head to the side.

"You're into that?" he asks.

"Lots of people like being spanked," I say coyly.

He rubs his face. I grin. He's probably hooked up a lot, but not with someone like me.

"Well." He motions to the side. "Flip over then."

I bat my eyelashes playfully, but a tingly sensation spreads across my arms and legs. I like getting my ass spanked—who wouldn't?—but the hookup is acting so hesitant, and I know it won't be enough. He must think the only place he can righteously spank me is my ass.

I flip over to my hands and knees anyway.

"Hit me," I demand. "Hard."

His cock enters me, then his palm meets my ass cheeks, soft, then again, softer. So rhythmic, it's almost comical. My mind drifts in boredom, and I'm not inside myself anymore.

I'm underneath Crave while he chokes me from behind.

Be a good little fuck hole and take me, he had said.

The fuzzy images of a crowd of people surround us, like we're performing a ritual on a sacred night. Candles flicker at the edges, illuminating their faces, but I can't see anyone's expression. There's no clear detail. There's only Crave, hidden inside of his bondage mask.

A fingertip rolls down my spine. I shiver back to reality. The hookup stops.

"Are you okay?" he asks. "Was I too hard?"

"Don't stop," I say.

I moan, and the hookup's pace increases. The same rhythm. A thrust, then a spank. Thrust. Spank. Switch sides and repeat. My head controls the situation again, transporting me back to the vision with Crave. Now I have no interest in even stealing from this hookup. I'm distracted. I want something else.

Your mind is on Crave because you need to ask him for help, I tell myself. *He'll have better luck with the police, and with his background, he'll be able to steal from the police department better than you can.*

These are excuses though. They're not the real reason I'm bored of this monotonous hookup right now.

I want something more. Something harder. Something rougher. Something that doesn't let me think. Something that rips every thought and calculated action out of my brain until I'm merely a sexual object being used for pleasure.

I want Crave.

Chapter 10

Crave

On the video feed, the latest conquest hits Rae's ass like a set of bongos. A drum. An instrument. Not a woman. Not a person. An object. Her lips pinch, her annoyance obvious. That primal need goes straight to my balls. The filthy bitch probably doesn't see the objectification from this angle, but I do.

She glances at the camera lens in the corner of the room, and those eyes penetrate me down to my core. My cock twitches.

Finally, she flips over, lying on her back again. She grabs his hand and puts it on her throat, forcing him to choke her. She squeals in delight and fake fear, but he loosens his grip. He pulls out his limp dick. A scared little boy.

What's wrong? Rae asks. She sits up.

His posture stiffens. *I just—*

She kneels on the ground, swallowing his limp dick in her mouth. He tilts his head back. His cock comes back to life.

I smirk. My little girl can't help herself. Even if she's using him, she *has* to make him come.

The leather mask lies on the seat next to me. My truck is parked in the back corner of her apartment lot again, with a clear view of her building. I rub my dick through my pants. I shouldn't be getting off on her sucking another man's dick, but I don't care. It's not like he'll live for much longer. She won't either.

The hookup pulls out, coming into his palm. Rae yanks his hand forward, licking up his white spunk. He deflates into exhaustion. She keeps licking.

I gotta— he spins toward the bathroom. Rae slyly smiles at the camera, like she knows I'm watching. She flips through his wallet, pulling out a handful of bills. A few seconds later, he comes out of the bathroom, drying his hands on his pants.

He starts, *Did you want to get a burger—*

I've got this podcast I'm working on, she says. *Thanks, though!*

I click off the phone's screen then watch the stairs. The conquest exits, whistling with his hands in his pockets. He gazes up at her bedroom window like he's lost in a daze. I understand that. It's not every day you meet a woman like Rae.

He drives off.

It takes about an hour for Rae's bedroom windows to darken. Then I check her surveillance feed to make sure she's asleep. When she hasn't stirred in twenty minutes, I head up to her apartment. A neighbor with their work apron on waves to me on the communal stairs.

"What's up?" I ask.

"Nothing much; you?" he asks.

"Same."

Once I'm alone outside of her front door, I slip the mask over my face, zipping the back closure to tighten the leather, then I unzip the opening on my lips. I use my key and slowly shut the door behind me.

Inside, I keep my boots inaudible. Snores drift from her bedroom.

I creep toward her.

Rae lies on her side, her ass sticking out of the comforter. Her oversized shirt bunches around her stomach, her thong pressing against that sliver of pink flesh.

A black circle on her purse catches my eye. It's darker than the rest of the bag. I lean closer. The spot is no bigger than a button.

A camera lens.

I don't have a video feed to this lens, which must mean it's a different brand that uses different software. But it's the same purse Rae brings to the Galloway House.

Rae stirs, rubbing her eyes. Within seconds, she's back to snoring.

I turn back to the hidden lens on her purse. The little girl must think she has so much dirt on me, but she has no idea that I have her password. Most people use the same one for every login. I quickly scan her laptop and find a surveillance app I overlooked before. The login works for it. Later, I'll collect that footage, and I'll be able to prove our mutual depravity. She thinks she'll be able to blackmail me, but we're cut from the same cloth.

I smile at the lens, my lips framed by the zipper's teeth. I hope it's recording now.

Turning back to the sleeping girl, I run my fingertips along her pussy so gently, a chill runs down *my* spine. I'm not a soft man by any means, but the idea of being here—right where I can fuck and kill her while she sleeps—is invigorating, even for someone like me. I pull her thong to the side, exposing her bare skin, and those pussy layers stack up. Curly hair. Supple skin. Ripe and waiting.

I stick a gloved finger between her pussy lips. Irritation bubbles inside of me; there's no skin-to-skin contact, but I'll have that before the experiment is over.

She groans. That annoyance drifts away. My bulge grows.

I should stop. If I want to keep Rae in the dark about my ability to get inside of her apartment, I should leave now. She'll never know I was here.

But there's something about *letting* her know that gets to me.

I stuff my finger in, then pull it out with a slick pop. The juices crawl down my glove, and I lick them off: sour and fresh, mixed with leather. I don't desire pussy or cock; I crave being the predator. I need the *threat.* I relish in the power of forcing myself onto a person, even as they die. And yet there's something about tasting *her* that makes me lick my lips.

It'll be a shame to kill her one day. She has so much potential; all she needs is a little push. Inevitably though, I'll lose interest. I always do.

But I'm not bored yet.

I kneel down, stuffing my mouth to her pussy, my masked nose in her ass crack, rubbing against her hole. My fat tongue flickers across her folds, and the zipper scrapes against her slit. She wiggles her hips—the zipper must be tickling her—and she grinds her ass into my face, her arousal smearing my mask and lips.

The fucking cunt on this woman.

I grab her hips, pulling her to me, feasting on those delicious, wanton, slutty little holes. Her cunt is slick, slopping against me, and I thrust my hips forward, knocking into the bed frame, jostling her in bed. I don't stop. I lick up, tracing her pussy lips up to her ass crack, then I tongue-fuck her dark hole.

She moans. Rolls over. Her lips smack.

I could go right now. *I should.*

Or I could let her know that I'll always be watching her.

I stand over her then, positioning myself so that I'm the first thing she sees. Her eyelids flicker open. She blinks, then focuses on the mesh screens covering my eyes.

She screams.

I pin her to the bed with my weight, pinching her nose shut and covering her mouth. Her eyes are frantic. She whimpers into my palm.

"You're going to listen to me very carefully, Rae," I say. I let go of her nose and mouth, and instead, I grab her neck, choking her the way she tried to get her conquest to choke her a few hours ago. "You belong to me. Every time you give someone else pleasure. Every time someone else touches you. It's only because *I* am letting them fuck you. Do you understand me?"

Her eyelids flutter. I tighten my grip. She nods frantically.

"Then say it," I growl.

"I'm yours," she sputters.

She pulls at my hands, but the little girl is no match for me, and she never will be. Her eyes bulge, and my dick strains against my pants. I thrust against her. There's too much fucking fabric between us. I squeeze harder until she only has seconds left.

"You're going to kill for me one day," I say in a low voice.

"You're going to die for me too. And fuck, I'm going to enjoy every second of it."

Her eyes roll to white, her muscles loosening. Unconscious.

I smirk at the camera lens on her purse, then I move quickly, leaving her alone. Once I'm on the communal stairwell, I rip off my mask and stuff it in my pocket. This time, I don't run into any neighbors on the stairs.

In the truck, I gaze at her building. She stands on the top stair near the rail. Her eyes glaze over my truck as she adjusts her pajama pants. I'm too far away. She has no idea that it's me.

She goes back inside.

I sniff. The scent of her cunt lingers on my lips, but it's not sex that I want. It's blood. *Her blood.*

But I'm not going to kill her yet.

I download a few hookup apps, using the same info I copied from her surveillance programs. After two failed attempts, the login for the third app works.

Are you free? I want to fuck now, she typed.

I click on the conquest's profile, then download his default photo and use a reverse image search to find him.

The conquest—her hookup, DrummerBoy420—lives in Pahrump, but his picture is uploaded to one of the Las Vegas resort websites. A cabana boy for rich and wild cougars. He's young and fit. He must make a good chunk of change at the resort. He's Rae's age, and I'm way fucking older than her.

Aww, what is it? my mother's voice asks. *Are you jealous, little boy? Jealous because she asked that man to come over and not you?*

I'm not jealous of this man for sticking his dick inside of that little girl. That would mean that I'm insecure about my place in this world, but I know, without a doubt, that *no one* will ever be able to get to Rae like I can.

He's just a dick she's using for a cheap thrill.

I put the key in the ignition and start the truck. The engine roars to life, loud enough that Rae can likely hear it in her bedroom.

The mind is a funny thing. When it has no connection to the people it sees, the suffering makes no difference.

But if Rae *knows* the man that's dying, it will be different for her. It's why I love killing people when they're together. They fight for each other's survival, then dissolve into dying defeat, and it's like taking a breath of fresh air after being choked unconscious.

When the time is right, I'll kill DrummerBoy420 while Rae watches. The need for survival, the fear of death, and the thrill of murder will rush between her legs. I'll force her to endure that inevitable lust.

She won't be able to deny that we're the same.

Chapter 11

Rae

It's late—almost midnight—and the Galloway House blocks the moonlight. The tattered curtains are stagnant in the upstairs windows. I try to picture my father standing there, peering at the empty desert. Did he bring my mother here? It would have been risky, bringing his mistress to his home, especially if his wife could have caught him. But there would have been a thrill to it too. The chance of getting caught and watching the chaos unfold. *That* feels familiar. I'll have to ask my mother about that.

I unlock the padlock with my copy of Ned's key and stuff the bulky lock near a cactus bush. It's late—hours past the mall's closing time—but you can never be too careful about who's watching.

I stand in the entryway and shut the front door behind me. I should go upstairs and see if there are any clues about my father's life and death, but Crave won't be up there.

He's the reason why I'm here.

In the basement, I don't hide my footsteps this time. The stairs creak. Crave leans against the wall, a dim light hanging from the ceiling above him, illuminating his rugged form and his eyes shrouded in black cloth.

My body tenses, every muscle ready for anything Crave throws at me.

A need fills me. What will he do next?

Is that what Crave is to me? A sexual fantasy?

No—he's more valuable than that.

I swing my purse around, making sure that the lens is aimed at him.

"You know I record everything in my apartment, right?" I ask. He doesn't know that the cameras don't film while I'm sleeping. "I have footage of you breaking in. I know you looked at my purse."

He clicks his tongue in amusement, like this is a game between the two of us. My stomach squeezes, each butterfly crushed into a pulp.

"Always the blackmail," he says. "There are worse things. You should just kill me."

Kill him?

I shake my head automatically. "I don't kill people. I'm not—"

"What?" he cuts me off. "You're not *what,* exactly? You're not stupid enough to kill? You're not smart enough? Or are you too good to get your hands dirty? Are you too dumb to get away with it?"

His lips pull apart, revealing gleaming teeth. "You're not like me," he murmurs. "That's what you were going to say, wasn't it? But you'd kill in a heartbeat. You're just scared of getting caught."

I roll my eyes and exhale. "That's right, Crave. I'm *not* like you."

"You wish you were like me." He grins. "Tell me something, little girl. If you found your 'father's killer'"—he lifts his fingers in the air, mocking me with air quotes—"what would you do to him? If you had the chance to kill the man who stole your family from you, would you do it?"

"All I want is to find out what actually happened to my father," I scoff. "This isn't about murdering anyone."

Crave's boots clunk on the floor, each step reverberating in my chest, his shadow creeping over me like a burned layer of skin. I hold my ground and force myself to stay strong.

"You really think Michael Hall is—" Crave stops, laughing to himself. "No—you think Michael Hall *was* your father?"

I scrunch my nose. "Why wouldn't he be my father?"

"Did your mother show you a picture of him, or are you doing all of this on hearsay?" His voice gains pitch slightly; he's entertained by his own words. I ball my fists at my sides. He goes on: "You know, your bitch mother must be a liar, keeping secrets too. A whore who spreads her legs for anyone who can make her feel something. Like mother, like daughter."

I don't care if he calls my mother a bitch. It's a word. It doesn't change anything.

But why does Crave think *I'm* a liar? Does he know about Vegas? About getting fired?

How could he?

I search his bondage mask. My mind travels back to the night I was fired.

Who the fuck is Michael? I screamed.

Your father, my mother whispered.

Was my mother lying to me?

No. Crave is wrong. He's just messing with my head so that I question everything. I know I'm right. For my entire life, I've wanted to know who my father is, and my mother kept it from me like she was holding a treat over my head. Now that I'm this close to finding him, I'm not going to back down.

I'm not a violent person. I'm aware of my size disadvantage compared to Crave, and yet I can't stop imagining punching him in the face. Tearing off that stupid leather mask. Bruising his eyes until they're puffy and red. Laughing in his face and saying, *Who is the little girl now?*

"Do you even have a DNA sample?" Crave asks.

I grit my teeth. "What are you saying?"

"Your mother probably didn't even know who she was fucking. Just like you."

And that's the last straw.

I race toward him, my fists swinging. I connect with his chin, but then he darts to the side. I stumble forward. My shoulder impacts the wall, and he grabs me from behind, pinning me to the wall's surface.

"Feisty," Crave teases, his motor oil scent surrounding me. "Is your mother like that too? Or did you get that from your father?"

I swing my neck around as much as I can and spit into his face. The glob of saliva lands on his leather cheek, clumping like an egg white. He snarls.

"Fuck you," I hiss.

His fingers curl into my ribs, digging between the bones. Pain spreads across my body, and I swear it's like he's stabbing my lungs. I curl into myself, and he throws me to the floor. I flip over, struggling to crawl, the cement biting into my knees. He grabs my foot and pulls me back, my shirt bunching up under me. The brittle floor scrapes my skin.

"What the fuck?" I scream.

He climbs on top of me, twisting our bodies until he's on top, holding me in place. Metal cuffs—where the fuck did he get those?—bite into my wrists. He locks them above my head. He stands up, and I roll over, pushing myself up on my bound wrists—

Whump! His steel-toed boot smacks the side of my stomach. I cough. He steps on my fingers, and the pain surges to my temples. I wail.

Leather and fabric slide against skin. Is he taking off his mask? I quickly look up.

He changes into a new pair of black gloves. I pant. Frantic nerves swell in my head. I have no idea what will happen next.

"Roll over," he says.

"What am I, a fucking dog?" I snap.

"Roll. The. Fuck. Over."

"You're standing on my fingers."

He lifts his boot. Blood rushes to my fingertips, filling me with warmth. I start to twist my body, complying with his orders. Then I push myself up again, ready to run for the stairs—

He grabs my stomach, pulling me back. Metal pins spike into each point of contact with him, and I squeal. He turns me around, manipulating me until I'm on the ground underneath him again.

"The hell is that?" I cry.

"Spread your legs," he demands.

My neck stiffens. It's stupid to refuse the demands of a murderer, but I know he won't kill me. If he was going to, he would have done it last night, or the first night, or even ten minutes ago, but he hasn't yet. I shake my head furiously. Crave grips my thighs, pulling them apart. Thin spikes breach the sheer fabric of my stockings, jabbing my skin.

"Spread your fucking legs," he murmurs. "Or I will bleed you dry right here."

I whimper. My legs spread. My brain is empty, stuck on survival. On primal instincts. On lust.

Get him to fuck you, I tell myself. *If he fucks you, then you'll be safe.*

But how does that even make sense?

A blinding light flashes. I squint my eyes. After a few seconds, my pupils adjust.

Crave holds my phone over me, the flashlight on the maximum setting. The bright bulb illuminates his mesh, turning his eyes into hollow globes.

He rips off my stockings and thong with his free hand, leaving the skirt bunched up at my waist, then he lowers the flashlight, illuminating my pussy. I bring my legs together, and Crave smacks my thighs with those spiked gloves.

"What? You don't like it when you're not in control, little girl?" He tilts his head. "You only like fucking people when you can use *them.* But you can't use me. I'm the one who uses you. I'm the one who owns you now. Isn't that right, little girl?"

My cheeks flame. "I don't *use* people."

"No, you just steal from them."

Chills cover me from head to toe. How does Crave know that? Has he been watching me without my knowledge?

He unzips his pants, stroking his pierced cock with the same needled gloves, the metal jewelry shifting across his hard length. My mouth salivates, my pussy muscles clenching.

He wants me so badly that he's handcuffed me. He's kneeling on the ground and using a flashlight to see my pussy.

I'm powerless and powerful at the same time.

You're fucking crazy, I think to myself. *You can't be turned on by something like this. He's fucking with you. Using you. Tricking you. You don't hurt people. He does! He's hurting you right now. Messing with your head.*

I have to be angry. He has no right to do this.

"Are you stalking me now?" I hiss.

"Me stalking you?" He drops the phone, and the flashlight beams toward the ceiling, giving us extra light. "Is that what you call those surveillance cameras you put up in your own apartment?" I twist to the side, refusing to face him. He continues, "What, little girl? Are you afraid a big bad man will steal from you, just like you stole from him?"

He leans down, licking my clit, slurping it up. The sensation sends shivers up and down my body. He lifts up, still leering at my pussy.

"God, what a selfish little cunt," he murmurs. "You're the one who fucked those idiot men and stole their credit cards, who doesn't see people for anything more than objects. But you're an object too, aren't you, baby? You're just a little toy to be fucked and broken by a man like me. And one day, when I have no use for you, I'll throw you away. Kill you like the rest of them. And you'll love it, won't you? An object discarded. At least your death will give me some amusement."

Desire incinerates all the logic in my brain, replacing it with tension. At the same time, my blood pressure rises.

"Fuck you," I say.

"You may hate me, Rae. But this little thing?" He pinches my pussy folds between those spiked gloves. The sharp pain jolts through me. "This meaty little thing needs me. Wants me. Yearns for me." He traces a finger down my slit. "You're sopping wet, little girl."

"Go fuck yourself."

"That's what this pussy wants, isn't it? A little cunt like yours, desperate for my rough hands." He adjusts his touch, pinching a new area of skin, and the pain trickles through me again. "You're so used to controlling everything, dictating every consensual thing in the bedroom, that now that you're with me—a man who takes what he wants—you can't help it, can you? You're so wet, it's disgusting."

My insides churn with so much molten rage and desire that I can barely think.

A spiked leather finger pushes inside of me and scrapes against my flesh. He's cutting my insides. My brain is blinded by swirls of white and black shapes, a Rorschach Test changing inside of me. Right to wrong. Pain to pleasure.

This is wrong, I think. *Wrong. So wrong. You're going to get hurt. You're going to—*

"You can't do this," I cry. "What if I get an infection? What if—"

His finger curls, those tiny daggers of pain increasing with intensity, the pressure mounting as he hits that tender spot. Warmth floods my veins, my toes curling.

"Do you think I fucking care?" he snarls.

The needled thumb teases my clit, and his inserted finger massages my inner nerves.

"Please," I whisper. My voice is weak. I don't know what I'm trying to ask for.

"Admit you want to kill people, and I'll make this all go away," he says in a low voice. "Say that you want to kill me. To kill strangers. That you want to kill simply to see what it's like. Admit that you're a killer, Rae, just like me. You just haven't had the opportunity yet."

Fire bursts through me, my body tightening in anger. I don't *want* to say that. The phone is still there, and the camera device on my purse—wherever it is—is recording this.

My face is boiling. I'm overwhelmed.

I don't want to kill him. I want to him to fuck me.

I don't want to kill him. I want him to hurt me.

I don't want to kill him. I want to destroy him.

I don't want to kill him.

I don't—

"I don't want to kill you!" I shout. "I wouldn't risk my life for your death. You're not worth it."

His laughter is instant, raw, deep, and it quakes in my chest. He inserts a second finger into my pussy, and I squirm, those needles digging into my flesh.

"All right," he says. "We'll do it my way instead."

"What?"

He inserts a third gloved finger. My core muscles spasm, and I swear he's scooping out my pulp.

"The fuck is that?" I squeal.

"These are vampire gloves," he says. "They aren't meant to be used like this, but I knew you'd enjoy them."

He takes his other hand, pinching my folds around his three fingers. The needles pierce my skin.

I bite my tongue, tears stinging my eyes. "I—"

"Such a meaty thing, isn't it?" he mutters. "It's surprising you don't get embarrassed by it. Or is that why you're so desperate? You thrust your meat hole out onto any dick that will fuck you."

Summoning the anger inside of me, I thrust my hips forward.

"At least I don't hide my average genitals behind metal," I snap.

His tongue snakes across his teeth. Winged-creatures flutter in my head, spinning in circles, trapped in a cage.

"Oh, little girl," he says. "My sweet, sweet little girl. My dick may be average, but you liked the way I ripped your throat apart, didn't you? So much that you rubbed your ugly little cunt on my boot."

He adds a fourth finger. The spikes are smashing against my inner flesh. The sensation is full and sharp, the pressure splitting me at the seams. Liquid drips down my face, and I can't tell if it's tears or sweat. A bead of something streams down between my thighs, and I lift my head. Is it blood? Arousal? Sweat? I can't see what it is. Crave's four fingers, bundled together, are all I see.

He's going to fist me with those gloves on, isn't he?

"Get off of me." I squirm, shoving my feet toward him, but my legs spread wider.

"This giant meat hole didn't even have to warm up to take my four fingers. But we can't have your pussy blood staining my custom gloves." He salivates, then spits a glob into my wet, gaping hole. Tears blur my vision. He shushes me. "It's okay, baby. You can make this all go away if you just admit who you really are."

I close my eyes, willing this to disappear. To wake up with relief that this is just some fucked-up, wet dream.

But I like it.

"I bet this used-up pussy can take more," he says. I open my eyes. Pleasure flames inside of me while pain radiates from my core to my head. My whole body quakes. He readies the final finger for insertion.

"You can't fit that thing inside of me!" I scream.

"I can. And I will," he says. "Relax, or this will hurt."

He pulls his fingers back enough to add his thumb. I suck in a breath. I count in my head to distract myself from the pain. I quickly lose track.

I could tell him what he wants to hear. I can admit that I want to kill too. Words don't mean anything. They're just sounds. It doesn't mean I will actually kill someone.

His knuckles push through, crowning over my pelvic bone, his wrist bruising my hard muscle. My brain expands, every drop of blood inside of me rushing to the surface of my skin. My vision goes white. A garbled noise, something like a grunt and a cry, bursts through me.

"Is it in?" I wail. "Oh god, please, let it be in—"

"Look at how easy that was," he laughs. "What a good little cunt, taking a fist like this. No wonder you're so desperate for attention that you fuck any man who takes an interest in you. They probably can't feel anything."

That's *not* true. He knows it. Men *like* fucking me.

Don't they?

"I hate you," I scream.

"They'll never know you like I do," Crave says. "They'll never be able to take you like this. You need someone like me. A killer who doesn't care about what you want. A maniac psychopath who will rip you apart and force you to endure every fucking second of it."

He leans forward, his lips so close to mine, I can smell his scent. Burnt. Oil. Musk. The slightly sweet taste of his breath.

"You're mine, Rae." He moves his fist, his knuckles like insects eating me alive from the inside out, the sensation stunning me.

Is it pleasure? Pain?

"You're not a person; you're a possession. My fucking possession," he says. "Nothing more than my flesh. My blood. An object to use however I want."

The pleasure seeps through me, and I convulse. A contorting body, muscles spasming, squeezing around his gloved, spiky fist, my body pulsing with fire. He bellows, his howls like the cracks of a cannon. My mind can't concentrate. I am pure sensation.

Eventually, the tension recedes.

Crave removes his fist slowly. As his knuckles caress the opening, I whimper, curling into myself. The spiked gloves *should* hurt, but I'm so over-sensitized that I don't feel anything.

I turn to my side. I wasn't supposed to like that.

He pulls my hips until I'm lying on my back again. Then he pulls out his dick and fucks my gaping hole. I can barely feel him.

"You're so goddamn loose," he says, still pounding into me. "A sloppy little cunt."

His head throws back at those words, and his cock explodes inside of me. He switches hastily to his hands and knees and licks between my thighs, eating each drop of depravity that leaks out between us. My hips twitch forward. It feels good. Almost soothing.

When he lifts himself up, clear fluid and spots of red mark his lips. My cum, his cum, my blood, his saliva.

He spits it all into my mouth. Without thinking, I swallow it. His lips part, his tongue skimming across his bottom lip. Heat rushes between my legs.

Why does this turn me on?

He unlocks the handcuffs, and reflexively, I curl into myself again.

"Don't hide from me," he growls.

"Go fuck yourself."

He grabs my face, pulling me until our eyes are locked. Maybe it's my eyes adjusting to the darkness, but I swear I can see those black, cavernous eyes staring down at me, warning me with a single look. I'm so lost in his gaze that I'm numb to the pressure of his needled fingertips on my cheeks. My stomach rolls with nerves.

"You may have video footage against me," he says. "But you want me, don't you?"

Without hesitating, I nod. I *do* want him. I know I do. He's the only person I can't figure out. And maybe that's all he is—a challenge, a game, a puzzle—but I can't get enough of him.

Crave stands, then goes to the corner of the room, removing a small water bottle with a broken seal. He lifts it to the dim light. The liquid is tinted yellow, like an electrolyte drink. I doubt Crave wants me to stay hydrated though.

"What is it?" I ask.

He hands the bottle to me. "Poison."

"So this is your way of killing me?"

He snickers. I roll my eyes. I take the bottle, holding it up to the light to see the toxins.

It's a clear, yellow-tinted liquid. Completely unthreatening.

"I'm not going to drink that," I say.

"You wouldn't use a knife. Not a baseball bat. Not even a gun," he says. He grabs my chin, forcing me to look at him again. "But poison? That's more like you. Watching someone die on the inside. The agonizing waiting period of knowing that you didn't have to lift a finger. They'll disintegrate before your eyes, giving you their power."

He closes his mouth zipper, then ascends the stairs, his shadow disappearing. I study the bottle, my nervous system in overdrive. An overwhelming urge burns inside of me. I want to tell him to stop. To explain what he means. To confirm my own thoughts about whether or not he's right.

Would I poison someone?

Would I enjoy watching them die?

I imagine my mother drinking from the water bottle, watching her fall to the ground in the hotel lobby, the tailored staff members rushing to her side. Would she call out for me with her last breath? Would she suspect I had poisoned her, the daughter of a killer?

I imagine Ned drinking it too. Collapsing in the food court. Death by food poisoning. *Literally.*

By the time I center myself, the stairs are empty. I hastily stuff my underwear and stockings into my purse, fix my skirt, and rush to the front and back doors on the ground floor. Cacti and rock formations loom in the darkness. The stars light the sand for every nocturnal predator, but there's hardly enough visibility for people like me.

The desert is empty again. Crave is gone, and yet, I can feel him staring back at me.

I don't want to kill Ned or my mother. That's not me.

But as I look into the darkness, I imagine it.

Chapter 12

Rae

The next day, I stow my purse in the boutique break room, then I meet Penny in the food court. My shift doesn't start for a while, which is a good thing. My brain is filled with fog from last night's chaos. A bubbly, know-it-all teenager will distract me from those thoughts…maybe.

"You're ten minutes late," Penny says. "We barely have enough time to go over everything."

"Sorry," I mumble. "I was—"

Penny launches into an explanation about the town's crime history. I try to listen, but my thoughts wander. I think about what Crave said: *Watching someone die on the inside. They'll disintegrate before your eyes, giving you their power.*

I've always liked power.

I imagine killing Penny with the poison, telling her it's an electrolyte mix. Could I take her life?

No. I couldn't. I'm not a killer, and besides, most criminals get caught, and I don't think my mother could save me from prison.

Penny drones on, and I gawk at the surveillance cameras on the ceiling of the mall. Black orbs with red lights, like scorpions waiting for the right time to strike.

I'm almost positive Crave has access to the cameras in my house, and I get this feeling that Crave has been watching me for a long time, longer than when I first laid eyes on his masked face in the Galloway House.

It's not like Crave has anything on me. Ned doesn't know that I sometimes hook up with strangers, but it's not like Ned has any right to be mad about it. He eats me out and buys me lunch sometimes. We're not in a relationship.

I should do something about the cameras though. Change my password. Uninstall them. *Something.*

I know I won't do anything.

Maybe I like knowing that Crave is watching me.

Jerking off to me.

Examining me.

I shake myself out of those thoughts; Penny doesn't notice me zoning out, but I need to focus. Crave isn't my main concern; my father's murder is.

"So you've done everything?" I interrupt her.

She raises a brow. "What do you mean?"

"You've interviewed everyone. You've talked to random people. You've looked at the evidence."

"Well"—she shrugs—"I haven't looked at *the* evidence. My dad won't let me. But I have—"

She explodes into a list of the people she's interviewed. I can't concentrate though.

If she's already done everything, then what can we do now?

If the killer is still around on the anniversary of these murders, then he'll want to revisit his victory site, right? That's what the TV shows and books say. He'll possibly want to relive it too.

"What if we do something on the thirteenth?" I ask.

She wrinkles her nose. "Like what?"

I tap my lips and scan the room. A group of teenagers laughs as they go into the antique store.

I turn back to Penny. "A party."

"A party?"

"Hear me out." I put a hand on my chest. "What if we host a party on the thirteenth to bring people into the house? We can say it's a haunted house or something, and talk about the murder-suicides and *our* theories. If the murderer is still around, he'll want to be there, right? To see the power his legacy still holds over the town. He may even want to correct us."

My mind buzzes forward. It's a crazy idea. Crave will *have* to attend the party to see what we do and say in his territory. And maybe, just maybe, I'll get to see him without his mask.

My heart thuds in my chest, my eyes wild. At some messed-up point, this stopped being about my father and started being about Crave.

It's about both of them, I tell myself. *My father and Crave. They're intertwined. Crave represents the house, and that's where my father was killed.*

"Why didn't I think of that?" Penny smacks her head. "The killer would be too proud to let it go, especially if we taunt them with incorrect details. Most serial killers are overly confident and proud. They wouldn't let us say the wrong thing."

"Exactly!" I grab her hands, clutching them in excitement. "We could set up the decorations like the murders. It would add authenticity and bring people in—"

"And the murderer would want to act it out!"

"What if *we* act it out?" I shout. "We can show the way we think it happened. Whoever it is, they'll be too proud to sit back and let us dictate their victory. They'd *have* to step in."

"I can interview more people!"

"I can too," I say. "I'm not that good at it, but I always get these feelings about people. And if I get an instinct, you can interview them too—"

"And the killer will have some sort of signal, right? A hint that leads us to the truth."

"Exactly!"

Penny spirals into ideas for the party, and I take mental notes of the things we need to do: clean, decorate, invite.

And make sure Ned is on board.

A sliver of wonder throbs inside of me, burrowing into my waist like a tick. If Crave shows up without his mask—if we taunt him, and he's the killer—will he expose himself?

Crave could be my father's killer, *or* Crave can help us figure out the truth. If Penny and I dress up like victims of the murders, we could get Crave to get dressed up too. He could even come in his mask. No one would suspect him. He could use his expertise to help me find the killer.

An arm wraps around my shoulders. I startle.

"Hey, beautiful," Ned says. He nods to his niece. "Hey, Penny."

"I'm beautiful too, thanks," she says.

"Of course you are." He gives her a quick hug. "What are you two scheming up now?"

"It's not a scheme. It's a plan, actually," Penny corrects. Then she tells him our idea, leaving out the location of the party. Ned smiles patiently. He must already know what we're going to ask him. My body goes rigid as old doubts about Ned come rushing back.

What if Ned's patience is an act? A way to trick people into thinking he's innocent?

What if Ned is my father's killer?

What if Ned *is* Crave?

Crave and Ned are around the same height, but they smell different. They have similar body shapes, sure, but Ned wouldn't do those things. He's the kind of person who sets up rodent repellents instead of lethal traps.

But Ned has never let me near his cock. He always claims it's about my pleasure. Could he be hiding piercings down there?

"Well…" Penny elbows me. "Ask him."

"Ask me what?" Ned asks.

I scan Ned's face. His expression is well kept, like he knows he belongs here. As if he owns this mall, this town, and everyone in it.

A killer would be that confident too.

A ball of tension forms at the base of my spine, and I spit out the words before I can reason with myself. "Can we host the party at the Galloway House? We'll clean it. Decorate it. Make sure it's safe. But we still need your approval."

His nostrils flare slightly, letting out some air. "That place is a wreck."

"Come on," Penny says. "We'll clean it."

"We'll take care of everything," I add. "We just need the key to the padlock and your trust in us."

Ned inspects me, his blue eyes full of trepidation and longing. He rubs the back of his neck like he wants to help us, even if he knows he shouldn't.

"Uncle Ned," Penny whines.

"Shouldn't we let it go?" he asks. "That stuff happened a long time ago."

I gnaw on my tongue. I should tell Ned about my connection to the case, and maybe even ask him to help me retrieve evidence from the police department, but I don't want Penny to know that Michael Hall is my father. I want this to be about the crime; that way, she'll be more willing to help me.

But we need Ned's approval to do this. It won't work without him.

And I need to see Crave in the light, even if he's still wearing a mask.

"This could really help the podcast," I say.

"The truth deserves to be told," Penny says.

Ned studies me, then Penny. She must be like a daughter to him. Her father—his brother—is a cop, and even *she* wants to find out the truth.

Ned smiles. "All right."

"Really?" Penny asks.

"Really," he says. He winks at us. "I knew you two would be trouble."

"Good things are always trouble," I tease.

"We have a lot of planning to do," Penny says. She turns back to me. "Let's meet again. When do you work? I can meet you here before or after your shifts."

We figure out tomorrow's meeting, then Penny gives Ned a hug and bounds toward the exit. I race after Ned, tapping on his shoulder before he gets to his office. I clench my jaw until my cheeks redden, feigning embarrassment.

"Penny's father is a police officer, right?" I ask.

"Yeah, why?" Ned says.

"Do you think your brother would let me have a DNA sample from the Michael Hall case?"

Ned's lips pinch together. *Crave is just messing with your head,* my brain reasons, but I can't help it; the words are already out there.

"I just want to make sure, you know?" I explain. "A paternity test or whatever."

"A paternity test?"

His eyes trail off, studying the gray tile. Melancholy pulls down his lips, like he finally understands why I'm so obsessed with this case. Why I can't let my father be a killer. Why I have to prove my mother wrong, or I'll never forgive myself.

"And you don't want to ask Penny?" he confirms.

I shake my head. "She doesn't need to know about my reasons for all of this."

His chin bobs, his eyes glossy with thought. "My brother doesn't really do things like that, but I'll see what I can do."

"Are you sure? I don't want to impose," I say, regurgitating the line I know is expected of me.

Ned takes my hand. "You deserve to know."

I blink, emptiness creeping up my chest. I squeeze his hand back, then let my hands fall to my sides.

"You're too kind," I say with a flat voice.

It's true though; Ned is *too* kind. I never trust people who are nice. There's always another intention they're hiding beneath the surface. I know, because that's what I do too. And it's probably why I like Crave. He's a killer. He lets his violence embrace every word and action. You know exactly what to expect. On the other hand, you never know when a nice person will turn on you.

"Anyway, I've got to go check on the food court," Ned says.

"Work. That thing. Right," I joke.

"I'll catch you later. I'll talk to my brother and let you know."

"You're the best."

For the second time today, I wonder about Ned. The idea doesn't make sense at all, but I can't stop myself from wondering. Could Ned be Crave?

They're the same height. And Ned could change his voice under the mask. But the cock piercings don't add up. Ned hides his dick, sure, always putting his sexual attention on me, but I'm certain he would never do something like that to his genitals.

Instead of heading to the boutique, I wander inside of the antique store. Dust floats in the air, the stale scent of old books swaddling me in their perfume. Rusted gadgets. Tin cigarette cases. Picture frames. Used decks of cards from the casinos. Even a vintage chicken ranch sign.

I don't know what I'm doing here though. Am I shopping for props? Decorations?

A white nightgown, lined with lace, hangs from the top of a booth. A pink bow embellishes the neck, with little flowers embroidered into the lining. I trace my fingers over the nightgown.

My mind fills with the leaked crime scene photos.

Miranda Hall hanging in the noose. Blood leaking down her thighs. Her nightgown had little pink flowers too.

This nightgown could have been hers.

I can wear the nightgown and pretend to be the strangled wife, Miranda Hall. My fingertips tremble over the bow. It's a simple material reminiscent of that time. When things were softer, kinder.

Or maybe they weren't.

"Ain't you supposed to be at the boutique right now?" a hoarse Southern voice asks.

I swing around. The mall cop ogles me. A clean, soapy scent, heavy with cologne, permeates from him, like he's covering up his gym stink. His round eyes narrow at me like I'm the scum under his gym shoes. His tongue runs across his bottom lip, reminding me of a hissing snake. My neck stiffens.

The fucking creep.

"My shift doesn't start for another hour," I say. It's a lie—it starts in ten minutes—but he doesn't need to know that. "I didn't know mall cops also kept tabs on the employees."

"I keep tabs for Ned," he mutters. "He's a good man, and I know you ain't faithful to him. I've seen your hookup profile."

I huff through my nostrils. Like that matters. Everyone has a hookup profile these days; the mall cop is just making an educated guess. And even if he *has* seen my hookup profile and I haven't seen his, then that means I denied his sexual advances. The mall cop is jealous.

"Ned knows too," I lie.

"That so?" he says. "Makes sense. Ned knows a child like you is an easy fix then."

A child like me?

I ball my fists. The mall cop is older than me, yes, but I'm not a *child.* I'm a fucking adult. I know what I'm doing, and I own my mistakes. It's part of why I was so irritated by my mother's reaction when I was fired. *You're just like him,* she had said, as if my dead father was the sole reason for blame, when she had watched me steal from guests for years before I was caught.

At the end of the day, this mall cop—a *mall* cop, not even a real police officer—is in his forties, working at the mall. He's the one who's no better than a child. A teenager could get his job.

"Ned would fire you if I asked him to," I say.

"Do it then," he says. His eye twitches, almost like he's trying to wink, and I scowl in disgust. "Get me fired, and I'll make sure he knows about RaeRae69."

I roll my eyes, though inside, my stomach is rolling. That is my username.

I don't know if Ned would fire the mall cop for me. It's not like I have proof that the mall cop is harassing me—my dumb ass left my purse in the boutique break room—but the mall cop could have screenshots of my profile. If he knows my username, there's a good chance that he has real proof of my escapades.

Would that bother Ned?

No. Ned wouldn't accuse me of anything; he knows we're not dating.

And yet I wouldn't be surprised if his feelings were still hurt.

"It's so nice to see you again, but I should get going now. What was your name again, *officer?*" I ask with fake kindness.

"Officer Gaines," he says. He puts his hands on his hips right near his stun gun, proudly reminding me that he's armed. What a fucking joke. "You best remember that."

I laugh, ignoring his little weapon. It's not even a taser.

His tongue flicks over his lips. I hold back a grimace. I imagine the mall cop drinking that poison bottle Crave gave me. Maybe the mall cop would have a coughing fit, and I'd be there, right by his side, to offer him more of the "sports drink." *Here,* I'd say. *It'll make you feel better.*

Then the sad little mall cop would crawl on the floor, his lungs and throat closing in on him, desperate for an antidote. I'd know that it was me, *all me,* who took his last breath. I'd sit on his face, and he'd gasp into my pussy. He'd be suffocated by a so-called child.

I walk past the mall cop to the cashier at the front of the antique store, taking the nightgown with me.

Maybe I am more like Crave than I'd like to admit.

Chapter 13

Crave

That night, I wait in the corner of the basement. Rae's shoulders peel back, stiffer than usual, an attempt to make herself bigger than she is.

She must be trying to get ahead again. Clever girl.

I tug the metal zipper on the front of my mask. Rae's eyes gloss over, entranced by my lips.

"Hello, little girl," I say.

A subtle breath swells in her lungs, a hint at her desire. It must be odd to hear those words, "little girl." A woman without a father. Small. Taken care of. But not in a way she imagined. Not in the way she wanted.

Each finger, one by one, slowly loosens on the strap of her purse. She slides her grip down so that her hand rests below the camera lens, the recording eye staying fixed on me.

"The mall owner is going to get the DNA evidence for me," she says. "I'm going to get it tested."

"Oh?"

"It'll prove that Michael Hall is my father."

I vaguely consider questioning why she thinks Ned can get her evidence like that, but the interesting part is that she thinks she's ahead of me.

Still, I can't resist fucking with her.

"Good for you," I say.

She crosses her arms. "What's that supposed to mean?"

"I said those things about your mother being a slut to mess with you," I say. "You let it get to your head. I don't know shit about you or your mother. Why would I know whether or not Michael Hall is your father?"

Her eyelids flutter. Her lips part, opening wider to say something, then they pinch shut.

I grin. I'm cracking her facade, one chip at a time.

"You're such a dick," she says.

"And yet you keep coming back here," I say. "So tell me, little girl. What's the real reason you're here?"

She pauses for a moment, carefully choosing her words. "Like I said, I'm going to prove you wrong."

"Always proving people wrong," I tsk. "You want to prove that I'm wrong about your blood relations to a dead man?" My boots thud forward. Her arms cling to her sides. I hammer my weight into each step, my presence booming. "But there's something else, isn't there?"

She stays firmly in place, holding her ground. My boots echo through the basement. Her eyes trace me as she figures out her next move.

I stop right in front of her. I'm so close, I can breathe on her. She licks her lips.

"We're hosting a murder-suicide anniversary party here," she says.

"An anniversary party," I say with amusement. I stroke my hands down the sides of her arms. She shivers.

"I figured you'd want to know."

"I won't plan any murders that night, then," I tease. "Unless… your guests would like the show?"

She stiffens, then continues: "The party is on the anniversary of all six deaths. The Galloways and the Halls."

She thinks she's going to bring out the killer then. I click my jaw.

"How smart," I say. I squeeze her shoulders. She avoids my gaze, but her chest expands; she can't help but lean into my touch. "Another excuse you're telling yourself. A fake reason to explain why you're here." I put a gloved finger under her chin, lifting her up, until she's finally looking into my mesh-covered eyes.

In this mask, she can't see me, and I can't truly see her. It's fitting. One day, I'll reveal myself. She'll have no excuses then. She won't be able to lie to herself.

"You know the real reason you're here," I murmur. "Don't you?"

Her eyes flicker across mine. I can imagine it from her point of view: the dark, cavernous eye sockets; a figure; a creature; something you know should look human; something you know breathes and bleeds like you; a morbid fantasy; a monster you want sexually; and you tell yourself it's okay, because at least he's not *real.*

I clutch her throat just enough to remind her of her place. She groans, startled by the contact, and her noise oozes with lust. She stands on her toes.

"You know what you want," I say.

She licks her lips, finding her strength. "If you think you know what I want, then take me," she bargains, her voice husky. "Take me exactly how you want."

A warmth flows inside of me, like a gust of heat from a car's engine. The girl is trying to regain the upper hand. To prove that she can control me with her sexuality like she controls everyone else. She knows I like being in control too, but she thinks if *she's* the one who gives it to me willingly, she'll be able to manipulate me back.

I know exactly how to mold her too. I love this game with her.

"Beg for it," I demand.

Those misty brown eyes blink at me, wavering with desire. Then her whole body is quivering, amping it up, *pretending* just for me.

"Please," she whispers.

I keep still.

"Will you take what you want from me?" she adds. She pulls at my gloved hands. "Crave?"

I let go of her neck. She immediately gets down on her knees. She fumbles around, crawling like a dog.

"Please," she says.

"Use full sentences. I can't understand you like that," I snap.

She lowers her head. Her lips are inches away from my boot. I could lift my toe, and she'd be kissing them.

"Please use me," she says.

I grab her red hair and shove her face until she's smothered against my boot.

"Stick out your tongue," I say. Her pink muscle slithers out. I angle her so that she's dragging her tongue across the leather. "There it is. That's it." My dick grows, and I rub it through my pants. "Lick it up, you dumb slut."

She moans, her body languid, her hips circling in lust. I spit, the drop landing on the top of my other boot, and I move her head, using her hair like a leash.

"Go on now. Lick it up," I say. She licks leisurely, her tongue like a snail inching across my shoe. "Good girl," I mock. "Doing everything I tell you." My tone fills with agitation to ensure that she knows I've caught on to her game: "Did I do it just like you thought I would?"

She stops, twisting her neck to look at me. "What?"

"You think I want to use you like this."

She huffs. "I don't—"

"Fuck yourself then," I demand.

After a second of confusion, her instincts take over: she's back on her haunches, spreading herself wide. Her hand shoves down the front of her thong, her skirt crumpled around her. She rubs her clit like her life depends on it.

"Eager to please, aren't you?" I ask.

"Please," she begs.

I smirk. "Because you asked so nicely."

I pull out my dick, the erection rock solid from the anticipation. She has no idea what's coming next. God damn, it hurts, but I strain, using my muscles until the piss fights the erection. The yellow stream crashes into her, ammonia wafting in the air.

Her jaw drops. She lunges out of the way. I step in front of her. Cornering her. Her eyes race, but her legs spread again as the piss soaks into her clothes.

"Beg for it," I repeat.

"No—"

The stream trickles over her chin and neck, and as she closes her eyes, disgust falls over her face. Still, her hips inch forward, her piss-soaked pussy humping my boot.

"Look at yourself," I say. "You're grinding on my boots again." I fist my dick harder, each ring of metal tight against my flesh. "What a little trash whore."

"Crave," she moans, and for the first time, the begging is real. "Please—"

"You watched me kill people. You didn't turn me in. You let me fist you with a spiked glove."

"Let you?" she wails, but the slut keeps rubbing herself off on my boot.

"You licked spit from my shoes. Licked my boots like a shoe cleaner. You just let me piss on you, and you rubbed your hungry little pussy on my boots like you were *grateful* for it." I lean in closer. "I could tell you to eat my ass, and I wouldn't even have to try very hard, would I? You'd stick out your tongue like a hungry little bitch and let me sit on your face."

"Fuck y—"

I reach down, pressing my gloved hands against her pussy. The arousal oozes out, a different, slimier consistency than the piss. She curses under her breath, but it's a lie.

"Would you eat my ass, little girl?" I ask. She writhes harder into my hand, smashing my fingers between my boot and her pussy. "You'd like that, wouldn't you? Licking a stranger's asshole. Feeling me fuck myself while you lick my asshole clean."

"No—"

"Your cunt says differently."

I shove my hand down her skirt and thong, inserting my finger into her pussy. She moans. I use my finger like a hook and drag her closer to me. "A little, bottom-munching whore like you loves to eat ass, doesn't she?"

"Crave—"

"Beg me for it."

Her eyelids flutter again. Hesitation.

Irritation simmers inside of me. She knows what she wants; she just has to admit it.

I remove my hand and stand up straight, taking away the friction she desperately needs. Her bottom lip trembles.

"Crave!" she screams.

"Admit that you love every way I take you. Whether it's eating my ass. Fisting you. Fuck—" I laugh. "Even if I wanted you to fist *me.* You don't care, as long as I use you."

"Crave—"

"Tell me you want to lick my ass."

"Crave, please—"

"Tell me, or I'll never touch your dirty little cunt again."

"I do," she cries. "I do. I swear I do—"

I fall to my knees in front of her and slam her back to the ground. In a few quick movements, I rip off her clothes and shove two fingers inside of her. She shrieks in pleasure and pain—she may still be sore from the vampire-glove fisting—and her lips quiver again.

"I want to eat your ass," she cries. "Let me eat your ass—"

I slap her clit. She convulses. I curl my fingers toward, bringing the little girl closer to explosion.

"Say it, bitch," I growl. "Admit you'd love eating my ass."

"Please let me eat your ass!" she screams. "Use me. My body is yours. I want to eat your ass—"

I rub her clit furiously with my gloved fingertips, her pussy clutching my other hand as I curl into that spot. I curl and rub and stab into her until her body tenses, a sudden wave of power rippling through her. Her body constricts around my fingers, and that fluid gushes out, drenching the leather. My cock twitches against my leg, and I keep fucking her cunt with my hands.

"Stop," she cries. "No. I can't—"

She scrambles away from me. I hold her down, forcing her to take my pleasure and pain. She comes again and again, the uncontrollable cum leaking out of her body, gushing out like a fountain, her own acrid ammonia ripe in the air around us.

Once I'm satisfied that she's empty, I pull out my fingers. Her eyes search lazily, too cum-drunk to know what to do with herself.

Even after all of these years of being desperate for a thrill, she's never been fucked like this.

"Let me—" she starts to say.

I shush her. I brush the hair out of her eyes. "It hurts, doesn't it?" I ask.

"What?"

"To know that I'm in control. No matter what you do. No matter who you pretend to be. No matter what you tell yourself, I could do *anything* to you, even kill you, and you'd like it because I'm the only one who understands who you truly are."

Her lips press shut, studying me, and it's like stealing a pacifier from a baby.

A vibration rumbles. She finds her purse. My eyes catch on the button-sized camera lens.

Her purse was recording her getting pissed on and begging to eat my ass. I love it.

She turns off the alarm, then glances at the stairs. The soft morning light comes down the steps, inching toward daybreak. She still has to shower before work.

"Go," I say.

"Why?" she asks. "I could stay."

The subtext of her words: *Tell me to stay with you.*

"You need a shower," I say. "You smell like a bathroom."

"You're such a—"

"What?" I smirk. "You like that I pissed on you, don't you?"

She rolls her eyes. "No."

"You like that I degraded and fucked you, and that I still want to fuck you right now. And that makes it all okay, doesn't it?"

She sighs in irritation, but her eyes linger on my crotch. It must kill her not being able to make me come.

"Not tonight, little girl," I tease.

Her eyes trace the stairs again.

"You need to be gone on the thirteenth," she says. "Unless—" She lifts her shoulders, gaining her confidence back. "Unless you want to come to the party."

"Not my scene."

"You don't want to miss out on the fun, though."

She walks up the steps, leaving me behind.

She *wants* me to come. To make my appearance. It's not like it's a Halloween party—there's no excuse for me to wear my mask. What would she do if I came? How would she explain who I am?

I could always show up in the flesh.

Chapter 14

Rae

While the rest of Pahrump is Anywhere, U.S.A., the graveyard on West Street is deserted. Bitter. Desolate. And yet it's one of the only places that feels real.

Off to the side, Penny wanders the grounds, shouting to me about the different burial plots. I'm listening, but as soon as I find the grave we're searching for, my mind loses focus.

Weeds grow around Michael Hall's grave. His stone is flat, dirt smudging the surface in the shape of a footprint. Even the groundskeeper doesn't care about what happens to a murderer's final resting place.

A fresh bouquet adorns the neighboring grave, and balloons decorate the headstone to the other side. I dust my hand over my father's stone, clearing it off. The epitaph reads: *A good man who did what was right for his family.*

Family has always been a strange concept to me. I was raised by a single mother who put me through one of Clark County's only private schools, paid for my college, and made sure I had everything in my grasp to find a good job in upper-level hospitality management, just like her. She did everything for me. Even if it's just us—a mother and a daughter—I should be able to easily call us a family. My mother loves me.

I check my phone briefly. Red notifications dot the screen.

Today, I have two missed calls from her, and that's not counting the other calls, voicemails, and texts I've ignored since moving to Pahrump. I can't bring myself to call her. I just don't care.

If Michael Hall—a man who killed his own wife, and perhaps didn't even know he had a child—can be called a family man, then what's keeping me from calling my mother and I a family?

The word "family" never fit us though. Even before I learned about my father's past, there was always suspicion lurking in my mother's gaze, like she knew instinctively not to completely trust me. And maybe she had a right to feel that way. After all, half of my genetics were controlled by a man capable of killing his own wife. Maybe it's not that far off to think that one day, I might become the same as him. A woman capable of killing my own family.

The gravel crunches. Penny shrugs her shoulders, then kneels down and pulls a weed next to my father's headstone. The roots hang down from the plant like blood vessels.

"I guess if the government says you killed people, you're not worthy of proper maintenance," she says.

"I guess not."

We both pull up weeds and lie them down in a pile. I appreciate the sentiment. Penny doesn't care about Michael Hall's criminal record; she still wants to honor and respect a dead man by doing this small act.

My phone buzzes in my purse. Penny snarls. I elbow her side playfully.

"It's your uncle," I tease.

"That's even worse," she chokes. "Why don't you marry him already?"

I playfully smack her arm. "Trust me; we aren't there *yet.*" I answer the phone: "Hey, Ned."

"Hey, beautiful," he says. His voice drops: "Listen, I talked to my brother, and he can't get anything like that from the Michael Hall case. I'll keep checking and see if there's another way to get that kind of information, but it's confidential, you know? I tried to explain the context, but he says they get requests like that all the time, and he can't let a DNA sample slip—"

My mind goes blank. I'm outside of myself, sitting on top of the mortuary building, looking down at Penny and a girl named Rae. Nothing is real.

I can't confirm that Michael Hall is my father.

But Crave was just messing with me. He said so himself.

What if Crave is right, though? What if I'm chasing the idea of someone who doesn't have any connection to me?

What if I've been chasing Crave for no other reason than the fact that he excites me?

What if this is all for nothing?

"I'm so sorry, Rae," Ned says, interrupting my thoughts. "I tried to make it happen, but it's legal stuff, you know?"

"Thanks," I say. I clear my throat; I need to appear more grateful. "Really, I appreciate it. You're a good man."

Michael Hall was a good man too.

Another man. Another lie.

"This isn't over yet, okay?" he says. "I'll keep working on it. My brother has to know something."

"Sure."

I stow my phone in my purse. Penny lifts a brow, reading the mood change. She doesn't ask me about it.

My phone buzzes again. I answer immediately.

"Hello—"

"This is the Pahrump Police Department," an automated voice says. "Due to unforeseen circumstances, we've had to cancel your appointment with the sheriff. Please call back to reschedule—"

I hang up before the message finishes. An unsavory taste lingers on my tongue.

The timing is strange. It's as if Ned, his brother, and the sheriff discussed my interest in the case somehow. And maybe they did. Maybe they're all in on this, and this is another attempt to hide what really happened to my father.

Or maybe it's a sign that I'm supposed to let it go.

The breeze chills the bare skin on my neck. I pull my cardigan tighter around myself. Penny studies the headstone thoughtfully. She picks up some dried twigs.

"Why do you think they were killed?" I ask.

Her eyes trace mine, her expression different from before. Maybe she's trying to read why I'm actually asking. It's a sudden change in tone, I know that, but I'm not sure what I'm supposed to do now. Asking her seems like the best way to figure that out.

"Some things are the way they are," Penny says. "There is no reason. No nature. No nurture. People are just in the wrong place at the wrong time. It is what it is." She lowers her eyes to my father's gravestone. "That's the only truth that helps me make sense of this stuff."

I cling to that word: truth.

The truth is in my DNA, and part of me is scared of that. What if I never get the answers I'm looking for? What if I'm related to Michael Hall, and he really *did* kill his wife? Or what if Crave is right—that I'm not actually related to Michael Hall—and I don't have any excuse for the way I am? What if my fucked-up thoughts don't have any direct cause? What if this is who I am for no reason at all?

"Hey," Penny says. She puts a hand on my shoulder. "Are you okay?"

I straighten my posture. There's no point in bringing Penny into any of this.

"I'm fine," I say. "I guess it's kind of weird to be so absorbed by this dark stuff sometimes."

"I get it. Totally," she says. "Let's just focus on the party for now. Are you finished cleaning?"

There's still a window that needs to be replaced, but after spending all of my free time in the Galloway House, the wall is patched up and both floors are finally clean enough for a party.

"Then we'll start decorating soon," she says.

"And the guests?" I ask.

"Everyone's coming. It's going to be packed."

"This is—" I stop. I'm at a loss for words. I don't know how to feel about it.

"Exciting," Penny finally says.

My stomach flutters. I'm not sure if "exciting" is the right term for it, but I fake a smile and go along with it. On the surface,

I'm eager for it. This party has the potential to give me the answers to my questions. If my mother—someone who loves me—can keep me at a distance due to blood that I supposedly share with a killer, then proving that he's a *victim* will give me the ability to prove my worth, and give me the opportunity to shove my innocence in her face.

But with each day that passes, my mind is increasingly on overdrive, sensitive to every subtle change in the atmosphere. A party like this may drown me even deeper than before, leaving me with more questions than ever.

"It's getting cold," I say. "Let's head back."

We walk back to the car, and I make a decision for myself: whether or not Michael Hall is a murderer or a victim, it doesn't change anything. He's still my father, and the truth matters to me.

There's nothing I can do to change my past.

Chapter 15

Crave

Rae drives her sedan with a blonde teenage minion in the passenger seat, not noticing my truck following them. White trucks blend in around here. Mine isn't the only one on this street.

The two women drive into a neighborhood to take the teenager home.

I drive forward, taking the highway to Las Vegas. Off to my other job.

Tourists tend to prefer rideshares, but the digital trail would make things difficult for me. Luckily, taxis are still frequent in Sin City. My boss lets me come and go as I please, and he doesn't know I'm using a fake name nor did he give my "background check" a second glance. I keep the taxi's back windows tinted, and I keep the front windows at thirty-five percent density, distorting my visibility from outsiders. The tourists' cell phones ping the service towers, but once you toss their devices in the desert, the cops are as lost as sharks in a sandpit.

This next victim isn't a tourist, but everyone who lives in this town is the same. They hustle through the daily grind and earn themselves some cash to spend on cheap sex and booze. Once the right time comes, I park across the street in a strip mall parking lot, where I've got a perfect view of my next victim's favorite spot. The titty club he frequents is a shack, especially sitting next to the giant hotels and resorts on Flamingo. It must have good-looking strippers and cheap booze inside. I keep my roof light off, a taxi driver on his break.

A rideshare drops off DrummerBoy420 in front of a strip club. He checks both ways before entering the building. And like clockwork, DrummerBoy420 exits the building three hours later, drunk and satiated.

I put on my leather gloves and drive over, pulling up in front of him. He usually orders a rideshare. Tonight, I'm faster.

Are you going to make your little plaything watch this time? my mother's voice asks. *You're letting her control you again, aren't you?*

"I'm controlling *her,*" I mutter.

DrummerBoy420 wrinkles his nose. I jump out of the car to open the back door for him before he can tell me no. Capturing Rae's latest conquest is another way to manipulate her into being a little killer for me.

He blinks, unable to focus on me. "Uh—"

"Taxis are cheaper than rideshares, man," I say. "You look like you need a ride."

"I do." He bobs his head. "I don't have cash. Do you take card—"

"Don't worry," I interrupt. "As long as you're not driving drunk, it's on me."

"Thanks, bro."

He falls into the backseat, then slides to the middle. The scent of fast food stinks up the cab. He belches, and I lock his seat belt for him.

"Thanks," he mumbles, his eyelids heavy.

Right as I push myself up from the backseat, I switch the child lock on the inside of the car door to engage it before slamming the door shut.

In the front seat, I ready the needle, then turn over my shoulder.

"Where are you headed?" I ask.

"My girlfriend's," he says. "Henderson."

"You're a local, then," I say. "Don't forget to put on your seatbelt."

His gaze drops to his lap. "You already—"

I lurch between the front seats and stab him with a hypodermic needle. The sedative plunges into his veins. He fumbles, but he's so drunk already, he loses consciousness within seconds.

I unlock his seat belt. He flattens on the backseat. Then I find his phone, power it off, and drop it on the asphalt. My tires crunch over it. About twenty minutes later, we park the taxi next to my truck, near the industrial buildings off of Sammy Davis Jr. I transfer him to the bed of my truck.

He sleeps the entire time.

When we make it to the Galloway House, it's past the mall's hours. Rae isn't here yet, but her jasmine perfume—that overly floral, synthetic scent—floats through the house. I carry him in an oversized duffel bag through the kitchen and down to the basement.

I pull him out of the bag. I flick the next needle, then squirt it into him. There are enough sedatives to keep him dazed until we're ready.

You're getting her presents now, my mother's voice says. *You're a pussy-whipped little boy.*

This time, there's no anger. Instead, I grin. This isn't about giving Rae another conquest to fuck. This is about pushing her into her rightful place.

Parked outside of her apartment building, I check Rae's cameras. On the screen, she's sleeping face down. I turn off the surveillance cameras. Then I let myself inside of her apartment.

I scrawl a note and leave it on her nightstand, close enough to where she sleeps that she'll lose her mind knowing that I was here again without her knowledge.

Since she first slid into the backseat of my taxi, I've seen that lack of human connection in Rae's eyes. She doesn't see others as real people; she sees others as objects, even me. Above all else, she needs the thrill—going against society's order—to feel like she's alive. We're the same that way.

She just doesn't know what she's capable of yet.

I chuckle to myself, then head back to my house to get ready for the day. Our little game won't resume until tomorrow night.

DrummerBoy420 will sleep through the day, and when the moon comes up again, Rae and I will play with him together.

"Perhaps it is a present," I say to myself.

It's not about pleasing her though; it's about pleasing *myself.* Playing with my little girl, seeing exactly what she does, and discovering how her mind works entertains me. She may not be able to kill him yet, but she'll like the idea.

I'll make her admit it too.

Chapter 16

Rae

I've got a surprise for you, THE NOTE READS.

There's no signature attached to it, but I know who it's from. I clutch the paper in my hands, squeezing it until it crinkles. It's like I can feel Crave there, writing it.

A surprise from Crave can be anything. I don't know him well enough to know what kind of gifts he would surprise someone with.

"A surprise isn't a gift," I say to myself, but as I look up at the Galloway House, the excitement burrows inside of me. I can't ignore it. Still, I clutch my purse to me, comforted by the fact that my handgun is inside.

Crave is nothing more than a murderer, I remind myself.

"A murderer I've fucked," I say out loud.

And blackmailed.

A murderer who has fisted me.

And pissed on me.

My pulse increases as I reach for the doorknob. The surprise could be pleasant or horrific, but the truth is that whatever it is, he did it *for* me. And that means he wants to please me. Or, at the very least, he wants to see my reaction.

And if he's trying to get me to react, then that means I have power over him. It may not be sexual power, but it is some kind of power. Which means I can ask him for help with getting the evidence from the police station.

The basement stairs moan under me. It's dark this time. A steady breath whispers from the corner of the room.

A figure looms in the darkness. My heart rate quickens. At the bottom of the stairs, I check my phone, making sure the hidden camera lens on my purse is recording. Then I turn back to that shadowy figure.

"You have something for me?" I ask.

"How many people are you fucking?" Crave asks.

I cross my arms over my chest. Why does that matter? It's not like we're in a committed relationship.

It's not good to make a killer jealous, my brain warns.

Yet my heart drums inside of me, pushing me forward to see exactly how much I can taunt him.

"Are you jealous?" I ask.

"Do you want me to be jealous?"

I snicker. Of course, he turns it back on me.

"No," I say. "You'd jerk off to it."

"I get off on a lot of things, little girl. Do you think me watching you fuck other men is one of them?"

With other, normal people—people like my mother—it's always easy to flip around the circumstances until they think *they* are the guilty ones.

Crave knows our interactions are a game. He likes dragging out agonizing answers from me.

I can get back on top though.

I'm here for more than his "surprise." I'm here to trick him into stealing evidence from the police. There are plenty of ways I could ask for his help, but acting like I need him seems like the most effective.

"I need your help," I say, making my voice weaker than before.

"What do you want me to do exactly?"

"Get the DNA samples from the police records."

He steps closer. My mind erases, filled with his scent. He towers over me, his boots stomping on the floor.

"Your little mall owner couldn't get it for you?" he mocks.

"No," I whisper.

"What a pity."

Our shoes touch, and a jolt of anticipation tingles over me. The overwhelming need to touch him surfaces on my fingertips. I want to feel him. I want to feel him and know that I can have power in this situation too. I want to see *him* react.

Instead, that faceless bondage mask stares down at me.

"This isn't about finding your father anymore, is it?" Crave says. It's not a question, though. It's a declaration, and inside, I know he's right. "It's about you trying to find your place in the world, to pretend like you *mean* something." He chuckles, then tangles his gloved hand in my hair, using it to guide me to his leather face. "But you're back to square one, aren't you? A blank slate where the only person who *wants* to be connected to you is your mother." He laughs. "No, not even her. Because that's why you're here, isn't it? Not even your mother wants you."

Chills crawl down my spine. My mother calls me every day and tries to make it right. And yet, there was an unmistakable expression on her face when I was fired. Fear that I was like my father. Regret that she hadn't done anything to stop me. And guilt for giving me life.

Is Crave mocking me, or is he trying to help me find my truth?

"What if your father is alive?" he asks.

Did Crave kill Michael Hall? Does he know who my father was?

That would be crazy, I reason. *Crave doesn't care about my father.*

"What if your father never wanted you?" he asks.

My blood cools, tiny pieces of ice floating in my heart. Crave's grip tightens in my hair.

"Tell me, Rae. What do you truly want? More than anything."

My senses pinpoint with adrenaline: our heavy breathing, the tick of each heartbeat in my blood vessels, the light sweat on Crave's upper lip, his motor oil scent lingering in the air, the brush of his breath on my face.

Maybe I want revenge. Maybe I want to show my mother that I'm not that bad.

Maybe I want to prove that I'm worth something, even if it's only to a dead man.

Maybe what I want is something less noble than that.

Admit you want to kill people, Crave had said. *Admit that you're a killer, just like me.*

Maybe Crave is right. Maybe I want to feel like I'm capable of overpowering another person like that.

Maybe I want to feel alive for once.

"I want to kill my father's murderer," I say. My words are full of air, my brain testing it out. My chest coils up. It's there in those words, that honesty. I'm outside of my body, looking down at myself. A young woman standing in front of a masked killer, and I'm not sure who I am anymore.

A penetrating sigh escapes Crave's lips.

"It's progress," he says. "But it's not enough. Your words imply that you want justice." He licks his bottom lip, and my core surges with need. "Is that the lie you need to tell yourself right now?"

"I—" I stutter, unsure of what to say. "I don't know."

"Justice like that comes with a price." He bends to me, our lips almost touching. "Are you ready to pay for it?"

My eyelids flutter; I'm desperate for his lips to touch mine. If there's nothing else in this world—if I'm the daughter of a mother who reluctantly claims me and a father who murdered his own wife—then maybe, just maybe, I want to experience that violence. That blood.

"Yes," I whisper.

He shoves me back and strides toward the back of the room.

Emptiness envelops me. I wrap my arms around myself. What the fuck did I just admit to?

The lights flicker on.

A man lies on the ground with duct tape over his mouth. His skin is mottled red, as if he's been exercising. His face is so plain that it melds with all the other faces of the world. And yet, I recognize him somehow.

His moan hangs in the air, muffled by the adhesive gag. My heart pounds, drowning everything out. The realization surfaces.

The guy from the other night. The one who didn't want to

spank me unless it was my ass. My recent hookup from the dating app. What was his name?

What's he doing here?

What is this?

What am *I* doing here?

Why—

"Hrrhhhf—" the hookup groans.

Two gloved hands grab my upper arms from behind. I startle, jumping out of my skin. A masked face curls over my shoulder, his leather cheek pressed against mine. His gloved hands push my palms down between my legs.

"Fuck yourself," Crave whispers.

My mouth trembles open to resist, but my cold fingers snake down into my underwear, pressing against my pussy lips.

"What are you going to do with him?" I breathe.

"I'm going to kill him," he says. "And you're going to get off on it."

No. This can't be real.

It doesn't *feel* real.

"He didn't kill my father," I say. "He's my age. He couldn't—"

"I never said he killed your father," Crave says, his voice even and steady. "I said that I'm going to kill him and you're going to get off on it. Unless—" He smirks, his lips curling at the edges of the open zipper. "Unless *you* want to kill him yourself."

Before I can process his offer, I'm declining. No. No. *No.* This isn't me. I can't. This isn't right.

My eyes dart down, searching for something, and I see that button on my purse strap. The camera. I'm recording this. I can do the right thing. I can give the footage to the police.

What will the police say when they watch it? Will they say my reactions are a survival mechanism? A way to cope?

If I try to stop him, will Crave kill me?

And if I watch Crave—

Crave lifts bolt cutters off of the floor.

"Don't," I whisper. The word comes out hoarse. Ineffective.

Am I even trying?

"Calm down," Crave laughs. "Don't get yourself too worked up yet."

Crave kneels down and cuts the man's hands free from his bindings. The man grunts and tries to crawl, a legless ghost worming toward me. I scream. Crave steps on the man's head, keeping him still. Then he leans his weight on the man's skull, crushing him.

The man looks strong, but he moves like he can barely function. Did Crave drug this man?

Crave scoops the man's fingers between the plier blades.

The man screams, his cry muffled by the duct-tape. He flicks his hands around. Crave puts the fingers right back into the scissoring blades.

"If you fight me, this will be much worse," he says.

The man cries into the floor, but he stops moving. Crave curls his lips. He's enjoying this, everything from the way the man squirms to the power it brings him. He's a god right now, playing with this man's life and death.

And I watch in fear. In confusion. In complete and utter fascination.

Energy stews in me. At the same time, I'm paralyzed.

I should stop Crave. This man did nothing wrong.

Is this Crave's revenge? For seeing me fuck another man?

Why can't I move?

The bolt cutters clip shut. The harrowing scream slices through the basement like a fire alarm. My fingernails jab into my pussy lips.

The man's wailing stops.

I feel it then. I'm wet.

What is wrong with me?

"Save him," Crave taunts.

He throws a knife along the floor. It stops at my feet. Red crust lines the sharp edge of the blade, dried from some past act of violence. I wheeze. My throat is dry, my fingers vibrating with adrenaline.

"Be the hero you say you are," Crave says. "Save this innocent man and kill me. Oh, little girl," he murmurs, his voice pulsing with lust. "Make sure you kill me. Because if you don't, I will come after you, and I will make you regret it."

I don't move.

I can't.

You're afraid, my brain reasons. *That's why you can't move. Because Crave will kill you if you do anything like that. You can't save this man. You can only save yourself.*

Those reasons are lies. Crave won't kill me; I know that. Not now. Not like this. I know this with my entire being, even at the bottom of my stomach.

Crave tosses his head back, his laughter rumbling through the basement. The man's labored breath increases to a dangerous rhythm. Crave's dick bulges in his pants, his erection evident. Is he excited because he's about to kill this man, or because he knows I'm getting off on the murder just like he wants?

"You have your phone," Crave says. "Call the police."

The man's whimpers intensify. My body is light, loosely tethered to the ground, arousal booming in my veins.

This is Crave's surprise. He's killing someone so that I can watch.

He's doing this for me.

"No?" Crave asks.

I realize I'm shaking my head. My fingertips glide over my clit furiously, my body acting on its own desire. I can't stop myself from playing with myself.

"No police, then. No rescue," Crave says. "So sorry, DrummerBoy420." Crave bends down to his victim. "I guess I chose a little slut who likes blood as much as I do."

"No," I say, my voice frantic. "No. I'm doing this because—"

Crave snaps the bolt cutters again, slicing the back of the man's neck. Tendrils of muscle and nerves spool out, pink and red spaghetti noodles hanging down to the floor, the white fragments of spine exposed, like an open Pez dispenser.

My heart beats in my ears. I should do something. I should help this man. I should—

"What, little girl?" Crave asks. "Are you too turned on to help him?"

Those words throw me out of my stupor. I rush over, clutching the man's neck. He's warm. Hot, even. And his blood is warm too, like a spa. My knees soak with the liquid, and I slip, my ass landing in the pool of blood. It soaks through my underwear and warms my pussy lips.

"Is this what you call saving him?" Crave murmurs.

I grab the man's head. I try to make him right again. To put him back together, like a broken toy.

But he'll never be fixed again. It's too late.

Crave kneels down beside me, shoving his gloved hand down the front of my skirt. He cups my pussy, his gloved fingers sliding along my folds so easily, my whole body aches.

"I'd say we have some bloody lubrication here if you need it," Crave rasps. "But you don't need any help, do you, baby? You're wet. Fear and adrenaline and your own fucked-up desire to watch people die makes you feel things, doesn't it, Rae? You were made for this. Just like I was."

My body thrusts against his palm, and he laughs.

"No. Not yet, little slut," he says. He pulls me up by the hair until I'm on my knees again, like a pathetic mortal kneeling before her god. "You need to get cleaned up before you come."

He pulls out his cock, and those metal rings and bars gleam in the light. He twists the head of his cock, pointing it down toward me. My cheeks flush, knowing what's coming.

Move, my brain screams. *Don't let him do this.*

"Open your mouth," he demands.

I wait for the screams. For the urge to stop this. I don't have to do everything Crave says. He's right: I can call the cops. I can deny him. I can take the footage of him killing this stranger to the police right now.

Instead, I open my mouth.

Piss washes over my tongue like hot tea. The taste is slightly bitter, like a lemon pith steeped in metallic water. My clothes cling to my skin, and my eyes are glued to Crave's dark, cavernous eye sockets. His tongue flickers over his bottom lip; he's salivating for me.

My mouth is wet too, full of his urine.

I swallow it down, taking everything he has. Disgust is inside of me, but my molten arousal is stronger.

"Drinking my piss. What a good little toilet whore," Crave says. His tone is a mix of mockery, desire, and utter revulsion, somehow unified into a declaration of praise. "You want some more?"

My eyes roll into the back of my head at those words. He grips the back of my skull, positioning his tip at my lips, and I let his liquid wash over me. He's close—so fucking close—using me like this. I'm a toilet—his human toilet—but my mind is so full of him, full of need, full of fucked-up desire that it doesn't matter that I'm a literal toilet. I want him to use me. I want to be everything and nothing to him, and I want all of him inside of me.

He did this for me. Killed a man for me. He's pissing on me to prove that he can, and to make me understand how much control he has.

It's *all* for me.

Once the last drop drips on my tongue, arousal returns to his cock, filling it with tension and blood. He kicks my chest just hard enough that I fall back on my wrists. Then he kneels down, pinning me under his body.

I should get away. I should crawl. I should leave. There are so many things I *should* do right now. Instead, I scramble out of my clothes until I'm naked, and I wrap my legs around his back, pulling him closer to me, using my limbs like a cocoon, a spider encasing her prey.

He lines his cock up with my entrance. I should tell him to get away from me. It would be the right thing to do.

But I don't.

"Fuck me, Crave," I say. "Fuck me. Please, please, just—"

"I'll take what I want," he says in my ear, his voice so low that I have to stop my whining to hear him. "And I'll take it when I want. And if that means I want to piss in your mouth, if I want to fuck you, if I want to kill you, or if I want to torment and tease you while forcing you to watch a man die, then I will get exactly what I want." His voice is so calm, so untouched by emotion, that it thrills and terrifies me. It's like he doesn't feel anything at all—

no remorse for killing this stranger, no guilt for making me watch —all he feels is his cock inside of me. "If there's a blood cell left in your body, it belongs to me, Rae. And right now, you're my stupid little toilet whore."

His dick gores into me, splitting my pussy apart, his metal piercings scraping against me. My vision swirls. I'm covered in piss and blood and my own arousal, and Crave's sweat is drenching through his clothes. The cement ground scrapes our bodies; neither of us cares.

Crave's cock is a violent extension of his body, and it makes me feel everything at once. The pain in the back of my head. The pressure of his weight. His breath hot on my neck. The mix of ammonia and metal fragrant in my nose.

"Say it, Rae," he murmurs. "Say that you're only alive right now because I'm letting you live."

"You own me," I rasp. "My life. My death—"

At those words, both of us convulse, our bodies twisting together like thorns and vines braiding into each other, tangling up until everything explodes and it's only us. *Just us.* Crave and me and our fucked-up existence of life, death, blood, and rebirth.

The orgasms subside. My head throbs. I relax, letting my body melt back onto the hard floor.

Crave pushes himself off of the ground.

This would be the part where a typical hookup would want to cuddle or get a quick meal together. Crave simply stares down at me as if I'm an insect and he's debating whether to smash me with his boot or to let me crawl into another hiding place.

The half-decapitated body lies a few feet away from us. Crave's mask clings to his face, his lips loose. His expression emotionless. The damn mask covering everything up.

I stiffen, then push myself to a standing position too. My body is covered in filth.

"How am I going to get back to my car?" I ask.

"You'll figure something out."

Irritation floods me; he doesn't care about things like that, but he's also got a mask to hide himself. He knows it too.

Then a sense of strength wells up inside of me. I'm not scared of getting caught. If I can survive this—live through getting off to murder, then fucking the murderer—then I can get back to my car. I don't need a mask like Crave. My mask is my own face.

Still, I came here for a reason. I need his help.

"Get the DNA samples for me," I say. "I've already tried talking to the police. I even asked Ned to help me." I lift my shoulders. "They won't take me seriously. Maybe you can get them to tell you something they'd never tell me." A hint of anger flushes my skin. "You're a man. They'll listen to you more than me."

"You trust the police?" Crave asks.

I furrow my brows. "They're always hiding something."

"I'm hiding something too."

I tilt my head. I've only seen Crave's lips and cock. I don't know what he looks like, or if "Crave" is his real name. And yet, I trust him. There's nothing hiding in his words. No lies. No hidden truths. He's a bloodthirsty killer who—for some reason—hasn't killed me yet.

And I hate to admit it, but after tonight—after he forced me to watch what happened to that stranger from the hookup app—I trust him even more. It's like he made me look into a mirror to see what he already knew was inside of me: the desire for violence, for the passion he dedicates to me, for the fact that he killed a man for me.

Maybe I like that about him.

"You'll figure something out," I say, repeating his words back to him. I pull out my phone to remind him of the footage, and that sends another rush through me. It's a dangerous and delicate balance with him. I can still give the footage to the police. At the same time, all it would take is those bolt cutters to my neck, and Crave could have that blackmailing footage in his possession.

"Clean this up," I say. "Penny and I are supposed to decorate tomorrow."

"Or what?" he asks. "Are you afraid she'll find out the truth about you?"

I wave him away dismissively, then I walk up the stairs, pretending as if I have the final word. He's right, though. It's not about cleaning up a murder scene, or the fact that I let more crime happen in Penny's hometown, or the fact that I'm using her for a fake podcast.

Penny doesn't know—no one does, besides Crave and Ned—that Michael Hall had a child. *Me.*

At the top of the stairs, I search the kitchen as I try to remember what supplies I stashed here. I dig a trash bag out from under the kitchen sink, ripping a hole in the bottom so that I can poke my head through. I giggle at myself. I'm a literal trash bag now, and I can hear Crave's words in my brain: *What a little trash whore.*

As I walk to the car, I don't think of the repercussions. My head is in the clouds, and right now, I know Crave will help me. After what we did tonight, he knows he has to. I have footage that will put him in jail.

I'm innocent, though. Sure, I got off on it, and I can admit that I *liked* my surprise. Especially how it proved that Crave is just as entwined with me as I am with him.

But I'll tell the police it was for my survival. I haven't hurt anyone.

Crave did it all for me.

Chapter 17

Crave

As I walk through those doors to the Pahrump Police Department the next morning, comfort washes over me. Wearing the same jumper as their regular maintenance worker, the police don't notice me.

From the outside, it must look like I'm kissing the ground Rae walks on. It's more complicated than that, and it's part of the plan.

"Where's Bill?" the secretary asks. Bill must be the regular maintenance worker. I keep my head lowered.

"Sick. Diarrhea," I mumble. "Came to fix the vents. Shit's leaking in the back."

"The back?"

"Evidence collection or something?"

"Oh, right," she says. She hands me a key ring, then points to the bullpen. "That way."

I swing around and slip through the half-gate. A few of the cops acknowledge me, and I keep my eyes lowered, like I'm rolling over in submission to their authority. The evidence collection is unstaffed. In a town like Pahrump, some officials are too proud to handle their evidence any other way besides the traditional means, and now I've got a key.

The evidence collection room is quiet. Plastic bags lean out of cardboard containers like arms struggling for a way out. Dates are written at the bottom of each row. I peel through each one until I find it.

Galloway House, Hall, Murder-Suicide.

I pick through, then find the vial of Michael Hall's forensic evidence. I stuff it in my pocket, then spin around, scanning the cardboard bins with different crimes. I grab another vial out of a random container and stuff it into my pocket. It's not from the Galloway House, but I don't care. Then I grab another, and another, until I've got five vials labeled with different crimes. Rae may have nothing to do with any of the samples, but it'll be fun to fuck with her frame of mind, pretending like all of it leads back to her.

Out in my truck, I open my phone and click through the surveillance app.

Rae sits at her computer in a loose shirt, typing on the keyboard. My skin crawls, irritated at how much I can't stop myself from watching her, and at the same time, my dick twitches to life.

I just stole for her. And damn it, I stole from the *police.* It's a huge risk, and a stupid one, but in the end, it'll make her think she has power over me.

Then I'll rip the rug from beneath her feet.

Blood rushes to my groin. I want Rae to fall for me. I want her to think that I love her too. And when I rip that away from her, what will she do? Will she kill me? Or will I finally kill her?

A few hours later, when Rae heads to the Galloway House to decorate with Penny, I slip inside her apartment and find her gun. I empty the bullets and drop them in my pocket. I write her another note and leave it on her desk. Then I clear my video activity from her surveillance feed and leave.

Back at my place, I turn on the encryption software on my computer and log into the dark web. I find an advertisement for carpet cleaners—black market code for hitmen—located on the west coast. We exchange information and make a plan to meet at a fast-food restaurant in Primm in a few hours.

By then, it's evening. I order a nine-piece chicken nuggets and a coffee, this time asking for mint flavored creamer. It tastes like pure syrup, and I enjoy knowing it tastes like the creamer in Rae's fridge.

Each day, I'm a little closer to controlling her, to ruining what's left of her good girl persona. And fuck me, it's like killing for the first time.

I spot two muscular men in the back corner with sunglasses on. The idiots stand out.

"You're the carpet cleaners?" I ask.

The first one bobs his head. "You must be our next home owner."

I slide into the booth across from them, opening up my chicken nuggets. I pop one in my mouth.

"What's the damage?" the second one asks.

They don't need details. They just need to know where she'll be.

"You know the Galloway House?" I ask through a mouthful of meat. One of them nods, and the other wrinkles his brow. "It's in Pahrump. Gotta get it cleaned tonight."

"You got a picture of the stains?"

I pull out my phone, scrolling through the image gallery until I find one of her. In the photograph, Rae is smiling, posed in a maroon blazer and a pencil skirt, the same picture she used on the resort's website before she was fired.

That is, before I *helped* her get fired.

"Looks like a snobby bitch," the first one laughs, breaking into my thoughts. "She turn you down, man?"

A mix of anger and satisfaction surges through me, like my nerves are full of electricity. I'm not an attractive man, but I never pretended to be. I'm an ugly fucker, but for the most part, I'm the same as any other person in this fast food restaurant, in this small town, in this country, in this entire world. And that's what makes me terrifying. I'm not pretty. I'm *normal.* And I'm underneath her skin. A bondage mask tricks women like Rae into thinking Prince Charming is hiding under the fabric, ready to lift her up and save her. In reality, I'm a monster, inside and out. And one day, I'm going to cut her open and show her that underneath that normal person disguise, she's a monster too.

"Can you do it?" I ask.

"We'll take care of that stain for you," the second one says.

We talk about the funds, and I give them a down payment in cash. Then I shake their hands and leave the building, tossing my trash in the bin as I go, like a good human being. I didn't even litter this time. Though I'll admit I agreed to a final amount that I don't have. I'm not worried about it. It's not like they're going to come and kill me for not paying up.

Either way, I *want* this to happen. I want to see what Rae does when she has to defend herself. Will she take the first chance she gets to kill them, or will she stumble in fear, too afraid to fight back? Will they kill her, or will she kill them?

I lick my lips and get back into my truck. I can't wait to find out.

Chapter 18

Rae

This time, Crave's note is in my pocket. A chill runs through the air, and I pull my hoodie tighter around me. It's not just the winter weather, though. The Galloway House has a presence, and its claws are ice cold in my flesh. With each step I take closer to that basement, it's like I'm becoming a part of the house.

Crave's note reads: *Meet me at one a.m.*

The words are scrawled on the back of a grocery store receipt. The fact that he chose an old receipt from my trash can seems purposeful, like he wants to reiterate that he can come and go as he pleases from my apartment.

I don't need confirmation anymore. Crave is definitely watching me. Maybe even right now.

My feet crunch over the dirt. The padlock is gone now. Ned gave me my own real key, without knowing that I already had one. We agreed that I could keep the gate unlocked for the time being since I'm preparing the space for the anniversary party. It's the logical thing to do.

It makes things easier for Crave.

I open my purse, a sigh relaxing out of me as my eyes settle on the gun. Crave hasn't hurt me—not in an unpleasant way, at least—but that doesn't mean whatever this is with him is risk-free. Last time, he openly killed a man while I watched. Crave could kill me tonight.

Or maybe I'll kill someone tonight.

Inside of the house, there's a new canvas cover on the old couch. Newspaper prints hang up in picture frames on the walls. Caution tape lines each door. We started decorating, and it's clean now.

I sniff; there's something in the air that I don't recognize.

A stranger is here, and it's not Crave.

A tingling rush flutters over my skin and disappears. I bite my lip. I'm imagining things. If anything, it *is* Crave. At the very worst, it's Crave with another victim.

My pussy clenches, my fingers wandering over the old wallpaper, imagining his leather gloves touching my bare skin.

"Crave?" I ask.

I glance toward the basement. The door is closed.

I reach for the handle. It's locked.

What the fuck?

Burned fast food seizes my nostrils. I snap around.

A hood slams over my head.

I scream.

A set of hands grabs me, pulling me around. I thrash, desperately trying to twist out of their grip.

"That's right," a man says. "Dumb cunt was here, just like he said."

Like he said?

"Didn't say she was a screamer though."

I kick—hitting what I think is a stomach—and the hands drop me. I scramble forward, flinging the hood off of my head and reaching for my purse. My gun is in there. I can defend myself. I can—

"Yeah right, bitch."

A foot kicks between my legs; pain assaults my core. A punch whacks me in the head, and my vision blurs. The hood comes over me again. Everything is dark fabric. I wheeze, and another punch lands on my back, the air knocked out of my lungs. My wrists are pulled into a binding, then my stomach is pressed against the couch. I kick again and hit the furniture. Their laughter vibrates around me.

"You dumb cunt."

Each of my legs is strapped to something—it must be the feet of the couch—and I'm spread wide. They pull the hood from my head. My heart pounds.

Two brown-haired men, overly muscular, carrying rifles, line each side of me. One tall, one short.

I search their eyes for proof. Is the tall one Crave? If I saw Crave, *really* saw him, I would know, wouldn't I? There would be a primal connection.

One of them *has* to be Crave.

Or this has to be a joke. A new trick he's playing on me. That's the only way this makes sense.

Their eyes aren't right though, too light to be his. And they smell like cigarettes and french fries.

My lips tremble. Crave isn't here.

A pain radiates between my temples. Crave wouldn't save me. I know that. But a small part of me holds onto the hope that he would at least spare me.

"Please," I whisper, tears filling my voice, though I don't know what I'm begging for. I want Crave to be here. I want his proximity and the fearlessness he gives me. I want to absorb him.

But I'm alone with two strangers, and it hurts like a knife to the heart.

"Please let me go," I beg.

"We were told to make it painful," the shorter one says. "Let's break some bones."

The taller one slips behind me. Then a heavy object bludgeons my backside. The pain guts me, radiating in my fingertips and swimming back to my lungs. I cry out, closing my eyes, willing myself to be somewhere else. To find a way out of this.

I can't do anything though. I wail. Another strike. I hold my breath and shake uncontrollably.

Crave is watching from the corner. He has to be.

That's what this is. He's going to let them kill me. He *wants* to watch me suffer.

"No!" I scream. If I'm going to die because of Crave, I can't die like a pathetic victim that walked right into his trap. "No. No. No—"

A knife prickles across my skin. I scream.

"I bet she's a bleeder," one of them says.

Anger fills me. I'm not in control, and it scares me.

I don't want this. I don't want them. I want *Crave.*

The muzzle of a rifle settles on my temple.

"A bleeder and a screamer," one of them says.

"We'll have to tell him."

Him. Fucking *him.*

Everything tunnels. My only instinct is survival.

Crave is the key.

"Crave!" I scream. "Crave! You motherfucker—"

"Crave?" one of the men chuckles. He whams the heavy object into my body again. I scream Crave's name again and again. "Is that some kind of slang word?"

"Crave!" I shout. Desperation fills me. My voice strains: "Crave. Crave, *please*—"

A hard object dashes through the air, and the shorter man falls to the ground, blunt force trauma killing him cold. Another object lands near the couch, right by my hands. I scream, closing my eyes.

More motion. More noise. More everything.

I can't think.

"What the—"

The tall man swings his rifle toward the noise.

A black leather bondage mask clings to the assailant's face, the zipper shut. The dark eyes ominous.

"Crave," I cry.

The tall man shoots. The bullet rings in my ears. Crave launches toward the man—the bullet must have missed him—and whacks the rifle out of his hands. The two of them fight on the ground. I squinch my eyes shut.

Crave is here. He's saving me.

Will someone hear the gunshots? Are the cops going to come now?

I both plead that the cops come and cross my fingers that they don't. If the cops come here, Crave will get caught.

I don't want to die.

I don't want Crave to get caught.

I want to see Crave again.

I want these rifled men to die.

I want to kill them myself.

I want—

I pull my arms down and realize that my wrists are free. Crave must have cut them free right after he killed the shorter man.

I panic, my eyes frantic. Then I see the man—that tall, brown-haired, muscular man—with his hands around Crave's neck. Heat boils inside of me—anger, fury, then pure need—replacing that drive for survival. Crave hooks a punch into the man's gut, and the man lets go, giving Crave his breathing back. With a quick blur of hits, the man is on his hands and knees.

Crave will take care of these men. He doesn't need my help. I don't have to do anything.

But I want to do something. I *want* to help. I want—

The tall man crawls, using the couch as leverage to pull himself up. I growl, the sound so beastly, I almost don't recognize myself, and Crave kicks the man's back. The man stumbles into the nearby wall, using it to find his footing.

"Get the fucking gun," Crave orders, his voice muffled by the zipper. "Kill him, Rae."

My eyes dart around. The tall man pulls a knife out of his pocket. Raises it up. The man looks from Crave to me and sees his easy shot. Blood seeps from his mouth and a wound on his head. His cheek is swollen like a ripe fruit.

"I'll kill you first," the man mutters.

Crave won't let me die. He'll protect me. I don't need to kill this man. He's so messed up that whether or not I do anything, he'll die soon.

But god, I want to kill him.

My ankles are still tied to the couch's feet. I reach for the rifle. "You motherfucker!"

The man swings toward me, and at the last second, I lift the rifle, using it to block me right as Crave stabs him from behind.

The man stills, Crave's knife keeping him upright. Blood gushes out of the man's mouth, spilling onto me. The man gurgles.

Crave shoves his body to the ground, pulling the knife from his back. His shoulders broaden. His expression remains as empty as a blank canvas. He's utterly calm, even after all of that.

His gloved hands roam my wet skin. It should upset me, knowing how much I trust Crave with my life when he doesn't trust me with his real self. The leather is his cold disguise. His armor. His lack of trust in me.

And yet, comfort washes over me anyway, because he's here. He did this for me.

"Crave," I whisper. "You sav—"

He slaps my face. My jaw drops.

The truth hits me then; my body blazes with confusion and need.

Crave orchestrated this night. He left the note in my apartment. He hired those hitmen. He must have done it so that I would kill one or both of them, to prove that I'm a killer just like him.

And I was ready to. I could have told myself it was self-defense, and that may have been why Crave hired them in the first place, so that I would have justification for my actions.

Somehow, I still trust him with my life and death.

He didn't let them kill me.

Crave grabs the tall man's hair and yanks him up. His lifeless eyes stare straight ahead.

I should be scared. I don't feel anything.

I wait for Crave's next move.

He slits the man's throat right in front of my face, then adjusts his grip at the top of the man's head, draining the warm blood all over my body. He does the same with the shorter one, drenching me in their blood. It's like I'm being baptized. I'm not pure and clean, but I also know I'll never be the same again. Whatever this is, Crave has transformed me.

Crave moves behind me. Fabric shuffles against skin, sloshing with liquid. He grabs me from behind. A thin rope pulls around my neck. My belly tenses.

Then I realize it's a belt. Crave's leather belt. Make one mistake, and the belt could get stuck on my neck, killing me.

Crave will only let me die if he's the one to do it. And that thought thrills me.

The belt locks onto me, and his dick splits my pussy. My head spins with fear and lust and disgust. I want this so badly that it scares me. He's here. He didn't let me die. I must mean *something* to him if he's doing all of this to prove a point. To prove that I'm a killer too.

He unzips the mask's mouth.

"Weak little girl," he whispers, the condescension dripping from his words. "What a disappointment."

Each thrust is a punishment. His metal-ringed dick hits my cervix, causing pain to course through me. Tears streak my cheeks, and I swallow it down, absorbing it all, relishing in the fact that it's *him.* The man I want. The killer I know. The man who may have sent those men to kill me, but when it came down to it, he saved me. He killed them instead.

He let them hurt you, my rational brain argues. *And you failed him. You didn't kill either one of those men.*

No, I argue back. *He was always going to kill them for me. He only hired them because he knew I was strong enough to survive this.*

My entire body quivers in shock. All of it—the physical pain, these warring thoughts—should hurt. I trusted Crave to keep me safe, and he let those men hurt me. But it's more than that.

This must have been a test to see if Crave could trust me. If I really am like him. I may have failed him, but now I want to prove myself. Now more than ever.

I wish I had killed those men.

And that would make you a murderer, my brain screams. *Your mother would be right. You would be the daughter of a killer, just like she said.*

Those logical thoughts dull as the desert air skirts through the house, my skin freezing, my mind whirring with fragmented thoughts. Am I like my father? A murderer? Am I misunderstood? Will Crave continue to test me? Will I ever prove myself?

Crave's body crushes on top of me, both of us collapsing into the couch. My vision fills with stars as the belt tightens. My body tingles with numbness, his cock like the blunt arm of a cactus shoving inside of me. I'm not a person, not a body, not an animal, but a thing. A vessel. A possession. *His.* An object he can mold. A puppet he controls. And if I could only figure him out, I would control him too.

Everything goes black, and my hearing tunnels until his voice is all around me, like a million insects crying out in the desert night.

"You're nothing without me," he says.

Chapter 19

Crave

My cum drips down her legs. Blood and sweat cake her stockings like a layer of glue. Fingerprint bruises freckle her hips, and the belt hangs loose around her neck. If I gave it a few more minutes of squeezing, this shit would be over.

She's gone, but she's not dead yet.

You nasty little boy, my mother says in my mind. *Playing with that rat like it'll love you back.*

My mind is working against me, reasoning myself out of a situation that could put me in jail. For someone like me, it's both better *and* worse to keep someone around. Better to hold up the disguise of a normal person, but dangerous too. The closer they get, the more they know, and the easier it is for them to end your life in the free world.

The discarded needle lays to the side. Rae will be out until the morning.

I bend down, so close that I can see the pores on her nose. The jasmine perfume is faint now, doused by the stench of metallic blood.

I lift her head by the hair. "I'm going to kill you one day." I smirk. "Or maybe you'll kill me first."

I drop her head, letting her collapse back onto the couch. She moans in her sleep, and I cut all of her ties. Then I move her until she's lying on the couch. Was she that peaceful as an infant? As a teenager? Would she have bored me back then? Would I have strangled her before she became all of this?

Using my mother's voice, my mind mocks me: *You wouldn't have. You know why? Because you're fucking obsessed, and you're too much of a coward to kill her now.*

"God fucking damn it," I mutter.

I lean my knees onto the couch, right by her head. It wouldn't take much to crush her skull until she's nothing but pulp, and then this debate—to kill or not to kill—would be over.

And then I would be bored again. Another dead body to prove my supreme being. Another boring old serial killer.

But with Rae by my side, things are different. They're not as predictable as before.

I didn't expect her to call out and curse me.

Rae's brow creases and her eyelids flutter. She's dreaming. Everything is so easy for her right now.

I take off my mask. Clutch it in my hands. Another layer of my disguise leaving me.

I drop it onto her chest.

The moonlight is damp on her face, soaking her skin, and she's so peaceful, it's fascinating. I want her to wake up. To force her to see my real face. To be in so much horror that she doesn't know what to do with herself. To realize that she can't actually trust me.

She thinks I'm here to save her. To *help* her. My reasons for killing those men and not her are more selfish than that.

"You're weak," I say, but I know I'm not talking about her. I'm talking about me and my dick, about why I haven't killed her yet, about the fact that I know what will happen now.

If she becomes predictable, I'll have no use for her. And the closer I get, the more I can taste that inevitable end.

But it would be a waste to kill her now when I'm finally getting to know her.

I peer down at her. I'll let her keep the mask for now. She'll have to wait for her precious savior to return. She'll have to be patient when it comes to that ugly truth.

The truth is right in front of her, waiting for her to open her eyes. One day soon, she'll figure out the truth about how her father died, and that truth is far worse than any nightmare she's created for herself.

Chapter 20

Rae

An engine gurgles through the walls, then shudders to a halt. I groan, rubbing my eyes. A sharp pain throbs in the bridge of my nose. I pinch it, and the pain shifts behind my temples.

A door slams.

Light sears into my eyes.

It's daytime?

Shit. How late did I sleep?

I fumble around for my phone and try to ignore the red stains on the couch and my skin. Bruises darken patches on my wrists, ankles, and hips, and my body is sore as I move around. I find my phone and hold down the power button; an empty battery shows up on the screen.

A hard piece of fabric slides into my lap.

Black leather weathered around the edges. Sheer screens for the eyes. A zipper across the mouth.

Crave's mask.

He must have left it here for me on purpose.

I sniff it. Blood. Metals. Sweat. Oil. Musk. *Him.*

The night before comes flooding back to me. The rifles. All of that blood. The two men.

Crave sent two men to hunt me. To test me. And in the end, he still saved me.

I swing around. The bodies have to be somewhere. Everywhere I turn, the floor is empty and clean. Even the tile and walls are polished as if nothing happened last night. The only evidence is the red-stained couch and me.

I saw Crave kill two men last night. I know I did. Still, something about it doesn't seem real.

As I stand, the discomfort in my skull moves, my vision sliding across the axis. Each step forward is like I'm spiraling toward the ground.

The doorknob jiggles.

I step back. Who is it now?

The door opens.

Black hair. The widow's peak hairline. Proud shoulders.

The mall cop.

What was his name?

He closes the door behind himself. His eyes meet mine, then widen. I open my mouth to speak, but I cough uncontrollably. Panic swells in his dark eyes.

"Christ Almighty, what happened?" He reaches forward, offering me a hand. "Are you all right, ma'am?"

I finally catch my breath. "I—"

I hold on to the mall cop's hand long enough to steady myself, then I let go. What can I say without dragging Crave into this?

I start again: "These guys were trying to kill me, and I—"

"What guys?" He broadens his shoulders, taking up space to exert his dominance.

"I-I don't know," I stammer.

Fear trickles inside of me as I scan my surroundings. I'm familiar with the house—I've been here plenty of times—but I've never been alone in here with a man before. It's like last night is happening all over again.

Bullshit, my brain argues. *You're here alone with Crave all the time.*

With Crave, it's different though.

Isn't it?

"They tied me down," I say. "They were going to—"

I stop. The mall cop must think I'm traumatized. It's not that. I just don't know how much I can say. If law enforcement starts watching this house again, then my father's killer won't come to the anniversary party. And if that happens, Crave definitely won't be able to stay here. I won't be able to find him again.

But he'll be able to find you, my brain says.

The mall cop puts his hand on my shoulder like a father figure. Disgust wriggles down my spine. Older men are like that, aren't they? They think they can protect anyone younger or smaller than them.

I stay still.

"I know," the mall cop says. "Men like that should pay the price."

I nod, though I'm not sure why. How can the mall cop be rude to me in the antique store, but inside this house, when I'm clearly the victim, he wants to pretend to be my hero?

"You don't need to worry now, ma'am," he continues. "I'll take care of it."

I roll my eyes. *He'll take care of it?* He's so caught up in his own idea of masculinity that he thinks I need his help.

I don't need him. I need him to leave.

I need Crave though. And Crave needs me.

"Right," I mutter. "Thanks."

The mall cop spins around, latching onto my sarcasm.

"Excuse me, ma'am?" he asks with that accent so thick, it sounds fake.

I can feel Crave inside of me, egging me on. *You almost killed someone last night,* his imaginary voice says. *You almost died. Who cares about this chauvinistic pig?*

Maybe I can pretend this is another test to see what I'm capable of.

I bat my eyelashes at the mall cop. "What?"

"You don't think I can handle the situation around here?" he asks.

"I didn't say that."

"Then what are you saying, ma'am?"

We face each other, both of us staring so hard, that if our eyes were magnifying glasses, the house would catch on fire. The mall cop's narrowed brown eyes judge me down to my core, like he can see each and every female weakness inside of me.

I see him too. He changed from a helpful hero to a judgmental prick so quickly, it's funny. And fucking scary. He'll only help me if I submit to his dominant manly-man side. How cliché.

"It's just—" I say, putting on a show of reluctance.

"Spit it out," he growls.

"You're a mall cop."

A moment passes by, the anger visibly rising in the mall cop's shoulders.

"I'm Officer Gaines," he says, his voice low.

"You're not an officer of the *law*," I say. "You have no real authority. And even if you did, there were *two* men. They had me—"

"And what exactly happened to those two men?" He steps closer, clicking his jaw, his brown eyes scanning me like the eight tiny eyes of a spider, analyzing the prey caught in its web. "I see a blood stain. I see you. I don't see any men."

I huff through my nostrils, crossing my arms. "They must have run away after they attacked me. *I'm* covered in blood. I did nothing wrong."

"Whose blood?" He angles his head to the side. "Is this one of your games?"

I scowl. "I don't play games."

He puts his hand on his hip to remind me of his weapon. I roll my eyes—a stun gun can't do shit—but when I glance, I realize it's not a stun gun this time.

It's a pistol.

"There was no attack, was there, Miss Sinclair?" he asks, a smug expression on his face, now that I know he has a gun. "No fight. Just you, your loose cunt, and your lying little self."

He's barely taller than me, but I swear he thinks he's a giant, ready to crush me.

I glare at him. I want to squeeze his dick until it bleeds. He has no idea what I'm capable of.

Kill him, Crave's voice echoes in my ear.

An image flashes across my mind: me lifting the rifle from last night. Aiming at the mall cop.

If that gun was here right now, I'd use it.

"You have no idea what you're talking about," I warn.

"Don't I?"

His eyes linger on my skin, taking in each inch of me. I glance down. My torn stockings are hanging from my legs. My breath catches in my throat.

He raises his chin. "On your knees."

I scoff. "You're—"

"If you want me to forget this ever happened, you're going to drop to your knees and open that pretty little mouth of yours."

What the fuck is this?

He thrusts his chest forward, so proud, it's mind boggling. His fake plastic badge. His gym shoes, as if he has to run and catch people during his crappy little job. I want to laugh in his face.

"You don't know anything," I hiss.

"You're covered in blood, yammering about some crazy men, when there ain't no one here but you. Who cleaned up the bodies for you?" His jaw ticks. "I think you're smarter than your stubbornness, Miss Sinclair. I think you can tell exactly the precariousness of this situation. Besides, I'll tell Ned about how you've been stealing from the boutique *and* his office."

Blood boils under my skin. Officer Gaines laughs.

"That's right, girl," he chuckles. "I see you. I ain't stupid."

Rage crawls through my skull. Ned wouldn't trust Officer Gaines, would he? Officer Gaines has worked for Ned longer, but *I'm* the one fucking Ned. I'm the one with power.

I spit at the mall cop's feet. "Fuck you, you blackmailing pig," I snarl. "You're supposed to protect me."

"Oh, I think we're past that point," he says, his voice eerily smooth. "Now. On your fucking knees, girl."

I hastily grab my purse off of the floor, ripping the handgun out of it. I aim it at his head.

"Stay the fuck back!" I shout.

A grin spreads across his face. He cracks his neck to each side.

I pull back the hammer. "I'll shoot!"

"You gonna tell the police it's self defense?" His lips stretch into a smile, showing his teeth, and my heart pulses all over my body. "Self defense or not, it'll feel good to kill me, won't it?"

I close my eyes. This will be worth it. Ned will understand, and if Crave is around, he'll help me get rid of the body.

Yes, it *will* feel good.

The gun clicks softly, like a button tapping on a keyboard.

Officer Gaines thrusts out his chest.

I pull back the hammer and shoot again and again.

Nothing happens.

"No," I whisper. "No. This can't. I can't—"

He pulls out his own gun, aiming at my forehead. "I am getting real tired of waiting, Miss Sinclair. You don't want to see what happens when I'm impatient, do you?"

He grabs my shoulder, shoving me down with his sweaty palms, pushing me up against the wall. He unzips his pants and pulls out his dick. A layer of bumps and growths crawl over his cock like he has a disease.

I've always had good luck with this kind of stuff until now. If it looks off or smells weird, don't put it inside of you. If I do this, I may get infected.

Gaines leers down at me.

"Open your mouth now, pretty girl, and your secret will be safe with me," he says.

My shoulders shake. I spit at his ugly dick, and he grabs the back of my head, shoving his length between my lips. The tip tastes like bitter soap and his bumpy, unruly cock goes past my teeth until I'm pinned—my nostrils smothered against him—and energy rushes between my thighs. Warmth. Heat. *Need.*

No, I think. *This is rape. This isn't real. This is just self-defense. A coping mechanism.*

I bite down as hard as I can. He slaps my face. I loosen my jaw. He pulls out.

"That's how you're gonna play, huh?" he mutters.

He twists around like a tornado and lowers his ass onto my face, pushing into my face like I'm a seat cushion. My nose is plugged up, and his hairy ass cheeks cover me.

"Can't bite me now, can you?" he chuckles. "Lick my ass with that sweet little tongue of yours."

My core flames with desire. I picture Officer Gaines with a mask over his face and gloves on his hands. I erase his accent and replace it with a gravelly voice, pretending every word is coming from Crave.

Then I smell the soap and heavy, cheap cologne, and that fantasy is gone, replaced with reality. A seedy, disgusting man forcing me to eat his ass.

Heat lowers to my pussy. The unmistakable urge to get off. To thrust my hips. To take pleasure from this too. It's not about the mall cop. It's about the degradation. It's about *Crave.* It's about being reminded of the way Crave takes me—

But this isn't Crave.

Officer Gaines grabs the back of my head, digging my mouth into his ass crack, his hairy cheeks crushing me, the thick hairs scratching my face. My tongue reaches out, flicking against those ridges of skin around his puckered asshole, and he laughs.

"God, a girl like you must be hungry after all of that spilled blood, ain't you? Eat up, baby girl," he murmurs. "I'm afraid I can't let you go until your tongue is deep in my ass."

With my eyes up against his skin, everything is dark. I squirm against the floor, grabbing at my thighs. Stars fleck across my vision as I lose oxygen.

I can't do this. Not with him. Not now.

Do I have a choice?

Take him to jail, I think. *Let him rot in a cell.*

That's not enough. I need more. More violence. More revenge.

And to get more, I need to survive.

"Go on," Officer Gaines says. "My ass ain't going to bite you. Besides, a nasty little bitch like you would like that."

A shiver runs down my spine. I close my eyes, picturing Crave.

Play along, Crave's voice says in my mind. *Then we'll kill him later.*

I stick out my tongue, sliding it along the ridges of his textured ass. Salty bitterness on my tongue, the taste of soap and sweat. His natural musk drifts in the air, and he moans like a beast. My body covers in goosebumps.

"That's it," he says. "Eat my ass like a good little girl."

The friction of his hand against his dick breaks into a rhythm, encouraging me, and I stick my tongue out farther. If he likes what I'm doing, he'll come, and this will be over. I lick inside of those rings of muscle, his asshole squeezing my tongue, his body tightening as he gets off on using me. I hump my hand, and it feels good, and I don't care because I'm doing this for survival.

You'd like that, wouldn't you? Licking a stranger's asshole, Crave had said. *Beg me for it.*

No matter how much I try to deny it, some fucked-up part of me enjoys this. I love knowing that a man can want me so much that he forces me to submit. I feel powerful, like I can control him, even as he destroys me.

I'll get my revenge later. Right now, I need to give in.

"You dirty, dirty little slut," the mall cop murmurs. He lifts his ass from my face, and I gasp for air. His cock is bulging with purple veins, those callouses like scratched-off zits speckling his dick. It's the ugliest penis I've ever seen, and yet I still want it inside of me. I need to get him off as badly as every man I've been with, maybe even more than Crave.

It's survival. Pure survival, I lie to myself.

"You're a rapist," I snarl.

"Then why are you grinding on your hands?" he asks. My cheeks flush. I am grinding, rubbing my clit on my palm, practically writhing on the floor. I snatch my hands away, and he laughs. "Something tells me you'd eat my ass even if I wasn't blackmailing you. A little slut like you takes whatever she can get, ain't that right?"

"Fuck y—"

Before I can finish my words, he sits on my face again, this time resting more pressure on top of me, crushing me. My hands rub my pussy again so hard that my whole body ignites.

I don't care if it's wrong; it feels so fucking good to be used.

"You got something to say?" he laughs. He lifts up. "Go on. Tell me how you feel."

"Fuck you and your dirty ass," I pant.

"Got a mouth on you." He leans down and slaps my tit. "Now shut the fuck up and eat my ass."

And I do. God, I don't want to like it, but I do. It doesn't matter that he's disgusting or that I hate him so much that I want to kill him. He takes what he wants from me. He doesn't give me a chance to consider what I want. I'm so used to being in control, always using men for what *I* want, but with Crave and this mall cop—this disgusting, piece-of-shit man—I don't have a choice. Right now, the mall cop is so turned on that he doesn't give a shit about the consequences. I'm powerless, and he's going to take complete control of me. I'm under his spell, and he'll do whatever he wants to me.

And the worst part is he knows I like it.

"Tongue out," he barks.

I moan, sticking out my tongue, reaching inside those rings of muscle until I can barely breathe. His smooth ass hugs my tongue, and he pins me to the wall, pressing against me like I'm a toy he's using, rather than a human being. And maybe I am a toy. Maybe I like it that way. My vision darkens, and when he flips around, shoving his lumpy cock down my throat, I grimace, still sore from Crave. Officer Gaines groans like an animal, and I take it all, letting his cum drip down my throat.

His cock twitches one last time, and he pulls out. The bumps on his shaft rub against my lips.

"Now, that wasn't so hard, was it?" he asks.

I wipe my lips on the back of my hand, glaring at him, but I don't see the mall cop. I see his death. I imagine Crave ripping him apart, limb by fucking limb, until the wannabe cop is nothing more than a torso with a head.

"You're a dead man, you fucking bastard," I mutter.

"That so?"

The mall cop gives a knowing smile, like there's mutual hatred in our bones. Chills erupt all over me. He zips his pants and puts his gun back in the holster.

"We all die in the end, ain't that right?" He winks. "But you calling *me* a bastard? Something tells me your daddy didn't want you either."

I see red. My body seizes with the urge to grab his gun and kill him myself. Right fucking now.

"You're going to die one day," I whisper. "And I'm going to enjoy it."

"Oh, sweetheart." He grins like a jackal. "I hope you do."

He leaves me there in the living room.

Anger seethes inside of me. I don't move.

A car engine turns on, then rumbles away. He must be reparking.

A man like Officer Gaines is the exact wrong person to put in a position of authority, even if he's only the head of security at a mall. He can't get away with this, and if I tell Ned, he won't. Ned will fire him, and together we'll go to the police. It may take years, but eventually, Officer Gaines will go to jail, especially if I do a rape kit right now.

But jail isn't enough.

Images form in my brain: the leather mask clinging to Crave's skin. The mesh-covered eyes. A knife in his gloved hand. The thrust of the blade into the mall cop's stomach as I sit on *his* face, making him eat my ass as he dies.

There's something infinitely more satisfying about that scenario.

I won't tell Ned or the police.

But I *will* tell Crave.

Chapter 21

Rae

That night, I wait for Crave to show up in my apartment. I even go to the Galloway House. But like a tumbleweed scattering across the desert, Crave disappears. Even his mask—which I hid in my nightstand—vanishes.

By the time Penny comes to the Galloway House the following morning, I'm sitting next to the blood-stained couch. She gestures at the furniture.

"What happened?" she asks.

For a moment, I see Officer Gaines and those two brown-haired men circling around me like vultures. Crave stands behind them, a luminous shadow, their executioner waiting in the darkness.

"A decoration," I say. "I spilled a bottle of fake blood. Got it from that year-round Halloween store in Vegas."

"Authentic." She pinches her nose. "It reeks."

"We can light candles during the party."

"We'll need to. The blood and the candles will add to the atmosphere though."

Each day, we work on the final touches of cleaning, decorating, and inviting anyone in the area who may be interested. When they aren't receptive to Penny's invitation, I turn on the charm, and eventually, they all RSVP.

A week goes by like this. My mind is mush, too distracted by everything that's happened. By the fact that Crave is gone exactly when I need him. And still, each night, I go back to the house. I walk around the basement. I keep my gun close to my chest—double-checking that it's actually loaded this time—ready to shoot the hitmen or the mall cop.

Crave never shows.

Desperation crawls up my toes, bubbling between my ribs, until I stare at those cameras in my bedroom, knowing that he must be watching me.

In a frenzied blur, I invite Ned over to my apartment. He comes over immediately.

"You excited about the party tomorrow?" Ned asks. I pull him into the bedroom.

"Of course," I say. I toss my shirt on the ground. My breasts are in full view of the camera lens.

"Jesus," Ned mutters. "You're incredible."

I tug on his button-up shirt. "I need you," I lie.

He kisses my neck, his touch achingly slow. Goosebumps pebble my skin, but it's not Ned that I see. I imagine Crave's gloved hand pressing a knife to my neck.

Ned guides me to the bed. He pulls my thong down and leaves my stockings on.

I reach for Ned's cock. "Let me please you."

He pushes me away gently. "Worshiping your pussy pleases me, beautiful. This is about you." He kisses my inner thigh. "Let me take care of you."

Is he hiding cock piercings?

No. There's no way he's Crave. There couldn't possibly be such different people locked inside of the same person.

Right?

But Ned *is* hiding something. There's no doubt about that. And if I want to keep using him, I can't confront him right now. I have to pretend like I want him.

Ned's lips press to my clit, and my brain goes blank. Sometimes, my body is a commodity, and I can use it like a tool. An object. A vessel. A weapon used to get what I want from others. I knew from an early age the kind of power the female body had over others; why wouldn't I use mine to get what I want?

And yet with Crave, it's never like that. He uses me too, but he doesn't let me control anything. He *takes.* With him, I don't have to think. I can't; my brain doesn't work like that with him. I'm not in control, and I never will be. It's comforting.

Ned's tongue slithers down my slit. I close my eyes, imagining it's Crave. His zipper-framed mouth. His black-fabric eyes. His leathery touch.

"You're so beautiful," he murmurs.

The fantasy breaks. Crave would never call me beautiful, even in a situation where he's pretending to be a good man. I don't know if Crave finds me attractive, but somehow, our connection feels stronger than this thing with Ned.

I vibrate and moan, performing for Ned. When I open my eyes, he beams down at me.

"Did you enjoy yourself?" he asks.

It's obvious that I did; I made that clear, and yet he wants confirmation, that insecurity burrowing inside of him. He wants to please me so badly.

He's a man I'm supposed to want. He's got a decent fortune, a good job, he's attractive and tall, and maybe if I let myself relax, I can have a real orgasm with him.

But my memory fills with the image of Crave's mask, the flashlight trained on my pussy.

Such a meaty thing, isn't it? Crave had said. *You're so wet, it's disgusting.*

Crave doesn't hide behind kindness or sugar-coated words like "beautiful." He told me like it was, and he still wants me.

I glance up at the cameras. Crave's absence pisses me off, and I know that's what Crave wants. Everything he does has a purpose.

Ned leaves with a giant smile. Once his car exits the parking lot, I drive to the Galloway House.

New curtains hang in the windows. A clean doormat out front reads: *Welcome Home.* My inside joke to the killer.

Crave should be inside. I know he's not.

I check the basement anyway. I even switch on the lights.

It's empty.

"It's because of the party," I mumble. "He's waiting until it blows over. So he can have his space back."

It makes sense, but it doesn't comfort me.

At the apartment, I flip over in bed repeatedly. I can't sleep. All I want is Crave.

I find an old notebook and write a message. Then I stand on my bed, showing it to one of the surveillance cameras.

You want me too, my message reads. *I know you do. Admit it to yourself.*

I stand there, holding it up until my arms burn. Then I write another message underneath the first and hold it back up to the camera. The note is a challenge that will irk him, and that's exactly why I write it.

Stop hiding from me, it reads.

Chapter 22

Crave

I glare at those words. Me hiding from her? It's a fucking joke. She doesn't have that much power.

And yet the fact that I'm even doing this—watching her surveillance footage as she taunts me—proves something.

Rae isn't afraid of me. And I can play with that.

I look from the video feed on my phone to the DNA samples and paternity tests in my lap. Most of the DNA samples have nothing to do with the Galloway House, and yet, I still bought enough materials to test all of them so that I could show her the proof. The answer I already know.

She shifts her weight from leg to leg, then stretches her arms. Her muscles are getting tired.

Admit it to yourself, her message reads.

"I do want you," I mutter. "I want you like a toy. A possession. An object that I can keep and destroy. A piece of garbage that I can crunch with my fist."

Blood surges to my groin. In the darkness, she lies on her bed and stares at the cameras, waiting for me to do something. The note lies on her chest, exactly where I placed my mask the night I killed the hitmen.

Stop hiding from me, her note reads.

She thinks her metaphorical hands are wrapped around my

neck and dick, controlling me under her hypnosis. Perhaps some small part of me *is* under her control. It's part of why I've let her live for so long.

And it's also why I need to end this.

Tomorrow is her murder-suicide anniversary party where she can talk to people who will pretend like they care, when in reality, they'll gawk at her like a car accident. A gory train wreck. An animal in a cage.

She holds onto that party like it'll bring out the devil himself. Just like I hold on to these DNA samples, even though I know the truth.

These DNA samples, the hookup I killed, those hitmen I hired *and* killed—all of it is too much. The more entwined I become with her, the more I know that soon, I'll unravel and get caught. Even a girl like her isn't worth life in prison.

"Tomorrow," I murmur. "I'll kill her tomorrow."

Even if the party lasts into the morning, I'll be there, ready for it to clear out. She'll stick around, waiting for me to show up.

Waiting until we're alone is the smart thing to do, but the image of killing her in front of her party guests entices me. I could even kill the party guests right after her. It's not that hard to get an assault rifle in Nevada.

I can cut off Rae's head, just like Mrs. Galloway. Her skull will roll to the side, and I'll smile down at her corpse through my zippered mask while the party guests scream and the sirens howl in the distance.

This shit will be over, and I'll have the last laugh.

I close the surveillance app, then stow my phone.

Rae is nothing more than an obsession, but obsessions are dangerous; they poison different parts of you until your entire life revolves around that single object. I'm done with that.

I'm ready for death. I always have been.

It's time we both died.

Chapter 23

Rae

"Thanks for hosting this murder party," a stranger says as he shoves a six-pack into my hands.

I raise a brow. "You're—"

"Hey, bro!" he shouts across the room.

I gawk. "—welcome, I guess?"

Penny shrugs. "I guess he must have come from the flyers?"

My phone stays on the recording app. With the amount of people here, there has to be a new detail. But everyone that approaches me rehashes the same lines.

"Of course, I was here," one woman says. "I mean, I was only five years old, but I remember it on the news, you know? My parents wouldn't let me go to day camp that summer. It was this whole thing."

My eyes glaze over as the woman drones on about the vibes that summer, and I realize the fault is in this idea. A murder anniversary party is going to attract twenty-somethings who are out for a fun, spooky time. Party guests who did not commit double homicides as toddlers.

I sigh and glance at Penny. "This is—"

"—Crazy, I know," she says. "But the killer could still be here. They're always fascinated with publicity around their crimes."

I nod, because she's right. It's likely that the killer *is* here.

Somewhere. Maybe. We should be looking for older-aged guests, but my mind is unfocused. It has been for a while because there is only one *person* I want to see even more than my father's killer.

Crave.

I scan the living room. A woman sits on a man's lap, both of them right on the "decorative" blood stain, while a horde of twenty-somethings take vodka shots behind them. They cheer and slap each other's hands. My brain melts.

Crave may be here tonight. He may be in his mask, or he may come without a disguise. He could be my father's killer.

Of course he's the killer, my brain argues. *You already know he's a murderer. He even hired people to kill you. Why couldn't he have killed your father too?*

Sweat gathers on my brow. The noise increases, and my pulse races with it. I've never been in the house with this many people, and it's like suffocating on a crowded bus. My stomach churns.

"These crab cakes are killer," someone says.

I scrunch my nose. *Killer?* Did someone really use that word to describe an appetizer at a muder-suicide anniversary party?

Who brought crab cakes anyway?

"The tequila is out."

"Tequila?" Penny shouts. "Uh, excuse me. If you're not twenty-one, you can't—"

"Cool outfit," a young woman says. "Are you cosplaying as Miranda Hall?"

I glance down at the nightgown I bought from the antique store. With my pale foundation and the dark eye shadow circling my eyes, I definitely look like Miranda Hall's ghost. It seemed like a good idea at the time, a way to provoke the killer even more.

I don't respond. I walk toward the kitchen. The tequila may be out, but someone will have something to numb my senses.

A hand grabs my arm, and I ball my fist, ready to punch the assailant.

"Hey there, beautiful," Ned laughs. "I'm not going to bite."

I exhale slowly. Bite. *Hah.* I've been jumpy ever since the hitmen and the mall cop, but I haven't told Ned anything yet. I don't plan to.

"Sorry," I say.

"A little bit more of a turn out than you expected, huh?" he asks.

"That would be an understatement."

"You and Penny did such a good job. Look." He corners me, a business expression stretched across his face. "What if we charged for entry next year? Maybe we can make this an annual thing. We could make it a haunted house with the party being the main event. And with the ouija board—"

"Ouija board?" I gawk.

"Yeah. Crazy, huh? One of Penny's friends brought—"

Don't freak out, I think. I don't care about a ouija board—if it helps the event or provokes the killer, then *fine,* whatever—but right now, I'm out of my element. I can handle one-on-one interactions; they're easier to shift to your advantage. But when it comes to large groups of people, I'm out of my element.

I rub my brow. Ned's eyes scan me, and his financial ambition melts away.

"We'll use the profits to find out who killed your father," he says quietly. "All the funds will go to hiring a private detective or something. Here. I'll start a donation fund for this year."

He grabs a bowl from the table behind him, emptying the chips into another bowl, then he digs out a ten from his wallet, dropping it in.

I reach to stop him. "Just—"

His eyes are patient, waiting for me to tell him what to do. I blink rapidly. Does it matter if he collects donations?

Does any of this matter?

"Just don't tell anyone about my connection to it, okay?" I say.

"Of course not."

A woman with blue hair smacks Ned on the back. Ned offers her the donation bowl.

My head spins. I'm surrounded by friendly strangers, and I smile at them, but my heart palpitates. They could attack, and any one of them could be my killer. You never know who the person next to you might be. For all I know, Crave could be here too.

A person shakes my hand. Their lips move, but I can't hear

the words. My chest squeezes. It's like I'm surrounded by a group of animals that could stampede at any moment.

I'm suffocating.

I run outside, going past the open gate and up the dirt road. A few people smoke to the side, and I go past them too. Over the curb. Across the parking lot. Until I'm leaning against the exterior of the mall.

It's just people, I tell myself. *Normal people.*

My heart steadies, and eventually, my shoulders relax. But no matter how long I look at the Galloway House glowing in the distance, I can't let go of the feeling that my father's killer isn't inside of it. Not yet, anyway.

"What a fucking nightmare," I say.

A figure steps out of the shadows. A white polo shirt. Black slacks. A black belt. Broad shoulders. A widow's peak.

Officer Gaines.

A shiver runs down my spine. I wrap my arms around myself, tightening my grip as if I'm wearing a shield. I close my eyes, speaking wordlessly to myself, comforting my rapidly beating heart.

Crave will be here.

Crave will be here.

Crave will be here.

And he'll kill Officer Gaines.

"Nice costume," Officer Gaines drawls. He nods towards my nightgown. His hands are on his hips. This time, there's no gun though. It's just his regular stun gun. I'm relieved.

"Yours too," I mock.

He grunts. I shake my head. He doesn't have any power right now. There are too many people at the Galloway House. Too many witnesses.

I've been so obsessed with finding out where Crave is that I forgot why I wanted to ask him for help in the first place. I had planned to ask Crave to murder Officer Gaines *for me*, but now, I realize it wouldn't have been as satisfying to watch Gaines die. I want to kill him together. I want to kill Gaines *with* Crave.

Maybe it wouldn't be so bad if Crave killed my father. Maybe

I'm better off, more *powerful*, because of Crave. If my father was still alive, I would never have met Crave.

It's not like I knew Michael Hall. He's half of my DNA, sure, but he's nothing more than that.

And Crave means so much more to me than a sperm donor.

"You're right," Officer Gaines says, his voice softer than usual. He motions toward the house. "It's a nightmare."

I scrutinize him, waiting for the anger to boil under my skin, but the negative emotions fizzle. I don't feel anything right now. The mall cop doesn't have much longer to live anyway, and being here, standing with him, is still better than being around a bunch of strangers pretending to be my friend because I'm holding a murder party. Officer Gaines is a fucking rapist asshole, but he doesn't pretend to be anything else. I've seen his true colors, just like I've seen Crave's.

No, my brain argues. *Officer Gaines pretended to be good. He pretended like he was going to help you right before he blackmailed you into eating his ass. He's a security guard who turned on you the moment you were behind closed doors. He hides his true colors just like everyone else.*

I clench my fists. All of my thoughts are right, *but* I hide myself too. I don't feel guilty for tricking others, stealing from them, or even for the murderous thoughts I have about Officer Gaines. Why would I care if the mall cop pretends to be good when I know I'm going to kill him soon?

For now, I'll pretend to be good too.

"You're working tonight?" I ask dryly.

"Something like that." His upper lip twitches. "You?"

"Sure."

And with those words, it's almost like we're friends now, because we both work at the mall and we both hate seeing strangers crowd our space like that. Still, my skin crawls. I may be able to relate to him right now, but I still don't like him.

"I'm not letting you rape me tonight," I declare.

"And I suppose you're not murdering anyone tonight, either," he says.

I lock eyes with him. He studies me back. The power exchange between us keeps us tied together.

Me: a murderer in his eyes.

Him: a blackmailing rapist.

My eyes skim over his lips. My tongue throbs in my mouth, remembering the ridges of his ass. His hairy cheeks smothering me. Using me. Taking what he wanted from me.

"You enjoyed it," he says in a husky voice, as if he can read my mind.

"I wasn't thinking about you," I say.

"That so?" He chuckles. "You seemed mighty focused on sticking that dirty tongue deeper into my hole."

My cheeks burn, but I don't look away. I can't. That would show weakness. I want him to know that I'm not going anywhere. He will pay for what he's done.

"You won't get away with it," I say.

"I don't doubt that for a second," he says. Another chill runs down my back. I keep my focus on him, pretending to be unafraid. "But you'll enjoy that revenge, won't you?"

That hatred freezes inside of me, my chest opening up, letting Officer Gaines see my rotting heart. He knows he's a horrible person. He accepts that he's a blackmailing rapist. Embraces it, even. But he sees the horror inside of me too.

I watched people die. I never told the cops. And I'm planning Officer Gaines's murder. Maybe I am just as bad as he is.

Someone shouts. The crowds of people trickle inside of the Galloway House. My phone buzzes.

Penny texts: *Ouija time.*

I cross my fingers, pleading to the universe that something happens. Even though it's a silly party game, if it gives me one more detail, maybe I'll figure out what I'm supposed to do now. If finding my father's killer matters anymore.

"Looks like it's time for you to go," Officer Gaines says.

The house pulls me closer. A crawling sensation creeps through me with each step. At the gate, I look back at the mall, halfway expecting Officer Gaines to be following me, but there's no one. It's like he was never there.

A vision flashes in my mind: Officer Gaines's corpse lying in the darkness. Crave standing above him, waiting for me. Another surprise. A gift.

Soon, I tell myself.

The strangers crowd around the dinner table, tea light candles glowing around the ouija board, the planchette held down by Penny and some of the other guests.

Penny nods at me. I start to nod back, but the planchette moves, and Penny focuses on the board.

My mind glosses over. I go through the back door. The executioner's stone with the brown-black stain beams at me, streaked with fake red blood, the moonlight casting directly on it.

I sit on the rock and stare into the empty desert.

"Give us a sign!" someone shouts. "Anything!" Laughter erupts.

A shadow envelops me.

Black boots. Leather gloves. A mask. The zipper pulled shut over his mouth, like he has nothing to say. Those mesh-covered eyes focused on me.

Crave is here. Finally.

I stand, and once we're toe to toe, he fists my hair. I shudder. He maneuvers me until my stomach is flat against the stone. My hair falls down to the sides of my face, and he pulls up my nightgown, the clink of his belt sending chills through me. The leather belt pulls through the loops, and I melt into the stone, ready to accept whatever he gives me. To let him take and take and take.

His metal-and-flesh cock enters me, ripping a hole inside of me, my newly healed flesh torn to shreds again. The nightgown falls down, covering my legs, but there's no barrier when it comes to his cock and my pussy.

The edge of a sharp blade touches the back of my neck, and I can make out a long handle in my periphery.

My heart stops.

Crave holds an ax like the first murder in the Galloway House. The mother—Mrs. Galloway—was decapitated on this very rock. It's like I'm her ghost right now, and Crave is fucking me, just like my father raped his wife right before he killed her.

A gasp rings through the air. I keep my head twisted toward

Crave, my eyes locked onto the black holes of Crave's mask. I can feel people watching us; I don't care. With the long nightgown tucked around my legs, they can't see us fucking. Even if they could, I wouldn't stop.

A tingling sensation spreads through me. Crave is here. *For me.* And that means something.

He's my father's killer.

He has to be.

"Oh, wow," someone says.

"The spirits are coming!"

"Dad joke, not funny. Thanks—"

"That's not a ghost. That's the girl. The podcast chick—"

The lights from the house, from the candles by the ouija board, from the parking lot lamps—all of it grows until his leathery face gleams.

My brain fills in the gaps, conjuring the real Crave.

Crave killed my father. I'm the daughter of one of his victims. And I'll never be able to escape that.

Crave rests the blade of the ax against my neck, the pressure tickling me. He could kill me right here, right now, chopping off my head in front of everyone. He's likely considering it. Maybe he knows he'd be better off if he killed me too.

But I could also spin around and swipe that mask off of his face once and for all and expose his true identity. There would be so many witnesses. Someone would be able to identify him, and I'd have a face to attach to my videos. I could reveal him to the world.

He knows I have that power. That's why he's drawn to me.

Neither of us stops. We keep fucking. There's more power in keeping Crave to myself, using him like he uses me. We're each other's victims and perpetrators, and I won't let that go. Not yet.

"You killed him," I say softly. "You killed Michael Hall."

Chapter 24

Crave

"I know you did it," Rae whispers, her eyes filled with lust.

That takes me over the edge.

Each spasm of my cock brings me back down to reality.

I had a plan, and my hungry cock refuses to let that plan go into action.

Her lips are open, her eyelids heavy. I settle the ax on the ground.

"What are they doing, anyway?" someone asks.

"Is this part of the show?"

"Let's get back to the séance," a shrill voice says. "Maybe the ouija board will tell us why they're here."

The voices mumble, losing interest in the two of us now that the ax is on the ground. I pull out of Rae. She fixes her nightgown, sits on the executioner's stone, and waits for an explanation. For me to confirm or deny her accusation. I buckle my belt.

We don't say a word.

I walk into the desert until I can't see Rae or the house anymore. It'll be a bitch to hike back, but it'll be worth it to avoid the rest of the guests…and her.

I was supposed to kill her tonight. The fantasy was to do it in front of everyone. Logically, I planned to wait until everyone was gone so that there would be no witnesses. Another murder to sweep under the rug. Another victim that disappears into the vast desert.

Then Rae formally accused me of killing her father, and the plan was off.

A headache pulses in my skull. I peer over my shoulder, back at the town. I imagine she's sitting on that boulder, staring off into the distance, convincing herself she can still see my speck walking away.

She thinks she has her answer.

The next morning, I gather the DNA samples and their matching paternity tests. If I give them to her, she'll either have to keep fucking me, or she'll have to kill me.

Part of me is thrilled by that latter option. With her calculated nature, she may even get away with it.

Who are you kidding? my mother's voice mocks me. *You're the one who needs to fuck or kill her.*

Rae's voice interrupts: *You need me. Admit it.*

"Enough," I shout. Whether it's my adoptive mother's nagging or Rae's taunting, it doesn't change the fact that I *have* to fix this. I have to find a way to get what I want. And if I don't want to kill Rae right now, then I have to find another way to make her entertaining again.

My mask hangs on a wall hook. I punch it. The plaster cracks, breaking to the insulation, but there's so much empty space inside of the wall that it seems like an omen. A reminder that Rae and I are the same.

The mask falls to the floor, still fully intact. Leather is strong. I'm stronger.

Rae is stronger too.

I grew up without my biological parents. My adoptive mother hated me, and the rest of my adoptive family tolerated me. Rae never knew her father, and so, no matter what way you spin our histories, we share those same neglected roots. Her biological mother did her best, but Rae still ended up like me: a soulless manipulator, someone who lacks humanity, a person who only caters to themselves and their own desires.

There's something infuriating and intriguing about that.

Even if I don't give Rae the paternity results, she'll still think I'm here for her. Last night proved that to everyone, myself included. And these test results will be another declaration of my dedication to her.

I drive to Vegas to clear my mind. After a few hours of working in the taxicab, I find two young women in skimpy black dresses. They can't be more than twenty-five. One even has fake red hair and brown eyes like Rae. She's pale though, practically ghost white. Not tan like Rae.

"Can you take us to the Herbs & Rye?" the redhead asks. "Best late night happy hour, baby!"

"Giddy up!" the blonde says.

I chuckle. "Of course."

I get off of the Strip, and when the streets allow it, I take the ramp to the highway. The blonde rests her head on her friend's shoulder.

"Don't fall asleep on me. We're supposed to stay awake," the redhead says.

The road rumbles underneath us, and the billboards flash to the sides. The two women sway like palm trees; they're already drunk. It won't take long for them to pass out now.

I could kill them. Their murders may cool the tension in my gut. Give me the right frame of mind, so that I can figure out what to do next when it comes to Rae.

But killing these women won't undo fucking Rae in front of everyone last night. And killing Rae's look-alike won't make those paternity tests go away.

I drop the two women off at the restaurant, then turn off the cab light and park in a nearby strip mall. My neck tingles.

I open up the glove box and pull out the DNA samples, the testing vials, and the instructions. I spit into one of the tubes, my saliva mixing with the liquid at the bottom, more god damned proof of my obsession with her. With my DNA, she'll have the opportunity to link me to my other kills, giving her the ammunition to murder me from afar, like poison. With all of these test results, I'll be putting the ultimate gift into her hands: her paternity and my life.

But these test results will never be enough, and that goes for both of us.

I want more than to spit into these vials. I want to spit in her mouth. On her face. In her pussy. I want to cover her in my jizz and spit and slime and piss and mucus until she's unrecognizable. Until all I see is me. Until she finally looks in the mirror and sees *herself* for the very first time.

One day, she'll accept that we're nothing without each other.

I will too.

Chapter 25

Rae

I return to the Galloway House the next night. Crave doesn't show, and yet my mind is a blur of excitement and need. I tell myself he's just waiting until I'm bursting at the seams.

I don't know how much more of this I can take.

Does he think I'm going to try to kill him for murdering my father?

Is that why he's avoiding me?

"No," I say out loud. I smooth the comforter on my bed. "If he thinks I'm going to try to kill him, he'd just kill me first. He knows he can get away with it."

I write a note on a piece of paper, then tape it to the ceiling so that it dangles in the camera's view.

You're scared, the note says. *But I see you. The real you. And I still want you.*

More days. More nights. More thoughts of Crave. I can't think of anything else. Crave is a parasite, burrowing inside of my brain, controlling every thought. I knew from the first time I laid eyes on his bondage mask that he was a killer. Now, I know my father was one of his victims, and he covered everything up like a murder-suicide.

"So fucking what?" I argue. "I still want him."

Everything matters, my brain screams. *He killed your father.*

I look at the lens in the corner of my bedroom and point at the note. I never knew my father, but I *do* know Crave. And Crave sees more of me than anyone else has. More than Ned. More than my own mother. More than even I do.

At the mall, Penny comes by the boutique to update me on the audio recordings she took the night of the party. I lie, saying I'm going through my files too. Ned hugs her and kisses my cheek. He talks to both of us, and I automatically smile. He must not have seen me fucking Crave on the stone. That or he *is* Crave.

Either way, we go on like normal.

I buy rope from the hardware store and follow a video tutorial about how to tie a noose. It's how Miranda Hall—my father's wife—died. And maybe, in a way, it's how I'll end up killing myself too. If that's how Crave killed Miranda, then seeing me in a noose will excite him. It has to.

I hold up the noose to the camera lens, beckoning Crave to come after me, to burst through the doors and knock me down for provoking him

Nothing happens. I'm alone.

My phone rings. I startle. My shoulders sag when I see the caller: *Penny.*

"Hey," she says. "I meant to come by earlier, but I had an essay due. How did your files turn out? Anything interesting?"

I sigh, unable to hold my disappointment back any longer. I can't think about our fake project anymore. I have my answer. I know who my father's killer is.

I just need Crave to admit it himself.

"I think I need a break from the project," I say quietly. "Maybe we can get together to talk about it in a week?"

"Sure," she says. "I need the extra time for my classes anyway."

Another shift at work goes by. Officer Gaines judges me from across the lobby with his bulbous eyes. Neither of us moves.

I wanted to kill Officer Gaines with Crave, but now I don't even care about that. I just want Crave to know that even though he killed my father, I still accept him.

And I want Crave to accept *us.*

That night, I head to the Galloway House. A few soda cans still lie on the kitchen counter. Spilled alcohol sours the air. I head down the basement stairs and take off my sweater, resting it under my head like a pillow.

I sleep right where I saw Crave kill that first couple. I fall asleep with the noose in my hand.

When I open my eyes, a dark figure looms over me. I stand up. Crave cocks his head to the side.

I reach forward and unzip his mouth.

"I know it was you," I say. "You killed Michael Hall. It's why you're always here, isn't it? The killer always returns to where he feels most powerful."

He continues to stare at me, as if to ask: *Is this where you feel most powerful too?*

"You killed Miranda Hall while my father watched," I say. "You made my father watch you kill his wife. You wanted an audience, right?" I step closer, grabbing his gloved hands, and Crave bares his teeth, warning me to stay away, but I don't care anymore. I refuse to keep my distance. I need him. "You wanted to force him to acknowledge your strength, your power. I understand that." I squeeze his hands. "I record everything, even when I'm the one committing crimes, because it reminds me that *I* can control others. It's proof of what I'm capable of, even when I feel weak."

I hand him the noose.

"Here." I take the little lens off of my purse and toss it onto the ground. "I don't need that anymore. We have more of a connection than a shared love for violence and power. I know you feel it too."

Crave stays silent. My skin prickles.

"That's how it is for you, isn't it?" I ask.

His lips don't move.

Panic, then anger, flows through me, filling me with an uncomfortable heat.

"Say something!" I demand. "Say something, damn it! You killed my father, and I'm keeping that a secret because I don't care. I just want someone who sees me for who I am, just like I see you."

"I should kill you," he says.

A chill sweeps over me. It's true. We should kill each other for all the shit we've seen. If I kill him, it would be justice, and if he kills me, it would be insurance.

"I wouldn't blame you if you did," I whisper. "But fuck me first. Fuck me like you fucked her, because I know you did." I wrap his fingers around the rope, forcing him to grip the natural fibers. "I want to feel what it's like. I want to know what it felt like when she died." Tingling spreads across my face in a mix of pleasure and anticipated pain. "I know you want that too."

My heart beats in my throat.

"It may snap your neck," he says.

"I know."

"It will strangle you."

"I know."

"You might die."

"I know," I say. "I trust you."

His jaw tightens into a smile. "You're very, very stupid for trusting me."

"You're stupid for trusting me too."

His lips twitch. He knows I'm right. Both of us have each other locked in a place of danger, truth, and trust. No matter where we come out, both of us will either win or drown in the evidence of who we really are.

I put the noose around my neck. Crave goes into the corner of the basement and returns with a small stool. I stand on it, and he removes my clothes, then aims his cock at my entrance. He braces my thighs, and those barbells and rings cut me in half.

I hold his shoulders, supporting myself. I clutch the base of his neck, my fingers sliding across the zipper on the back of his mask. My mind races as he pulls me off of the stool, the noose constricting around me. My vision darkens at the edges, my pussy throbbing around his metal and flesh shaft. I don't know why, but I want everything that has to do with him. I want to be with him. I want to *be* him. He's a killer, and those urges are inside of me too.

I pull the zipper's latch, unzipping the back of the mask. Crave keeps goring me with his cock. Every noise tunnels in my ears, drowning out every logical thought.

His breath.

My wheezing.

The last ounces of truth.

He won't let me die. Not like this. I know that deep inside of my soul. He wouldn't waste a victim like that. Not with what we're capable of.

Still, my instincts fight. I flail. Panic surges inside of me, my thoughts swirling until there's nothing but survival and need. Because this is it. This is where I die. In a house where more than six people died. It's pathetic to find comfort in a man who killed my father, the same man who may kill me right now, but I finally feel like I belong.

"You think you're fucking the man who killed your father," he grunts. "What a dirty, pathetic little girl."

My pussy constricts around his violent shaft. It's true; I don't care though, because Crave is hard, and he's stabbing into me, and I've never felt more like myself than I do with him. A killer. The man who killed my father. The man who wants me so badly, he's willing to risk his freedom. The man who can still kill me right now. But he won't, because he needs me.

My muscles contract, and as I fall into the abyss of pleasure and pain, I rip off his mask. Crave gasps, sucking in cold air. My heart stops. He keeps thrusting. His jaw clenches as he growls into me.

Dark, bulbous eyes stare back at me. A widow's peak hairline. His teeth bared, jagged and raw. Officer Gaines.

Crave.

Chapter 26

Roderick Galloway

Age 9

"Why did you put it up there?" Gage squeaks.

I carry the ladder to the upper shelf by the rafters. Mrs. Galloway—I haven't been allowed to call her my mother since Gage was born—puts baskets of dead flowers up there, saying it brings life into the house. I don't know about that, but I do know that she never goes up there, not even to dust. The dead rat has been safe there for over a day now.

Gage's blue eyes blink up at me, so little and sweet. For a second, I feel good, like I'm the protective older brother I'm supposed to be. He doesn't get the difference between blood and adoption yet, so he still listens to me. Big brother perks and all.

Can I even call him a brother, though? I was adopted into the family while he was born into it.

"Look," I say. "I'm too heavy. It's better if I hold on to the ladder. You can go up there and see it. There's a rope up there. You can hold on to it if you get scared."

Gage's eyes zigzag across me, like he's not sure if he should believe me. He's four, but he can already tell that what we're doing is probably not allowed. It's annoying. It's not *really* a lie. He *is* lighter, and it is better if someone stays down here, making sure the ladder stays stable.

That's not why I'm telling him to do this, though.

"Trust me, okay?" I say.

"Mom will get mad at us," he says.

"Mrs. Galloway won't know if we do it quickly," I argue. "You want to see it, right?"

He scratches behind his ear. "Yeah. I do."

"It's really cool." I smile. "You can see the bones in its stomach."

"Really?"

I grin. "I'll be right here. Don't be scared."

"I'm not scared."

He straightens, eager to prove that he's cool like his big brother. He climbs the ladder, and I keep it steady at the bottom. My skin buzzes like I'm full of static electricity.

He stops at the second rung from the top.

"Roddy?" he asks.

"You see that rope?" I ask.

A length is tied to the rafter, long enough that it'll reach him. Gage puts it around his arm, hooking into it. It took me a while to figure it out, but it's just like the magazine I took from the grocery store.

The rope around the woman's neck.

Her eyes round, popping from her head like a bug.

The veins bubbling under her skin.

"No," I say. "Put it around your *neck*. It'll hold your weight better. It'll be balanced."

"Balanced?"

"Your neck, Gage."

Gage does as he's told, and the rope becomes a necklace.

"Okay," he says. "Now what?"

"Push the flower basket," I say. "The rat is behind there."

The basket shifts. He squeals with delight. My heartbeat drums inside of me.

"Wow," he says. "Gross! It's squishy. Rod, you have to see—"

I knock the ladder out from under him. The rope clings to his neck. Gage panics, his tiny hands clinging to the restraint, pulling it from his neck. He gasps. It's not like the rope in the picture—not as tight—and he gets his stubby fingers under it.

Why isn't it like the picture?

Does the type of rope matter? Or is it the knot?

I'll be so mad at myself if I messed up the knot.

"Roddy!" he chokes. "Help! Please—"

He dangles like a tire swing. My mind is fuzzy, like I'm underwater, looking up at the surface. His face turns pink. Then red. His fingers match. Everything swells like a balloon. His eyes widen, round, almost like that woman in the magazine.

"Gage!" a woman shouts, shoving me out of the way. Her flowery dress flashes past me, the same color as the dead flowers in the rafters. She grabs the little boy, holding up his feet.

"Mommy!" he cries.

Mrs. Galloway lifts him up. Gage wheezes. She glares at me.

"Get the scissors," she demands. "A knife. Something!"

My vision focuses on her. I imagine *her* in the rope. The knot around her neck until her skin pops like a water balloon. Her insides leaking everywhere, like fingerpaint and red slime.

"Roderick!" she shouts. "Are you stupid? Don't just stand there! Get the scissors! My baby could've died!"

Die?

I didn't want to kill him. I just—

I don't know what it was, actually.

How long does it take for someone to die like that?

"*Now,* Roderick!"

I startle and run to the kitchen. I scramble through the drawers and hastily grab the kitchen shears. I rush over, and Mrs. Galloway rips them from my hands, cutting through the rope in a few quick jabs. Gage falls into her arms and sobs like a baby. He snuggles into her boobs. She rubs his head.

"It's okay, baby," she whispers to him. Her eyes narrow at me like I'm dirty, like she knows it's my fault.

It's not. I told him to go up there, but he wasn't supposed to get hurt. I just wanted to see what would happen. I wanted to see if it would be like the magazine.

She points a finger at me. "You," she hisses. "Basement."

I hate going down there.

"Please, Mom," I whisper. "I didn't—"

"Don't call me Mom." Her eyes widen, the red lines around her pupils like bloody spiderwebs. "I'm not going to argue about this."

My chest hurts. I lower my head. She didn't even let me explain. My hands curl into fists as anger fizzes inside of me, my skin hotter than an oven. She assumes the worst of me.

Sometimes, I want to be that awful.

I can't let her win. She hates it when I question her parenting choices.

"Will you bring me dinner this time?" I ask. "Or are you going to let me starve again?"

She pushes Gage off of her lap and grabs me by the hair. I scream, and she shoves me forward. The door to the basement swings open. She pushes me onto the landing.

"Stay down there," she snarls.

The door swings shut.

Darkness surrounds me.

After I catch my breath, I walk down the steps, feeling along the wall so I don't trip this time.

Down here, my thoughts are all I have.

I think of Mrs. Galloway in the rope again. How long would it take for her to die? Probably longer than Gage. Longer than Mr. Galloway too. She's too much of a fighter.

Someone like Mrs. Galloway needs more than a rope. Something quicker. Something better. And she needs to be by herself.

She saved Gage, but no one should save her.

Age 13

The rat's body bends completely in half, and the insides ooze out onto my hands. It's nasty, and I do it for that exact reason. If I'm dirty, then Mrs. Galloway refuses to go near me. And when I get a good throw, I can hit *her* with the guts, and her disgusted face makes it worth it.

A bloody butter knife is under me, hidden from view. My latest attempt at a weapon. It worked on the rat, but will it work on a bitch like Mrs. Galloway?

It doesn't matter. Even if the butter knife doesn't work, she'll get what she deserves one day.

The basement door creaks open. Light floods in from the upper floor. I squint my eyes and cross my fingers that it's Gage. He always brings me sandwiches.

Mrs. Galloway steps into the light, her silhouette bulkier than normal, her dress stopping at her shins. One of her better dresses. It must be a special occasion. Lucky me.

"Pissed yourself again?" she scoffs. "You disgusting little boy."

I grit my teeth. Of all the things she calls me, "little boy" is the one that pisses me off the most. I'm thirteen years old, and yet she still refuses to see me as anything other than some little boy she can control. I guess that's what happens when you're adopted by someone who never actually wanted you in the first place, especially when you're replaced by the biological son she finally had.

She flicks the light switch. A single bulb flickers in the corner, casting shadows along the floor, lighting the shower.

"Get up," she orders. I stand, carefully moving the butter knife near the wall where she can't see it. "Wash yourself."

I turn toward the stairs. She points down at me.

"*Your* shower is there," she says.

I risk a moment to glare at her. The curly, teased hair. The shoulder pads. A pastel floral design on her dress. She really wants to show off if she's making me take a shower.

It's not really a shower. There's no curtain or doors. It's just a drain and a shower head. She had it installed so I could clean myself "like a proper man."

But a proper man doesn't stay locked in a basement for days on end.

She crosses her arms and watches me bathe. I consider jerking off like last time, just to make her sick. But getting to be outside—

in the daylight—is still better than being alone down here. It's worth behaving.

In the car, she hands me a box of saltine crackers. I devour the entire sleeve before we even hit the main part of town.

"Do you have to be a pig?" she asks. "Why can't you be more like him?"

One of my classmates crosses the street. Another teenager with black hair like me. I forget his name; he's in my science class, I think. Some kid with rich parents. An only child. It's hard to remember my classmates though. I'm not in school much. It's not like I get a choice.

"He's adopted too, you know that?" Mrs. Galloway says. "And he treats his family with respect."

And his family probably treats him with dignity, I think. *Not like a little rodent they hide in the basement.*

The words don't come out.

A while later, the station wagon slows. We reach two layers of gates with barbed wire at the top. *Nevada Southern Detention Center* is written on a red and white sign. A small box—almost like a standing closet—is right outside of the gates. A man comes out and checks Mrs. Galloway's ID. He glances at me, then waves us through.

Noise echoes in the hallways. We come to a big gray cafeteria with long tables, kind of like the tables at school.

A woman sits by herself. Her head down. A receding hairline with black strands.

"Hello?" Mrs. Galloway says. "Ms. Gaines, do you hear me? I brought your son."

The woman doesn't move. She faces the table.

"Ms. Gaines?" she asks. "Do you want your son to end up like you?"

Finally, the woman looks up. Her brown eyes are dark and regular, like they could belong to anyone. My eyes are like that too.

But her eyes are circled with bags and wrinkles. She's either old, or she doesn't sleep at all.

I don't know which is more annoying: being Mrs. Galloway's adopted reject or Ms. Gaines's biological spawn.

A hand bangs into the back of my head. I snap around, facing Mrs. Galloway.

"What?" I growl.

"How about you, Roderick? Do you want to end up like your mother? Your *real* mother?"

"Of course not."

"She's disgusting, isn't she?" The black-haired woman drops her chin again, and Mrs. Galloway lifts her nose. "No matter how bad it gets, you're still better off with us than you are with her." She clicks her tongue. "You should be grateful for that."

Mrs. Galloway escorts me back through the prison with a hand on my shoulder, as if she wants to show the inmates and guards that she'll protect me. It's just for show. The bitch only cares about her precious little Gage.

The station wagon is silent as we drive. For a while, we're the only car on the highway. I fantasize about ways to kill Mrs. Galloway—decapitation, burning her alive, a gunshot wound to the neck—and I crumple the cracker wrapper in my hands. It irritates her when I don't sit still, and I like grating on her nerves. Her reactions always energize me.

"You should be more grateful," Mrs. Galloway repeats. "I saved you from a life of poverty. If it weren't for me, you would've been a drug addict by now."

I stare at her blankly, then I laugh. I laugh so hard, I choke on my own spit.

"What?" she asks. "What's so funny?"

"You didn't want to save *me*," I say. "You just liked the idea of being a savior."

She faces me as she drives forward. If I provoke her enough, we may get into an accident. We may even die. It's exciting.

"You ungrateful little—"

"Look at yourself in the mirror, you dumb cunt!" I shout with amusement. "You can't save someone like me. You *made* me this way."

The brakes screech. The car lurches forward.

Mrs. Galloway slaps me across the face. The impact echoes in the station wagon.

Stars fleck across my vision.

"You were born this way," she says, her voice low and calculated. "Make no mistake, little boy. You come from a long line of trash, and that's who you'll always be."

I bare my teeth at her. Both of us leer at each other, the rage firing within us.

I never asked to be her adopted son, and yet she treats me like I'm her burden to carry. An outsider. A monster she has to keep in a cage.

One day, I'll tear her to shreds.

"Call me that name again, and I will make sure you regret it," she says in a low voice. She turns back to the steering wheel and puts the car into drive.

Once we're at the house, she forces me to walk in front of her. In the kitchen, she unlocks the basement door.

The butter knife is near the wall. I just need to get her near it.

"Come down with me," I say, using my thickest, saddest tone of voice. "Please, Mrs. Galloway. I don't want to be alone—"

She opens the door and kicks the back of my leg. I fall to my hands and knees. The door slams shut. The key twists in the lock.

Her shadow moves across the opening at the bottom of the door.

I stay on the landing for a while. My insides vibrate with frustration.

I need to stay calm. To be good. To stop giving her excuses to keep me down here. I need to play along and be the son she wants.

It's hard though.

A rat scurries across the cement; its steps soft like rain. There are so many of them in the basement, but she blames the ruined electrical cords on me. Always *me.* I'm the problem she needs to fix.

I need to fix her.

I walk down the stairs slowly, so as not to disturb the rats.

When they think I'm one of them, they forget me. Ignore me. It makes catching them more fun.

I need to do the same with Mrs. Galloway. Make her think I'm an obedient, loving son. That way, she doesn't suspect what's coming next.

I run my hand along the floor and grab the butter knife. The blade scrapes my palm, but it doesn't even scratch me. It won't hurt Mrs. Galloway.

But an ax will.

Age 15

In the backyard, Mrs. Galloway stares off into the desert. I wash our dishes in the kitchen sink, just like she told me to. That way, I can watch her from the window.

We're alone. Mr. Galloway and Gage are shopping for new uniforms. Gage keeps growing. He's tall, like Mrs. Galloway. Even though I've been good for a while now, they still get my clothes from the lost and found bin at school.

The small crowbar sticks out of my back pocket like a second spine. The ax is already outside. I check the silencer on my gun. It's funny how much you can get in a hardware store without the cashier batting an eye. An ax. A crowbar. Bolt cutters. The gun was trickier, but that was expected. The same gun seller gave me a discount on the hunting knife too.

I'm ready.

Easing through the back door, I creep forward, careful with my steps, using the same weight distribution that I do with the rats. You keep silent, and they keep to themselves, just like Mrs. Galloway. She's an infestation, a disease that's rotting inside of me. A sickness that contaminates everything around it.

I'm close now—close enough that I can smell her perfume.

A rock crunches under my foot.

Mrs. Galloway moves to turn her head.

I swing the crowbar into the back of her skull. She falls to the ground, the crushing thud of her body reminiscent of a teenage boy falling down the basement stairs.

I drag her by the hair, bringing her to the giant stone. It's flat and brown, an eyesore that she could never get Mr. Galloway to take care of. Back when we were little, Gage and I used to play with our toy soldiers on it. Knocking each of them down. Kill the soldiers. One by one.

Picking her up by the back of her dress, I lay her on the stone, her chest down, her head turned to the side. It's like she's on an executioner's block from the medieval period.

There's no judge or crowd to cheer me on, to say that I'm doing the right thing by getting rid of a scumbag like her. It's never been about justice though.

This is about my childhood dream coming true.

This is purely for me.

The hunting knife slides along her neck, the tendrils of muscle and esophagus popping into view. The nerves and vessels slop out like wet dog food. The knife slides back and forth, like a see-saw, and my mind wanders to her words: *You were born this way.*

Can a child be born with anger in their heart? Or is this the result of being removed from my biological mother? Am I the consequence of being adopted by a woman who never wanted me?

These questions are pointless though. The answers won't stop me from killing this cunt.

The knife stops, stunted by the spine. The bones are painted pink with blood.

The ax will be more practical now.

A car rumbles across the dirt. The engine cuts off. A door slams. I take the gun out of the holster, ready for them.

"Honey?" Mr. Galloway shouts. "Are you still out back? This kid has your genes. He's a weed."

"We had to go three sizes up," Gage adds.

The back door opens. The two of them freeze.

Blood covers me.

Gage runs, disappearing into the house.

"Roderick?" Mr. Galloway shouts. "The hell are you—"

I shoot Mr. Galloway in the thigh. He falls, his knees hitting the dirt like a wooden plank snapping in half.

"Argh!" he wails, then he crawls toward us. Is he trying to save his bitch wife?

"Sweetheart," he says to the mostly decapitated corpse. "Don't go. I'll get him, okay?"

I shoot him again, this time in the right shoulder. He falls back. My dick pulses, and I grab the ax off of the back of the house.

"Please, Roderick," Mr. Galloway wheezes. "You don't have to do this. We won't go to the cops. We—"

It takes one firm swing at her spine, and the rest of her head comes completely off. The mass drops to the ground like a bowling ball.

Mr. Galloway whimpers like a pathetic dog. My heart beats even faster. He knows it's over now.

I look down my nose at him like he's a piece of roadkill.

"Roddy," he whispers. "How could you?"

I put the gun in his hand. He's so weak, he can barely grip it. A sense of invincibility surges through me, like I'm growing in size. Mr. Galloway has always been taller, bigger, *stronger* than me, but never enough to stand up to protect me from his wife. And now, it's like I'm a giant compared to him. I never dreamed of killing him, but now that it's inevitable, I want to give him the chance to get rid of me. I'm not scared of death.

I hold up my empty hands.

"Do it," I say. "Kill me."

"She was your mother," he gasps.

I let my hands fall to my sides. I guess that righteous death isn't in the cards for me.

"She wasn't a mother," I say.

I bend down. I hold his hand and the gun to his temple. He blinks at me, the life draining from his eyes.

"They'll figure it out," he says. "They'll know you did it."

I smile. "I don't care."

I pull the trigger.

His body falls limp. More blood spills onto me.

I examine the area. Gage is here somewhere.

As I check the house, my bloody footprints leave a trail behind me. Gage isn't in his bedroom, the closet, or even Mr. and Mrs. Galloway's bedroom upstairs. He must be exactly where he thinks I won't check: the basement.

Even at ten years old, Gage is scared of the basement. He's never been locked in there, and yet he knows the possibilities. The unknown is always scarier than the reality.

The rats are quiet, hiding from Gage. I keep the lights off, letting my eyes get used to the dark basement.

His shadow crouches in the corner. Hiding like that, I see the baby inside of him. The little kid who used to look up to me.

He knows better now. Mrs. Galloway made sure of that.

"Come out, Gage," I hum.

He lurches forward, smacking into me. The force knocks the wind out of my lungs. I'm stunned, but not long enough to let him escape. I wrestle him until I'm on top, and I beat his head into the cement. He stills.

Eventually, his eyelids flutter awake.

"I'm sorry," he whispers. Tears fill his eyes. He's probably telling the truth. But what is he sorry for? Is he sorry that he never tried to use his beloved status to protect me? "Roddy, I'm sorry. I'm—"

Sorry is a word, and words can't save you.

"I'm not," I say.

I shoot him in the forehead.

I leave Mrs. Galloway near the rock for now. Then I drag Mr. Galloway to the basement, leaving him and Gage in a pile. Mopping up the blood trail takes forever.

No one checks on the house. The silencer must have done the job. Our house is out on the edge of town. Hardly anyone goes this way to begin with. I'm lucky that way.

I change my clothes into one of my better outfits, then I go to town, waiting for my look-alike to come out of the arcade. The boy heads to his car.

"Hey," I say.

He waves. "What's up?"

"You smoke, right?" I ask. "I need a ride. I'll give you some weed."

His eyes scan the street before turning back to me. "Where do you live?"

"The north side," I say.

He waves over to his car. "What kind of weed is it?"

His car crawls through the town. He says something about one of the girls from school—some bitch he's asking out to the football game or something—and I pretend like I know who she is.

His car pulls into the driveway, right next to Mr. Galloway's car. Gage's new uniforms are still in the back.

I hesitate in the passenger's seat.

"Is this your house?" he asks.

"You should come in," I say. "I've got to package it. It'll take a while."

"Package it?" he asks. "It's *that* fresh?"

"It's good shit. You can give it to—what's her name?"

"Stephanie."

"Right." I smirk. "It'll get her in the mood after the game."

He chuckles. "All right. You got me there."

He follows me inside. My ears throb. I open the basement door, then step to the side.

"It's down there," I say. "I'll let you go first."

As soon as he's in front of me, I kick him in the back of the knees. He tumbles down the stairs like a basketball. His groan echoes.

I close the door behind us.

"Are you okay?" I ask.

"You asshole," he coughs. "You fucking pushed me!"

I grab the gun from behind the stairs, then hold it up. My eyes focus on his form. I can see his head. I'm close now. Close enough that I can't miss.

"It was an accident," I say. After all, his death is an accidental necessity to this.

I shoot the gun. He collapses.

I switch on the light. A father, a ten-year-old, and a black-haired teenager. I wish I could've indulged in some of the techniques I've dreamed of over the years. But faking your own death doesn't leave much time for pleasure or exploration, and I need to focus on my plan.

Mrs. Galloway waits in the backyard, her head resting on the ground. That was the only murder I truly wanted: revenge and ambition wrapped in one glorious death. The rest were purely for survival.

I pull Mr. Galloway's body to the side, resting him against one of the support beams. Then I put the gun in his lap with his hand tucked underneath it, as if he killed himself. I scrawl a note about being a failure and deserving a bullet for each person he failed. I even smear the paper with his blood for effect. I douse the two young bodies in lighter fluid. Burned to a char, the cops won't be able to tell who is who. My look-alike will disappear, like so many kids our age.

And me, Roderick Galloway? He will have burned to a crisp. Another Galloway that came to a tragic end.

I hide behind a large cacti plant in the backyard. As the smoke rises up, filtering through the house, a car slows, then zooms off. A few minutes later, a fire truck shows up. Then the police. Sirens wail through the desert.

No one looks in my direction. It's like I've already disappeared.

A stretcher comes out of the house with a tarp-covered body. The cluster of people around the house try to make sense of the family murder-suicide. They run around like animals, searching for answers, tears and panic in their eyes, knowing they aren't immune to a tragedy like that; they could be next. I squeeze my shaft tighter, relishing in that power. *I* did that. I'm the one in control. The one who finally killed the bitch and her followers. *I* created that chaos.

I jerk off so fucking hard, a blister on my palm breaks open, the pus oozing over my shaft. The adrenaline lifts my head and dick so high, my hand doesn't even hurt. It's so loud at the house that no one hears me moan.

I stay in the desert, waiting until night comes. I don't know what happens next, but I'm not Roderick Galloway anymore.

Roderick is dead.

Age 19

Michael Hall has light brown hair and movie-star blue eyes. He's older, nearly thirty. But in boots, I'm as tall as him. I can pass for thirty. Add colored contacts and some hair bleach, and I fit right in with his family.

Now that he and his wife, Miranda, have moved into the Galloway House, there's been some repairs and renovations. A gray front door. Cheerful blue shutters. Yellow desert flowers in a pot on the front porch. Even the rats are gone. A new life for newlyweds. A real family.

Couples like them always settle into a big house and breed like rats until they've created an infestation for themselves. I don't have any children, but my own infatuation with the house seems to be like that. A disease I can't be cured of.

Living a normal life like Michael Hall seems different. Boring. Calm.

I've never had a calm life.

As Michael disappears into the casino to start his shift, a dark-haired woman with a small nose leans against the bar. She beams at me with watery eyes; she must be drunk already. The desperate air around her draws me in. She wants attention. An easy target.

I haven't killed anyone since the Galloways. Taking advantage of women doesn't count. What I do is violent, but I *don't* kill them. There's just something enticing about overpowering a woman, especially when you can make her feel small. Insignificant. A toy to be discarded. Something to play with until I'm bored.

Sometimes, it gets boring fucking them like this. Sometimes, I even date them first to see how far they'll go.

Tonight, I'm hasty. I've got a new piercing, and I want to see how it feels inside of her.

"Hey, gorgeous," I say with a wink. "What's your name?"

"Samantha," she says. I wave to the bartender, ordering us a round of drinks. "And you are?"

Tonight, I want to be someone normal. Someone with a family. A wife. Unborn children. Someone who can live in that house and have my perfect future wrapped up before me. Someone I'll never be.

"Michael Hall," I say.

"Thanks for the drink, Mikey-boy," she says. She laughs at the nickname. My blood curdles.

What a joke, I imagine Mrs. Galloway saying. *A stupid girl for a stupid boy.*

I blink slowly, getting that dumb cunt's voice out of my head. Samantha straightens, noticing my change in demeanor.

"You're beautiful," I say, giving her my best charm.

She blushes, turning away slightly. "You're just saying that."

I am, but I give her the practiced smile I've learned over the last few years. Pretending to be normal, like him.

"You have no idea how incredible you are," I say. "Let me show you."

Within an hour, we're heading back to her hotel room, and that itch burns inside of me. It started when I made my brother look at that dead rat and put the rope around his neck. It's the same crawling sensation that swelled up inside of me when I looked at Mrs. Galloway bent over that rock.

I don't have to hurt her. This drunk girl. *Samantha.*

I can get past it.

I don't have to kill her.

She pulls at my shirt, and I shove her against the bed. She gasps—both turned on and taken aback by my charm switching off. I flip her around, bending her over the bed. I pull her hair until her neck is taut for slaughter.

I picture an ax above that slender neck.

"Jesus Christ," she says. "You're going to hurt me."

I ignore her, pulling down her pants. She wiggles and pushes against my cock to convince herself that I'm *that* needy for her. That my aggression is part of our foreplay.

I want to kill her so badly.

"Hey," she pants. "I'm not on birth control. Do you have a condom?"

I press the head of my cock against her, my new Prince Albert piercing tugging at her opening. The ring represents Mrs. Galloway's death. Soon, I'll add more. One for each kill in that house.

The drunk bitch grimaces, and the head of my cock stings. Her warm cunt wraps around me, brutal and raw. I *should* be using a condom—not to protect her, but to prevent my piercing from getting infected.

But I don't care about an infection. I want to feel her pain.

"Ow. Shit. That hurts. Hey—"

She tries to turn over, but I dig my nails into her waist.

"Condom!" she shouts. "Condom!"

I hit the back of her head, stunning her. Her jaw drops open, and she lies against the mattress. Like a dumb little lamb, she stays silent. It feels good to invade her like this. To rip a woman's sense of autonomy apart.

Bent over a bed.

Over a rock.

Stabbing her from the inside.

Cutting off her head.

In my mind, Mrs. Galloway cries. My cock burns. The bitch squeezes around me. A woman's head—I don't know if it's Mrs. Galloway's or the bitch I'm fucking right now—drops.

I squirt my load inside of her.

I sigh. My dick squishes out of her. Her juices and my cum cover the head of my dick, but with a good rinse and some antiseptic, the piercing should be fine. And if not, I'll have the piercer look at it.

The drunk bitch cries into a pillow. It's irritating.

"Who are you?" she sobs.

Tears glisten on her cheeks. I could make up an excuse about my change in behavior, but her tears irritate me. Why cry when she knows it won't change anything? It's her fault for inviting me in here, and it'll be her fault even if she tells the cops. She should've known better than to invite a stranger into her hotel room.

Besides, I didn't kill her. I wanted to, but I'm not a killer. Not anymore.

"Why are you doing this to me?" she cries, her voice cracking.

I snicker, then look down my nose at her.

"What?" I ask. "You think this is about you?" I get in her face. "You're not special."

Her eyes shut. I sigh. I'm bored of her already. I need something more, and the drunk girl can't give it to me. I let myself out of the hotel room.

Months pass. More drunk girls. More nights where I'm good. I take what I want, but I don't take it *all.* I spare their lives. And that means I'm good. *Normal.*

But no matter how much I use them, it doesn't change how I feel when I park outside of my childhood home. The lights inside of the Galloway House are bright, almost as if there was never any darkness or violence inside of those walls. The married couple —Michael and Miranda Hall—live their lives as if that's exactly what they deserve.

I want to see them suffer. And I can't let it go.

Maybe I am a killer.

There's only one way to find out.

When the Halls are out for work, I put sedatives in all of their drinks. Then I wait in the basement for the night to come.

Once they're both passed out, I string the wife's neck into a proper noose, keeping her lying asleep in the bed for as long as I can. When I'm sure that the noose is the right length, I pull her off of the bed, letting it tighten around her neck. Hanging from the rafters, she wakes and begins to struggle. I plunge my dick inside of her as she twitches around. There isn't much texture with this oversized condom—the only rubber strong enough for my piercings—but she's a rag doll, slinging around, and her cunt has a literal death grip on my shaft.

It's a mistake to fuck her with a cock piercing. She'll bruise.

I'll use a knife later, I decide. Make it look like her husband got vicious there.

The husband opens his eyes, his mouth moving, but he's too drugged to do anything. Tears start to fall, and a sense of satisfaction washes over me, warm and comforting.

He watches me. His eyes glassy and blue. Acknowledging that I'm in control. That I have the complete and total power in this house. A god looking down on his helpless mortals.

When the wife's pussy loosens—relaxing into death—I come. I come so hard that my eyes go white, and everything blurs around me.

My head floats. My dick slides out.

I take out my pocketknife and jam it inside of her until the blood drips down, oozing like sludge.

I pull out Michael Hall's cock. It's bigger than mine. Anger floods me, pissed off that a perfect fucker like him also has a perfectly sized cock, but he's about to die, and it's not like his above-average dick will help him. I rub his wife's blood on his dick like he fucked her bloody cunt too. The fucker gets hard, staring at his dead wife. He closes his eyes in shame.

I smirk to myself. We're all fucked up, aren't we? We can't help it. Our bodies simply react.

The cops around here are tired, understaffed, and overworked. If they think this crime is unremarkable, they won't look any further. A murder-suicide isn't something they can prevent like other violent crime, and there's enough to worry about in Nye County. A suicide note will seal the deal. I can even print it out from their home office.

I start laughing to myself. It's the same day I killed the Galloways, almost like it's fate. The cops will be too distracted to connect it all; it helps to commit crime in an understaffed town like this.

I put the gun in Michael's hand. Tears run down his cheeks. He's too tired to say a word.

"Hold it like this," I say, helping him hold the gun to his temple. I have to clutch both of our hands around it. Eventually, he tightens his grasp. "There you go," I say using the same tone Mrs. Galloway used with Gage. "Such a good boy."

Then I pull the trigger.

Age 42

"Craven Gaines," Ned, the mall owner, says. "How's the Galloway House looking?"

The idiot mall owner shakes my hand like it means something, and most of the time, I return that respect. No matter how hard I try, I can't get a job at the police department, but Ned trusts me to do his private security. Sometimes, he even lets me carry a gun. Most of the time, it's a stun gun, like he thinks I'm a joke. A stun gun can't kill anyone.

But I can. And I *have.*

"Officer Gaines," I correct him in my fake Southern accent.

He pats me on the shoulder. "Officer Gaines, my man."

"I recommend a fence," I say. I put my hands on my hips, emphasizing the stun gun stowed on my side. "Security cameras. Something to make sure the kids aren't messing around over here."

"All for a little spray paint?"

I furrow my brows. It's a little paint for him, but a goddamn liability for me. The Vegas death tour buses finally lost interest in the Galloway House, but the local kids still think it's fun to play truth or dare in a haunted house. I can't have extra visitors when it's my favorite place to experiment with my victims.

"You don't want it to get worse," I warn.

Ned nods. "All right. Research it. Send me what you think is best."

I wander around hardware store, idly searching for a fence. But when I see a hacksaw, my mind wanders to her.

Raven Sinclair. Her first name fits inside of mine.

I picture her with a hacksaw on her neck, blood squirting from the incisions. A pocket knife stabbed in her gut.

I buy the hacksaw.

When I had seen Rae for the first time waiting for a cab on the Strip years ago, she reminded me of Michael Hall. Her smile was perfect, comfortable, the ultimate picture of hopeful youth.

That curiosity made me look into her life, which confirmed that she was sweetness and innocence personified.

At first, I wanted to analyze that. I promised myself I would keep my distance and observe her. With a mother who loves her, would Rae turn out normal, or would she turn out like me?

Now, I know. She is normal. Good. Just like *them.*

My fingers flex around the handle of the hacksaw, the urge to *do* something with her growing stronger by the minute. I've lost interest in her, but I'm not going to waste the knowledge that I've gathered; I'm going to use that information to kill her properly.

Good girls bore me, but good girls still deserve to die.

Evening comes, and I pick up an extra taxi shift. I put the hacksaw under the driver's seat, then I park the car on the curb beside Rae and her latest boyfriend. He opens the car door for her, and she slides across the back seat, her stockings swishing against the leather. She never leaves her legs exposed, always covering herself up with sheer stockings, the picture of purity.

The boyfriend stumbles in after her and immediately grabs her breasts. She smacks his arm playfully, then tucks her red hair behind her ear.

"You have to wait," she says coyly.

My skin crawls at those words. It's boring, how predictable she is. The experiment is over. The good stay pure, and filth like me rots. I don't need to keep her alive to confirm that.

I'll kill her tonight.

Chapter 27

Crave

present

The shock radiates across Rae's face as my cock explodes in pleasure. She twitches against me, bracing herself against my shoulders, too distracted by my identity and her survival to focus on the raw sensations.

My cock gives one last pulse inside of her, then I pull out. I use a pocket knife to cut her down. She falls to the cement, yanking the noose from her neck.

"You," she rasps. "It's you. You—"

"Mask got you fooled, huh, ma'am?" I say, in my fake Southern accent. I zip my pants. She scoots back like a crab, my cum squishing out from between her legs.

"How? I—" she whispers. "I don't—Why did you—"

"Why not?"

We stare at each other. The confusion is so palpable on her face, I can taste it. Bitter and sour, like biting into a cake and realizing you're allergic to the main ingredient. Watching her process the information is like pumping the energy straight into my veins.

"You forced me to eat your ass," she says. "You raped me."

"I raped you in that mask too, but it was fine when you thought I was some sexy masked vigilante, wasn't it, little girl?" I ask. "You enjoyed it. You enjoyed every fucking second of it. You even said you *wanted* to eat my ass. You fucking begged for it."

Her whole body crumbles into a ball of jerky vibrations. I lean against the wall, looking down at her with mild amusement.

It's funny how we hide ourselves from our own truths. Rae needed the mask to pretend like it was okay to fuck a man like me, because at least she could pretend I was a hot murderer underneath the leather. A man who would protect her even when everything went to shit.

I used to lie to myself too. I told myself I wasn't a killer. I simply killed my adoptive family because I was *forced* to. It was the only way I could survive.

Now, I know better.

"You are a monster," Rae stammers. She pulls herself to her feet, then backs away from me. "You used your position as a security guard to corner me. To protect this house. This—this place where you killed people!"

"If I remember correctly, you *like* that I kill people." I chuckle, then mimic her girly little voice: "I just want someone who sees me for who I am, even if you did kill my daddy."

"You disgust me," she spits.

With those words—those three little words—I'm back to that nine-year-old boy with hate growing in his heart, knowing that no matter how hard I tried, I'd never be enough for Mrs. Galloway. I'd always be the rat hiding in the basement. The diseased vermin. The pest she needed to get rid of.

But when it comes to us, Rae doesn't get a fucking choice.

I race forward, grabbing her hair. She claws at me, scratching my face. I whip her around like a ragdoll.

"Get off of me! You disgusting freak!"

I drag her to the shower stall. Turn it on. It whines, then gurgles out brown liquid before it clears up. I throw her inside.

"A disgusting freak," I murmur. "I like that."

"You are—"

I grip her neck, shoving her face under the water, watching her struggle as the water fills her lungs. She thrashes violently, a bronco at the rodeo with a desperate need to escape. But I'm stronger. Smarter. Bigger. No matter how much we're the same, I'll *always* overpower her.

I keep her there, struggling to fight under the water. Watching her take it. Seeing how much it destroys her to know the truth. Her masked man, her killer, her dream boy savior, is nothing more than the disgusting mall cop freak she hates.

Me.

She chokes on the water, her wet hair clinging to her face. Her red hair streams down her cheeks like trails of dark blood. I give her space to breathe as I shove my hand down between her legs and rub against her cunt.

"Look at you," I growl. "Sopping fucking wet. Getting raped again by your least favorite security guard."

"It's leftover from before I knew it was you," she hisses.

"Bullshit."

I drop her ass, letting her fall. She stumbles into the corner of the room, practically crawling for a way out. I grab my mask and stomp across the cement floor, then wipe it between her legs, drying her pussy with the worn leather. She snaps her teeth at me.

"The fuck are you doing?" she yells.

I unzip my pants, starting a new experiment. Her eyes glaze over as she gapes at my cock. No matter how much she wants to deny it, the bitch is fucking obsessed with my dick.

"I disgust you," I say. "Don't I, little girl?"

"I hate you."

I grab her by the throat, choking her until her eyes bulge. I bring her back to the running shower. Water pounds into the cement like a flash flood.

"You don't hate me," I say. "No, little girl, you fucking worship me. You know that I'm the only one who gets you. I'm the only one who will ever see the real you. I put on a leather mask, but you wear a mask every goddamn day, don't you, Rae? The good little girl who can do no wrong. Who dreams of killing and fucking and stealing and murdering and doesn't see anyone else as an equal. But I see you, Rae. I see down into your fucked-up little brain, and I know everything. I know how bloodthirsty you are. I know how hard you come when I use you exactly how I want."

I move us both under the water, then shove my dick inside of her pussy. She glares daggers at me, but it doesn't stop her from wrapping her legs around me, bringing me closer to her. The water pounds onto my back, splashing onto her face.

"Fuck you!" she screams.

"You and me? We're cut from the same cloth, little girl, but there's one big difference that you need to remember for the rest of your short life." I bare my teeth, thrusting viciously into her cunt. "I'll always have power over you. It doesn't matter if I'm Craven Gaines or Michael Hall or some stupid masked killer named Crave. You are made for me. From me. With me. And I will *always* own you."

She spits in my face. I clench my jaw. I pull my hips back, removing my cock, and her eyes drop, a frown pinching her lips. I rip off my gloves and shove a finger into her cunt. I slide in easily, her liquid need like blood gushing against my palm.

"Oh look," I murmur sarcastically. "What do you know? The bitch is wet, just like I thought."

She shivers, her body nearing that peak, and I slide her down until her face is directly under the water. She writhes, but I pin her down, forcing her to take it and drown as I finger fuck her used-up cunt. She coughs violently, and I pull her to the side, letting her find her breath.

I pull out my fingers and shove my dick back inside of her.

"I told myself I would kill you, but here you are," I snap. Her eyes water, her lips part, and her pussy squeezes around my cock. "I should've killed you a long fucking time ago, and you *like* that I haven't yet. You like that I've kept you alive. You think it gives you power over me," I growl. "Only if you keep me entertained, you little slut. Only if I don't grow bored of you."

I come inside of her again, and she convulses in relief from the agonizing pleasure, cresting over that final peak. Her entire body crumbles with need and arousal.

I pull out, then turn off the water.

The faucet drips softly, a sound I remember well. Both of us are soaked.

She sucks in a breath.

"You're not mad because it's me," I say. "You're mad because you know I'm right. We're the same, Rae, and it's always been that way."

She squints at me. She doesn't move.

I walk up the stairs.

In the parking lot, I contemplate going back and killing her. But that would be too easy. I could also chain her up and brainwash her the good old-fashioned way, forcing her to accept who we are. Neither of those options are as enticing as the new challenge in front of us right now.

Rae will accept her need for me, and it will be of her own volition. I'll make sure of that.

I take my knife to her tires and pierce the rubber. The act is on the security cameras. I don't give a shit; I'll erase the footage like I always do. For now, Rae will be stranded in Pahrump, chained to this stupid fucking town, like I am.

You did that to save me, a woman's voice pops into my head. *You don't want me to run away.*

It's not Mrs. Galloway's voice this time. It's Rae's.

My hands curl into fists. Is she replacing that old cunt inside of my head?

I turn toward the Galloway House.

"I'm going to kill you one day," I growl.

Then why don't you do it now? her voice taunts.

I smash my fist against her car's windshield. A spiderweb cracks along the glass. My knuckles bleed, the tiny cuts pooling like syrup.

I punch it again. And again. Until it shatters, leaving an opening for me.

I pull the DNA tests from my pocket. I use the blood from my knuckles to write a note on top of one of the results. The name is listed as John Doe. She won't *want* to believe who it really is, but she'll finally know the truth.

I didn't kill her father. Not like she thinks.

Chapter 28

Rae

Crave's footsteps echo through the house. Each step above me is like another cinder block smashing my chest.

I don't move.

Glass crashes outside. His distorted voice ricochets across the parking lot, like a crow cawing into the bleak desert.

I'm sitting at the bottom of the stairs with a million steps to climb. In a basement where I've seen him kill people. A masked killer that blended in with the rest of the people at the mall.

I need to leave. I need to run far away from here.

Ten minutes pass. Finally, I stand on weak legs. Put my clothes back on.

At the top of the stairs, I take off running to my car. I hold my breath.

The tires are flat. The windshield is shattered.

A headache screeches across my temples.

Am I upset that Crave is Officer Gaines?

Am I disappointed?

Or am I relieved? Relieved that he's been with me this whole time, even when I thought I was alone?

I scream, falling to my knees. The asphalt digs into my skin. I half expect Officer Gaines—*Crave*—to step out of the shadows and put me in handcuffs. To arrest me for being an accomplice to murder.

Then a paper flutters, landing on the dashboard. A stack of wrinkled papers is scattered across the front seat, each paper littered with glass shards.

I unlock the car, then carefully open the door, reaching over the glass to collect the papers. They're paternity tests. I asked Crave to get the DNA sample for Michael Hall, but I didn't ask him to test the samples. I stare down at the results, flipping through them until I see one I'm looking for.

Michael Hall. Probability of Paternity 0.00%

Not my father.

The next one is topped with a name I don't recognize; it has the same result. Then another. And another. How many DNA samples did he test?

Then I find a folded paper with his writing on top. The edges of the red letters are faded, like he was running out of ink. His neat handwriting reveals his note:

We're the same.

My heart thumps in my ears. Instinctively, I know what's there before I even read the results. I don't want to see it.

Maybe I do. Maybe I need to know.

Maybe I don't.

Is it better to live in the dark?

"Fuck!" I scream.

I rip it open.

John Doe. Probability of Paternity 99.999998%

The biological father.

My biological father.

I don't need to see his name there to know the truth. I shake my head so hard that I stumble, tripping over my feet.

Crave is my father.

No. He can't be my father. He probably took my own DNA sample and used it against me to freak me out, to fuck with my head on a whole new level. To make me think that we're related when it's not true. It's just me against me. Another twisted game to play. It has to be.

Crave can be Officer Gaines. It's disgusting, and I hate myself for wanting him, but I can accept that he's the mall cop who raped me. I can allow myself to like him with a mask on. Maybe I can even enjoy his actual face one day.

But he's not my father.

He's not my father.

He's not—

Tears burst through me. I'm not upset. I'm not sad. I'm not even mad or scared.

I'm overwhelmed.

I can't stop shaking my head.

I dial Penny. The call goes straight to voicemail. My fingers quiver, vibrating so hard, I accidentally dial my mother. I hang up and call Ned instead. He picks up on the first ring.

"Rae? Hey," he says. "Wow, it's late. What's up? Are you okay?"

"I'm having car trouble," I say. My voice cracks. I huff, trying to get the weakness out of my system. Then I let go of that strength, because Ned will be more likely to help me if he thinks I'm in trouble. It's better this way.

"Where are you?" he asks.

"I'm at the mall."

"I'll meet you out front."

I clutch my hands around myself and walk toward the front of the building, my eyes scanning the darkness, searching for that mask—for the mall cop's uniform, for Crave, for Officer Gaines, for whoever the fuck he is. It's inevitable; he's going to kill me now.

As soon as Ned shows up, I jump in his car, clutching the paternity results to my chest.

"I'm glad you called," he says. "I was hanging out with my brother. He's addicted to this new video game, and I swear, he made me promise to play with him for his birthday. I was bored out of my mind…"

His words fizzle to white noise. The street signs swirl into rainbow blotches. It's like I'm not here anymore; I'm simply a color.

Officer Gaines harassed me. Raped me. Looked down on me.

But is Crave right? When he forced me to say that I wanted to lick his ass, did I actually want what he was going to do to me?

Did he know he was going to rape me like that the entire time?

How can Crave be my father?

"Are those the DNA tests?" Ned asks, gesturing to my lap. "Did you find anything out?"

I shake my head vigorously. Ned raises a brow.

"That sucks," he says. "Gaines said you had a lot of results."

Results. *Gaines.*

"Gaines?" I whisper.

"Yeah, Officer Gaines said you got a lot of mail at the mall or something."

It doesn't matter if I'm Craven Gaines or Michael Hall or some stupid masked killer named Crave. You are made for me. From me. With me. And I will always own you, he had said.

Craven Gaines.

I bite my lip, then blurt out: "You want to come over tonight?" I sway slightly. "I just—I guess I want company."

No. I don't want the company. I don't even want Ned. But if Ned is with me, Crave won't do anything. Not until I'm alone again. And maybe there's something about Ned that's supposed to be comforting. He's the kind of man who will take care of me, who always respects me, who wants to do everything for me. He makes me feel like a bird kept in a cage, but at least that cage is safe. At least the master comes to feed the bird. The master even lets the bird out sometimes.

If Crave is my father, there's a chance he's stalked me my whole life. To Crave, I'm not a pet locked in a cage. I'm his prey.

He can't be my father. He just can't.

"Rae?" Ned asks.

He puts a hand on my thigh, and I jolt from the contact. The hairs on the back of my neck stand on end.

"I can't tonight," he says. "But do you want me to come by in the morning?"

My eyes glaze over. I nod. Ned checking on me is a good thing. Even if I don't care about him, he cares about me. If something happens to me, he'll report it. He'll make sure justice is served.

Won't he?

"Thank you," I say.

Inside of my apartment, I pace back and forth, gawking at the cameras on the wall. Then I physically unplug all of them.

I need to go.

I need to leave this place.

But your father is alive, my brain argues. *He's here. He's protected you all of this time. He's helped you embrace who you really are.*

"No," I say out loud. "He's been manipulating me this entire time. He's just messing with my head."

He wants you, my brain says.

I dial my mother. I blink, then squinch my eyes shut. With each drumming ring, my skin gets clammier. I've been clinging to the name Michael Hall since my mother first spoke that name.

But Michael Hall is not my father. My real father—Craven Gaines—may have killed the real Michael Hall.

The phone clicks. "Sweetheart?" my mother asks. "Are you okay? Thank god you're—"

There are a million things I could say to her about what I've been up to. About why I've been avoiding her phone calls. I could explain that I needed some time to myself to figure out who my father really was.

And fuck, I did find out.

"He's not the father," I say. "Is he?"

"Who's not?"

"Michael Hall," I say, raising my voice. "When I left, you said that I acted just like my father, Michael Hall. You meant the same Michael Hall who killed his wife, then killed himself in Pahrump the year I was born, right?"

My whole body vibrates with shock. I don't know if what I'm doing is right, but I have to know. I have to confront her.

"There are other Michael Halls, right?" I say. "Someone else who you had sex with. It can't be him." The tears gather in my voice. "It just doesn't make sense."

There's a long pause that pulls at my insides, each nerve ripped from the threads of my spine.

My mother clears her throat.

"Yes, that's the same Michael Hall," she says in a quiet voice. "Your father wasn't a good man, sweetheart, which is why I didn't want you to know who he was. But he *is* your father. Why doesn't that make sense?"

I tell her that I've been in Pahrump since I left Vegas. That I got a retail job here. That I've got an apartment. I tell her about the murder-suicide anniversary party, about interviewing locals, about wanting to know more about my father. I tell her about Ned and his brother, and how the sheriff canceled his appointment with me. I tell her about how someone stole DNA samples from the police department. I tell her about the paternity tests. I tell her I wanted to find out where I belong and why I am the way I am.

I don't tell her about Crave. The fake identities. The masks. I don't tell her that if the paternity tests are real, then I've been fucking my own father.

Tension coils inside of me like a spring, ready to smash into a wall.

"Then there's a chance that whatever you had tested is *not* his DNA, right?" my mother says, her voice so gentle, so trusting, that it scrapes my ears like nails on a chalkboard. "Even criminologists make mistakes, sweetheart. I wouldn't hold onto that knowledge like it's the absolute truth."

Truth.

I hate that word.

Are you afraid she'll find out the truth about you? Crave had asked.

That's the only truth that helps me make sense of this stuff, Penny had said. *There is no reason. No nature. No nurture. It is what it is.*

"Who is my father?" I ask, raising my voice again.

"Michael Hall," my mother says, her tone filling with aggravation too. "I told you that."

My eyes water. Panic fills my veins all over again.

I couldn't have slept with my own father. It's—

It's—

God, I can't even bring myself to say it.

"Why didn't you tell me years ago?" I cry.

"Do you think you would've been able to handle knowing that your father killed his wife and himself?" she snaps. "He was a bad person, Rae. He cheated on his wife, probably more than once, and he raped me. He *hurt* me. My guess is that he beat his wife too. But I didn't let the pregnancy get in the way of giving you a good life." Her voice cracks; I've hit a nerve. "He's dead. You're a good person. You've got so much potential. You've got your whole life in front of you. You don't have to let your past control you like this."

A good person.

Potential.

A life.

Have I somehow always let Crave control me like this?

Someone mumbles in the background, and my mother responds to them in a hushed voice.

"I've got to go," she says to me. "But come home, okay? We need you here. I talked to the general manager, and she says you can come back; you've just got to stay out of the rooms. You're on admin work only. Nothing with the suites or the penthouses."

I blink the tears away. There's nothing I can do or say. My mother only knows what Crave told her. He must have lied to her and pretended to be Michael Hall.

If we test our DNA again, it'll have the same result. Deep in the crevices of my soul, I know that.

"I worry about you," my mother says. "Come home."

"Okay," I say.

I hang up, then book a bus ticket from Pahrump to Vegas for the morning. I'll ask Ned to tow my car to a mechanic in Vegas. It'll be a pain in the ass, but I need to get out of this place as soon as I can.

I try to sleep. I can't.

I stare at the ceiling.

Crave is my father. Officer Craven Gaines. The sad little mall cop. A man who has been tricking me. Watching me. Hunting me.

And I walked right into his arms.

The logical part of me wants to be shocked. Disgusted. Ashamed. Mad at myself for falling for a man like him.

Another part of me is relieved. Comforted. A twisted sense of strength curls inside of me, knowing that Crave could have killed me long ago, but he didn't. I have some sort of hold on him too, just like he has a hold on me.

The lack of remorse makes sense now. The only guilt I've had was when I was caught. And that's why I never turned Crave in. I didn't care about the people he killed. I only cared about what he could do for me.

He must've known for awhile that he was my father. That's the only way I've lived for this long. Otherwise, he would've killed me sooner.

I look out my bedroom window, expecting to see him on the sidewalk.

The apartment parking lot is empty.

I search the cupboards until I find cold medicine. It's not a sleeping pill, but it'll make me drowsy enough to stop these thoughts. I need silence. I need to sleep.

In the morning, I'll go to Vegas. It'll clear my head.

I'll pretend like Michael Hall really is my father.

I'll pretend like Crave doesn't exist.

Everything will make sense again.

Chapter 29

Crave

The early morning light follows me into the apartment. In the bedroom, Rae lies on her back, an unusual position for her. She's completely gone, seduced by the cold medicine I saw on her counter.

She can't stand to think about what it means to be my daughter.

Society believes it's immoral to be intimate with our families. We can't fuck them—no, *never*—otherwise, our spawn will be cursed to wear our sins on their deformed bodies.

I got a vasectomy not long after I raped Rae's mother. The feeling of my piercings abusing my victims was too heady to give up, and in cases where I let them live, I didn't want to have to take care of any brats. I don't give a shit about society's rules, but perhaps one day, the knowledge that we can't have children will comfort Rae. Or perhaps it'll depress her, knowing that I never wanted her to be born in the first place.

I don't give a shit either way.

A sleepy grunt flares through her nostrils. The comforter lies loosely over her stomach, exposing the top half of her oversized shirt. Her eyes are closed, and there's an innocence to her. She looks like an angel. Even if she is twenty-five years old, she's nothing more than a child. Especially compared to me.

Family is nothing more than a prefabricated human need for survival. A bond that clings to you so that your group can survive the winter. But when you're adopted into a group where the parents hate you, the word "family" takes on a different meaning. It's not survival, nor is it a bond. It's a relationship that's chosen for you.

Samantha tried to save Rae. Tried to raise a child that would do good in the world. And by all means, she put in the time, effort, and love. That "familial love" was chosen for Rae before she was born. Even so, Rae still came looking for her father.

And she fucking found him.

Her laptop is open on top of her dresser. I drag my fingertips over the mouse pad.

A bus ticket to Vegas with an eight a.m. departure.

Funny.

She thinks she can run away, back to mommy. As if dear old Samantha is enough to save her from me.

My vision sharpens as I contemplate the years I've put into this insane experiment. I knew, from the day I found out about her existence, that I should've killed Rae and her mother. With the death of Michael and Miranda Hall, I needed to clean up the loose ends, including the one bitch I fucked while impersonating Michael Hall.

But curiosity won me over, seeing that dark-haired infant in the bitch's arms. I snuck into the resort's childcare center, posing as a maintenance worker, and I got the DNA sample for an acquaintance to confirm it off-the-record. With those results proving our shared blood, I knew what I wanted out of Rae.

An experiment. A daughter raised by a good woman. A woman who never intended to sleep with a man like me. How would our daughter turn out? Would she be good like her mother, or would the sadistic streak in her blood run so deep that she *had* to let it out? Would she end up being my girl?

I rub my dick as I look at her body. In the beginning, my fascination with Rae was merely scientific. It wasn't until I had her in my taxi the night I planned to finally kill her, that everything changed. The smell of her cunt and the devious look in her eyes intrigued me. She saw others, even me, as less than her. And I wanted more of that.

Her chest rises and falls, and her nipples are smooth under her shirt, like she's begging for my attention. By all definitions, she is my daughter. My blood. Half of my DNA. But it's not as simple as that. Family doesn't mean anything to me. Why should family suddenly mean something when it comes to Rae? We're simply bodies, and we both want more than "family" out of each other.

I pull the comforter down until she's exposed. The oversized shirt. Her thong. The makeup stains dry on her pillow.

I slide onto my stomach, moving myself between her legs. I pull the fabric from her pussy lips, exposing her slit. I tongue her folds, tasting her. Sourly sweet, like forbidden fruit. She moans, and it reverberates down to her thighs. Her hand grasps my hair.

"Little girl," I whisper, my words tickling her cunt.

She flinches sharply, then kicks me in the shoulder. I climb over her body and pin her to the bed before she can focus. Her eyes widen, shock huffing through her lips.

"What the fuck?" she screams. "You fucking freak!"

"You're not making that bus," I say. "You're staying here with me."

"No—"

I cover her mouth and press my hips down, my hard cock resting between her legs, the metal rubbing against her clit.

"This is who you are, Rae," I murmur. "Accept it."

She jerks her head to the side, desperate to get out of my grasp. I adjust my grip, pinching her nose and mouth in my fingers. Panic dances in her eyes as her face reddens, practically matching her cherry-red hair.

"Are you ready to accept it?" I ask.

She squints her eyes, and I chuckle, then I carry her across the bedroom to her bathroom mirror. I shove my hand down the front of her thong, the other hand clutching her throat, forcing her to face our reflection. My head leans against hers, and in my boots, I'm taller than her, like her masked killer, but the face is Officer Gaines.

She pants, her mouth hanging open, lust hazy in her eyes. I'm everything she hates and everything she wants, and *fuck*, my dick gets hard knowing how it gets under her skin.

"No," she whispers. "No, no, no—"

In the mirror, she sneers at me, her teeth bared.

I lick her cheek. "My little girl knows she's mine, doesn't she?"

She quivers, her body reacting to what she knows she shouldn't want. But my little girl can't help it.

"I don't want you," she says.

"You do." I breathe into her neck, nuzzling into her. "You like knowing that your daddy *knows* he shouldn't want you too. He knows he should let you go. He knows he shouldn't be following you for years. But you like that he can't help himself. Isn't that right?" She shivers against me, pushing her ass into my cock. My length strains against her, eager to be inside of her. "I told myself I was waiting for the perfect time to kill you, but as soon as I saw how much you liked watching people die, I knew you needed my help. I knew you needed the encouragement to try it for yourself. A daddy always helps his little girl shine."

She trembles. "Don't—"

"Don't *what?*" I snarl, curling a finger into her slit as I choke her, forcing her to watch her mirrored face as she loses oxygen. Her cheeks tint pink, then red, then purple. "Tell me, little girl. Tell me what you want. If you want me to stop, I'll stop right now."

I keep her locked in my arms, but I let go of her neck, giving her the ability to breathe.

"Tell me to stop," I repeat.

She squirms in my arms, her jaws snapping over her shoulder. She misses. Her juices slide down my fingers.

"Say it," I demand.

"Fuck you."

"Funny, isn't it? You won't tell me to stop," I say in a low voice. She stills, hanging onto my words. "Deep down in that fucked-up little brain of yours, you *like* that I worship your pussy. You like that I'm a killer. That I bring you bloody presents. That I hide behind a mask. You like knowing that I am your fucking father, because it means I've always been here, always watching you. You like knowing that you're mine. And I'll be fucking dead before I let go of you."

"I hate you," she whispers harshly, a tear running down her face.

"Then tell me to leave. Tell me you don't want me. Tell me to stop, little girl. Tell your daddy how best to love you," I mock. "And if that means you want me to go away, I'll listen, baby, like a good daddy should."

She shakes violently; the words don't come out. I shove another finger inside of her. Another tear. A delicious fucking tear. My tongue licks it up, tasting her salt, her skin, her trashy makeup. Her own disguise she wears so proudly for the world. But a mask like that won't hide her from me.

"So fucking wet for me," I say. "Your tears. Your cunt. Your brain can scream 'no' all it wants, but your sweet little pussy always says 'yes' to me."

"I hate you."

"You hate yourself. You hate that you still want me. Even as Officer Gaines. As your father. All I need to do is put on a mask, and you could pretend that I'm your dream man. Ain't that right, baby?" I change my voice to that husky tone I put on as Crave: "How does it feel, little girl? Knowing that I'm everything you hate."

I let go of her pussy and grab a knife from my pocket. I flick it open and hold it to her neck.

"Would it make you feel better if I wore a mask?" I tease in my gravelly, masked killer voice. Blood pools at the cut, and she whimpers into me.

"Crave," she says.

"Daddy," I correct. "Say it for me."

She sobs uncontrollably, still thrusting her ass onto my cock, begging me to take her.

"Crave, please," she whines.

"No, baby," I murmur. I taste her blood, that acrid, metallic substance slipping over my tongue, filling me with power. Euphoria washes over me in a blinding heat. Blood. Our shared blood. "Say it for me now," I whisper. "Call me by my real name."

I keep the knife on her neck and move my free hand into the front of her thong again.

"Daddy," she whimpers.

"I used to dream of killing you and your mother. You know that?" I ask. "If I had known about you while you were still in the womb, I would've killed you then. Two birds with one stone. A dead baby and her mother roasting under the desert sun. But I found you too late, so instead, I watched over you. Watched you grow. Saw you in the resorts. In the childcare centers. In the private schools. In the nightclubs. Took you in my taxi and even gave your last big conquest the surveillance footage to prove that you stole his firearm—"

"No!"

"—and got your ass fired. Look where you are, little girl. Isn't it funny?" I chuckle. "Daddy's here. You found me. Aren't you proud of yourself?" I lick the tiny stream of blood dripping from the shallow cut on her neck, and she shivers, her mound humping my palm. "And I still won't kill you, little girl. You're too amusing to throw away now. You're mine, baby. All fucking mine."

I flip her around so that she's facing me, her ass on the bathroom counter, and I pull out my dick, stroking myself. Her eyes are heavy, her pupils wide, her lips wet and open. Her tongue drifts across her bottom lip, and her hungry eyes betray her as she glimpses at my cock.

"Disgusting little girl," I say. She crumbles. I reach forward, holding her ass, squeezing her skin, relishing in the fact that she's literally my blood. Everything about her is mine. I click my jaw. "You and me, baby. We're disgusting, and we always will be. There's nothing we can do to change that."

She sucks in a gasp. I pull my gun from my holster, raising the muzzle to her temple. Her eyes water.

"Say it for me, now," I say. "Tell me the truth. If you have any last words, any last requests, you say them right now." I study her face, and she stills, so gentle, so compliant, so unsure of herself, that it fills me with excitement. Even Rae doesn't know what she'll choose right now. It's thrilling. She could choose anything, and that unpredictability fills me with anticipation. "What do you want from your daddy?"

Her brow crinkles. Her knees part. Her mouth opens.

"Fuck me, Daddy," she finally whispers.

I impale her on my dick. Her thong bunches up to the side of us as she wraps her arms around my neck, fear and desire coursing through her, every ounce of adrenaline running through her nerves, bringing her closer to me. Then vacancy subtly clouds her brown eyes, but I spot it. It's like she knows she needs more; she just doesn't know what it is.

Lucky for her, I know exactly what she needs.

The gun rests on her temple. She closes her eyes, losing herself on my dick. Her pussy constricting me.

Someone needs to die.

I could kill her right now.

I *should* kill her. I made my point.

Maybe it's not her who needs to die. Maybe it's me.

I've thought about killing myself before, but I'm not entertained enough to do it. Logically, I know the world would be safer without my DNA; Rae proves that. But I don't give a shit about the world or its people. I'd rather live just to see what I can get away with.

Still, I picture the roles reversed: Rae holding the gun to my head, killing me as I fuck her.

And I come.

She grimaces and pulls me closer. Our bodies are hot against each other. Our breaths panting.

I never wanted a kid. Rae isn't supposed to be here. But I won't kill her now. It's my choice. I want to see what she does in this world, even if she ends up killing me.

"You," she says, snapping back to reality, snarling at me once again. "You tricked me—"

A knock bangs on the door.

"Rae?" a muffled male voice asks. "I heard screaming. Rae? Are you all right? Open up! Let me in!"

I grin, immediately recognizing the voice.

Ned is here.

CHAPTER 30

RAE

I LUNGE FOR THE FRONT DOOR. MY HAND TWISTS THE HANDLE. Crave yanks me back. I stumble to the ground.

The door opens.

Ned's eyes widen.

Help, I want to say. *Run away.*

I stay silent on the ground.

Ned stares at Crave, his gaze seething. He steps inside of the apartment and broadens his shoulders, taking up as much space as possible.

I should warn him.

Crave will kill you, I should say. *You'll die.*

"You hurt her," Ned growls.

Crave's lips pull into the smile I know so well. When his mask was unzipped, it revealed this small glimpse of the real him.

I never saw Officer Gaines smile. Would I have seen the resemblance then? Or would I have denied that truth?

"I fucked her, you mean," Crave says.

"I'm calling the police," Ned shouts.

Crave bellows with laughter so hard, he holds his stomach. The clamor crashes through the apartment.

Ned and I gawk at him.

"What's so funny?" Ned asks.

A tingling sensation crawls from my stomach to the back of my neck.

This isn't good.

Crave cracks his neck. "I've got a better idea."

Crave barrels into Ned, his body slamming into the wall. The two of them pummel each other on the ground. Punching. Kicking. Grunts. Pain. A fist in a cheekbone. Blood spit on the ground.

I should do something.

I should call the police.

Crave's gun is on the floor, right outside of the bathroom. I could get it. They wouldn't even notice.

I should shoot Crave.

He's killed so many people.

Crave punches, his fists railing into Ned's face, a predator mashing his rival into the ground.

Crave has done so many horrible things. I know that.

But he hasn't killed me.

You're fucking crazy, my brain argues. *He's brainwashed you. Made you think you're special. You're not. He'll kill you too.*

I imagine a bullet colliding with Ned's head. The explosion of brain and bone and blood. The goodness of the world dripped onto a blank canvas. The meaninglessness of it all.

Crave smashes Ned into the floor. Ned's head bounces. His eyes go dull. Unconscious.

Crave turns to me. "Who is going to protect you now?"

I bare my teeth at him. "I fucking hate you!"

"You're a goddamned broken record." Crave scowls. "Admit it, Rae. Admit who you are. You thought fucking a masked man would take away your self-hatred, because I don't give a fuck what you want or what you did."

He leans his palms against the wall, caging me between his arms. Blood is smeared on his teeth. I bite my tongue.

"I see who you are, right down to your ugly core," he murmurs. "And I'm still here. We're the same, Rae. I'm the only one who will always be here for you."

My eyes frantically search him. Those bulging brown eyes. The clean-shaven face. His black hair.

It can't be true. He has to be wrong.

But I see myself in his face. Our shared brown eyes. My dark hair that I've dyed red. My hair hasn't receded like his, but I can tell we'll have the same hairline one day. There are even wrinkles around his eyes that I know I'll have too.

I may be his daughter, but I'm not a killer.

I can't accept it. I won't admit it. I refuse.

"Just because we share blood doesn't mean we're the same," I whisper.

"Don't it, though?" he snickers, a smirk painting his lips. "You were raised by a good woman. A woman I raped and got pregnant. A woman who gave you everything. And you still ended up here with me."

He grabs the gun off of the floor, and I back away, sliding along the wall until I'm pressed against the fold-up table. I broaden my shoulders, opening my eyes wide, daring him to shoot me.

He hands the weapon to me.

"If you hate me so much, then prove it." He puts his hands behind his head in a defenseless position. "Kill me. Ned will be your alibi. Say it's self-defense, and you can forget you found me. You and your mother can go back to thinking you were born from some fucked-up dead man named Michael Hall. You can move on and put a pretty little bow on your murder-filled past." He licks his teeth, the blood smearing clean from his white canines.

I hold the gun to his forehead.

Kill him, my brain argues. *He deserves it.*

"The truth, *our* blood, feels better though, doesn't it?" he asks. "It feels right."

I pull back the hammer.

"Do it," he demands.

I pull the trigger and flinch slightly. I shoot the wall.

I drop the gun and crumble to my knees.

I can't kill him. Not now. Not when I need so many answers.

"That's what I thought," Crave murmurs.

He turns toward the door and steps over Ned's unconscious body.

Blood boils in my veins.

His blood. Mine. Ours.

No. It's *my* blood. I choose my own path.

And I don't choose him.

"Go kill yourself," I shout. He stills, his back to me, his hand waiting on the doorknob. "I'm not a murderer like you, and I *never* will be."

His lips curl back. "But you thought about asking your masked killer to take care of that rapist, Officer Gaines, didn't you?"

My heart sinks. I wanted it so badly. I wanted to enjoy Officer Gaines's death *with* Crave.

My vision darkens. Is he right?

Crave chuckles. "I bet you even imagined fucking Crave on top of the mall cop's dead body."

Did Crave use his Officer Gaines persona to mess with me? To manipulate me into embracing my darker side? To show me who I really am?

The door closes behind him.

My breath pants in my throat.

Outside, a car engine starts.

I rush to the window.

A truck. Dark white paint. The kind of car that so many people have.

Crave—Officer Gaines or whoever the fuck he is—has always been here. Waiting for me.

Confusion and comfort and anger wrestle inside of me. I'm not supposed to be comforted by this.

But I am. I am. I like knowing that he's been here, watching out for me.

Ned groans, finally coming back to consciousness. My eyes stay glued to that truck. Crave drives away, leaving me alone with the truth.

Our blood. Our shared DNA.

Am I really like him?

Ned pushes himself up, grunting as he strains. He wipes his mouth with the back of his hand, blood dashing across his skin.

His eye is swollen and black, his nose bruised, and his lip is busted. He puts a hand on my shoulder.

My skin grows cold.

"I'll call the cops," Ned says.

Tears fill my eyes. There isn't a bad bone in Ned's body. He would never kill someone, even if meant protecting someone else. Every blood cell coursing through his body is undeniably good.

But me? I'm *not.* Even now, with everything that's happened, I still don't want anything bad to happen to Crave.

You'll hurt Crave by yourself, my brain promises. *You'll get your revenge.*

But it's a lie.

Ned continues: "I'll fire him. I'll—"

"No," I whisper. "Please." Ned's brows furrow with concern. I crack my voice: "I don't want to make this a thing. Not right now. Please. I just—"

My voice drifts off as if I'm in shock. But it's another act. A way to protect Crave so that I can take care of this on my own time. I can have Ned protect me later, in a way that I choose.

But right now, I don't want to give Ned that power.

"I'll have my brother watch him, then," Ned says. I gasp with anguish, layering on the tears. I am crying, but not from the fear of Crave. I'm crying because I'm overwhelmed. Because I can't face the truth of what wanting my killer father actually means.

Ned stiffens. He puts an arm around me.

"Okay, I won't," he says softly. "Please don't cry."

The clock ticks in the kitchen. It's past nine now. I missed my bus.

I need to go. I need distance from this. From Pahrump. From Crave. I need space to figure out where I fit in. If shared blood means anything to me.

To us.

"Can you drive me to Vegas?" I ask.

Ned kisses the top of my head. "Of course I can," he says. "I'll do anything for you, beautiful."

Ned helps me into my room and even stuffs different outfits into a duffel bag. When the police come to investigate the gunshot,

Ned lies to them, protecting me from their questions and from making this *thing* with Officer Gaines any bigger. After that, I get him a pack of frozen peas from the freezer. He holds it to his face and beams at me like he wants to give me the world. Maybe he does.

I should feel safe. Loved. Protected. Cherished. I should feel satisfied by a man like Ned, but I don't. Not even a little. Doing the right thing matters more to Ned than I do, and that's how it will always be. I'll always matter less.

Ned will never possess me like Crave does.

Chapter 31

Crave

I consider going to the Galloway House and staying in the basement until she returns. I think about hunting humans out in the desert. Finding another lucky set of hikers. All of it bores me.

Four days pass like that.

Eventually, I head to Las Vegas. I tell myself it's because I need the money; I can't show up at the mall anymore. But it's not about paying rent.

I drive the taxi up and down Las Vegas Boulevard, taking drunks to late-night diners. Business types to the right conference centers. Party girls to the hottest nightclubs. My mind mixes those flashing signs until all I see is her.

Wouldn't it be beautiful to see Rae die?

To force her to watch *me* die?

To make her kill me?

To have all of this end?

A few women in matching sequin dresses wave at me from the Cosmopolitan's ramp. They squeal at each other as they pile into the back of my car. One of them plays a pop song on her phone. They sing off-key and at the top of their lungs. They're unbelievably annoying.

You should kill them, Rae's voice says in my mind. *They have no purpose in this world.*

I lick my teeth, glancing at the women in the mirror. A blonde. A brunette. Another with an ombre hairstyle.

"You'd like that, wouldn't you?" I say in a low voice.

Of course I would, Rae says in my mind. I picture her sitting in the backseat of the taxi, smashed in between the sequined women. Rae's mischievous laughter echoes: *I want to watch what you do to them, then I want you to fuck me on their dead bodies.*

"You're a depraved little slut," I say, locking eyes with the imaginary Rae in the rearview mirror.

"Huh?" one of the passengers asks. "Did you say something?"

"Did you just call me a slut?"

"Where are we going again?"

"You're heading to the Linq, right?" I ask.

"Happy Half Hour!"

"We're gonna get freaking wasted!"

I laugh with them, pretending to be amused too, but my mind is on Rae.

Perhaps I told her everything too soon. It would have taken a while to get used to the idea that I'm the ugly security guard who "raped" her, but I know my girl; she would have gotten over that. I could've marked her too. Made her ugly like me. We could have had fun together, and she would never have known the truth about her lineage.

But Rae wanted closure; I simply gave it to her. I was curious. I wanted to see what would happen when she knew the truth. If she would embrace or reject me. Now she knows her truth is far more bitter than a sugar-coated lie.

I drop the women off at the Linq, then I search up and down Las Vegas Boulevard until I finally find her.

Rae stands on the curb, her elbow locked with a man who dresses like he's got money. Rae leans on him, using him for support. Drunk, or pretending to be. A coy smile on her face. Using him like she's used so many others.

The man hails my cab.

I should stop.

I could take care of her right now.

I could be done with all of this.

I keep driving. Killing her would be too easy. An organized mess of predictability.

The man scowls, shaking his fist at my passing car. Rae pulls him tighter, almost as if she knows it was me.

Maybe that's the reason I left her apartment that day. It was too easy knowing that I had control over her. Rae could play mind games with the best of them, but physically, I will always win. All I have to do is use my strength.

It's because you love me, the imaginary version of Rae scolds. *You love me. You always have. You can't kill me because you love yourself too much. You know I'm you.*

I roll my eyes at my inner thoughts. Some of that is true. I really fucking hate that I can't kill her. But I don't love her, nor do I love myself. I don't care about anything that much.

Rae is a possession. An object I created. A thing I own. And a psychopath doesn't love. He possesses. And if I keep her alive, then eventually, she'll possess me too.

Rae and her latest hookup turn into blurred dots in the rearview mirror. I keep driving forward.

One day, Rae will come crawling back to me. And when she does, I'll remind her that I've always been in control, and I'll do whatever it takes to keep it that way.

I have to.

Chapter 32

Rae

"You're not going to give me your number?" the man asks.

I smile over my shoulder. I don't remember his name, but I don't plan on saying it again. I wink at him, and he grins at me.

I turn back to the window. Down below, the Strip is majestic. A circus of lights. Millions of people with no real direction. A beautiful mess of humanity. And I'm floating above it all.

A month has passed since I left Pahrump, but it feels like it's been longer. The same nights. The same days. The same men. The same stolen possessions that don't mean anything to me. Not like Crave does.

"If I must," I tease. I grab the man's phone and type in the number for my mother's hotel.

He looks down at the number, then kisses my cheek. "I'll call you soon, Miranda."

I give him a quick hug, and a few minutes later, I close the hotel room door behind me, then take the elevator down to the casino.

I don't feel guilty. I don't feel powerful. I don't feel anything.

I ease through the casino and find my mother in the lobby. She waves me over.

"I got you coffee," she says.

I take the cardboard cup, and we walk through the twinkling slot machines, like a child and her mother in an arcade.

"How are you liking your new home?" she asks.

I bite my tongue, thinking over my words carefully. My mind gets stuck on that word: *home.* She's letting me rent one of her properties at a discounted rate. I can't stay at our penthouse anymore. I'm not even supposed to be in the hotel right now, but she wants to take care of me. She's a good woman, and with the things I've done, I don't deserve a mother like her.

Is that why I can't stop thinking about Crave? Because I think I deserve a father like him?

"I love it," I lie. "Thank you."

"You're still torn up about your father, aren't you?"

I stiffen. In a way, it *is* true, but not in the way she thinks. In her mind, Michael Hall is my father, and he's dead.

"Try not to think about it," my mother says as she rubs my arm. "Secrets like that can destroy you from the inside out. I don't want to see you hurt anymore."

My vision fuzzes at the edges.

Secrets. Destruction. My insides.

Crave *did* destroy me from the inside out. He showed me that the blood inside of me isn't just mine; it's his too.

In a way, my mother destroyed me as well. They both made me. Gave me life.

I never asked to be the child of a serial killer and a saint.

"How can I stop thinking about it?" I snap at my mother through gritted teeth. "How? How do I move on when my dad is a—"

Everything shakes around me. I try again: "When my dad is a—"

"It's okay," my mother says. She pulls me into her arms, hugging me like I'm a child again. Every time I stole from her flashes through my mind—the money, the jewelry, the perfumes, the credit cards, the way she knew it was me, and how she looked the other way because she knew she couldn't stop me. Nothing has changed; she loves me, even after all of this.

Her perfume—floral and expensive—stifles my nose, and I think about Crave. She's been with him. He chose her, and he didn't kill her. He kept her alive, even before he knew she had his kid.

Did he love her? Does he love her now?

Why did he keep her—*us*—alive?

Does it have to do with me, or just my mother?

Why does that make me jealous?

"I'm sorry," I say, pulling away from her. "It's been crazy lately. With everything."

Her eyes soften. "Tell me what you need. I'm here for you."

I study her. I don't feel anything. No warmth. No joy. No comfort. No love. She's my mother, the woman who raised me, but we're so vastly different from each other.

I should be grateful that she nurtured me. I'm not. I still ended up being a fucked-up person. I don't know if I would've turned out this way if I hadn't met Crave, but I know that no matter what I do—no matter which mask I put on each day—this need for power has always been inside of me.

"I need some space," I say.

"I understand," she says. "Don't—"

Before she can say anything else, I rush to the nearest bathroom and splash water on my face. The cold water chills me. I savor it. The remnants of my makeup drip down my face, streaking me in gray. I grab a paper towel and blot my face until I'm completely clean.

I have her button nose. I have their shared natural dark hair. But I have his brown eyes.

His blood.

There's a darkness inside of my heart that is *all* him. The thrill that needs more from people. More from life. A hunger that has always—and will always—belong to him, no matter how hard I try to resist it.

I pull out the small water bottle in my purse with the ripped-off label: the bottle of poison that Crave gave to me. Since I left Pahrump, I've kept it tucked inside of my purse. A reminder that I could kill him as easily as he could kill me.

If he hadn't told me it was poison, I might have consumed it.

It could have killed me.

It could kill my next hookup.

It could kill anyone.

And it could still kill *him.*

I stuff it back into my purse, then head to the parking garage. I should pack a bag, but there's an urgency rolling in the bottom of my stomach. I can't wait any longer.

I want to go *now.*

I don't have a plan, but I know I need to see Crave. I need to confront him for the last time.

I need to ask him for his birth name.

Chapter 33

Rae

A new padlock is chained to the fence around the Galloway House. I throw my purse and shoes over the gate, then I climb the fence. My bare feet cling to the links. It's painful, but it doesn't stop me.

I drop down to the dirt and slip back into my shoes. Crave may not even be here right now.

I walk forward anyway.

The house is different now that I know my connection to the place. Everything feels strange, like it's not as big as before. Like everything that happened was a dream.

Inside, the house is empty. Quiet. Everything is clean. The blood-stained couch is missing. There's fresh paint on the walls, and a clinical, fresh scent hangs in the air. Like someone's trying to cover up the past again.

I sit on the floor in the living room.

I'm back to where I started. I don't even know Crave's real name. I don't know how to find him.

A fist bangs on the front door.

"Hello?" a loud male voice calls. "Is someone in there? You're trespassing on private property. I'll call the police."

I walk toward the entrance quickly and open the door. Ned jolts, shocked by my sudden appearance. He pulls me in for a hug.

"Oh, hey!" he says. "I thought you were those teens messing with the house again. When did you get back in town? I didn't realize you were home."

Home. He thinks Pahrump is my home. If anything, the Galloway House is my home.

There's a lot of things Ned doesn't realize about me.

"I just wanted to see the place one last time," I say.

"I get that," he says. Like my mother, Ned still thinks Michael Hall—the supposed murder-suicide perpetrator—is my father. "You should've called me. I could've taken you out for a welcome-home dinner."

My lips curl. He's so nice, it's pathetic.

"Can I have Officer Gaines's info?" I tuck my hair behind my ear. "Sorry," I say. "I know that's weird. But can I?"

Ned's lips pull down. "Why?"

"I need to know where he is." I tap my lips and choose words he'll sympathize with: "So I can feel safe."

"Of course."

He sends me a text with Gaines's contact information attached. I click the file. The address opens to the map app, giving me automatic directions to where Crave lives. I know exactly where he is now.

If he's still there.

"What was he doing at your apartment anyway?" Ned asks.

I could tell Ned something close to the truth—that we were fucking—and Ned wouldn't fault me for it. He's too respectful of my independence for that. But there's another half-truth that will give me the best advantage.

"He was following me," I whisper.

For a while, we're both silent. It's strange that Crave had worked for Ned for years, and Ned never suspected him of anything evil.

I did. I *knew* there was something wrong with Officer Gaines. I never trusted him. I just had no idea how much was wrong, or that I *liked* that wrongness when it came from Crave.

Ned doesn't suspect anything evil about me either.

"Why don't you ever let me see your cock?" I blurt. It's out of the blue, but I don't care right now.

Ned blushes, glancing down at his waistband. "What are you talking about?"

"We had sex for months, but it was always you going down on me." I shrug. "I just want to know why."

"It's all about you," he says cautiously. "With everything you do for me, it should be your pleasure. You deserve it."

I tilt my head to the side. That she-comes-first habit made me think he was my masked killer at one point. It seems so obviously wrong now. Crave doesn't give a shit about my orgasms, nor do I care about his.

"You trust everyone, don't you?" I ask.

He gives me a lopsided grin. "You always have to believe in people," he says. "Otherwise, what are we living for?"

I laugh. It's insane how warm-hearted he is. His life has been one big pile of roses and rainbows.

Ned laughs too.

I gesture around. "The place looks good."

He rubs his forehead. "It does. We're still considering hosting the anniversary party here next year." He pinches the bridge of his nose. "Crap."

"What?"

"Do you have any ibuprofen? My head is killing me."

I open up my purse and find a small container of pills. Next to it, there's the label-less water bottle.

Maybe the poison was never meant for me.

Maybe it was another one of my father's gifts.

Maybe he always believed in me.

I hand Ned the pills container and the bottle. He pops three pills, then downs the entire bottle, his face twisting in a grimace as he finishes the drink.

Every drop. Down, down, down.

"What brand is this?" he asks. He crumbles the plastic. "It tastes terrible."

I lean closer to him. "I added a vitamin mix to it."

He wrinkles his nose. I watch him. What will happen? How

long will it take? Or is this another test? A final game orchestrated by Crave?

I want to fuck Crave for that.

Ned straightens himself, then lets out a long sigh. "So," he says. "What's next?"

"I should move back to Pahrump," I say. "Vegas isn't good for me."

"How so?"

"Well, it's—"

Ned grabs his stomach, lurching to the side.

"Jesus," he says. He grabs the wall. "Fuck. That hurts."

Ned never curses.

He wipes his nose. Blood smudges his pale skin. "What—"

His body begins to convulse. I peer down at him, watching every turn. Every twitch. Every movement of his body. It fascinates me. How long will it take for him to die? Or will he be in pain for a while? What will happen next?

"It's an allergic reaction," he mumbles. "Call an ambulance. Shit—"

He doesn't suspect me. Not even now.

I stand taller, towering over him as he falls to his knees. His mouth, eyes, and nose bleed as his body flails on the ground. So human. So natural.

Ned is wrong. Even if you don't believe in others—even if you only believe in *yourself*—there are other reasons to live.

Sometimes, that reason lies in the darkness. And sometimes, that darkness finds you.

Ned rolls to his side, vomit splashing on the floor. Black and red lumps mixed with green bile coat the laminate. It's beautiful in a putrid way.

I unzip his pants and pull out his cock. The shaft is small, like a pink hamster pup curled up. It could grow. It wouldn't be so bad.

Still, it irks me. His willingness to give me orgasms was never about me. It was about hiding his insecurities. Even someone like Ned can lie.

I honestly don't care about penis size. Sex has never been

about my pleasure; it's always been about getting what I want from others. Then I met Crave, and I learned that sex could be pleasurable for me too. Crave fucks me so good, he makes me forget myself.

I pull down my thong, then hike up my dress. I sit on Ned's face. He can barely move, the poison paralyzing him. It feels good knowing that he's dying now, and that it's not just the poison that's killing him, but I am too. My pussy is smothering him.

Part of me knows that this darkness was always inside of me. Now that Crave has entered my life, I'll never know if I would've turned out to be a thief who eventually grew out of her pick-pocket habit. I'll never know if I would've always turned out this way, with or without my father.

I'm okay with that.

I smear my cunt over Ned's face, painting him with his blood, his saliva, flecks of his vomit, and my arousal. Power fills my body.

I'm *alive.*

In my mind, Crave's mask fades away. Brown eyes glitter with greed. His entire focus fixated on me.

I always knew not to trust Officer Gaines. My mistake was trusting Crave.

But that's not a mistake anymore.

When Ned finally stops moving, I stand, lifting off of him. I look down at the corpse. A shell of a man. Everything good and pure and loving in this world. A man I should want to be with. Someone my mother would have loved.

Someone my father sees right through.

Someone I knew would never satisfy me.

I lick my lips, then check my phone again. I need to get rid of the body.

I'll ask my father for help.

Chapter 34

Crave

Rae drives through the mall's parking lot, then stops her car outside of the Galloway House. She'll come to me soon.

I turn off the mall's surveillance footage; Ned hasn't changed the password yet. He probably never will.

About an hour later, there's a knock on my door. I look through the peephole.

Rae stands with her arms crossed over her chest.

I open the door. She glares at me as if I owe her an apology. Maybe under other circumstances, I do. Right now, I don't speak a word. I want to hear what *she* has to say for herself.

"What's your name?" she asks. "Your real name? The one given to you at birth?"

I keep my gaze steady. Her lips pull back into a scowl.

"You don't call. You don't text," she says. "You push yourself into my life, and then you act like I don't exist. Do you know how annoying that is?"

She fidgets, and it's like I'm wearing a mask again. Hiding my reactions. Not giving her any clues as to what I'm thinking.

I'll never be like her conquests. She will never be able to manipulate me like them. I'll always be in control.

She turns away from me, her cheeks tinted pink.

"I need your help." She lifts her shoulders. "It's Ned."

A grin spreads across my face. She doesn't have to explain a thing.

"That's my girl," I say.

She wrinkles her nose, her checks flushing briefly before returning to their normal color.

"You know how fucked up that is coming from you?" she huffs in a forced angry tone. The upper corners of her mouth lift, showing that she loves hearing me say it. "You're my father. My *estranged* father. You can't act like you're proud of me."

I widen my stance. I'm not proud of her. I'm proud of myself. For finally getting my daughter to kill someone. For getting exactly what I wanted out of this experiment.

I angle my head toward my truck in the driveway.

"Get in," I say.

I don't tell her my plan. We drive to Vegas, and I let Rae mull over the possibilities in silence. And when we find a red-haired, tan-skinned girl, I send Rae over to her at the bar.

The two girls get drunk, buying each other shots. My girl likes playing with her prey as much as I do. I watch from the comfort of one of the slot machines, biding my time.

Rae grabs the look-alike's arm. "Come on," she says. "Let's go to a strip club. My boyfriend will take us."

"It's a male strip club though, right?" the redhead asks. "I don't know if I can handle seeing another pretty woman."

Rae winks, pushing her breasts together with her arms. Of course, this look-alike is falling for Rae's charms. Rae is a natural at tricking people; I wouldn't be surprised if she's seduced women before.

Rae motions for me to follow, and the three of us slide into my truck. Rae sits in the middle.

I lock the car doors.

"Hey, baby," Rae says. "You got anything for us to drink?"

Rae and I exchange eye contact. I nod toward the water bottles. "Help yourselves."

She hands one to the girl.

"Here," Rae says. "Hydrate, babe. This place—" she laughs to herself. "It's like nothing you've ever seen before."

"I've been to a male strip club," the redhead says as she gulps down the liquid. I smirk to myself, and Rae winks at me.

This time, the bottle contains a sedative. The redhead drinks enough that she slumps down, sleeping on Rae's thighs, snoring loudly.

I shift my hand between Rae's legs, my knuckles brushing the redhead's hair.

"You're evil," Rae says as she spreads her legs, giving herself to me. My thumb teases her clit, the redhead's hair tangled in my fingers and Rae's juices.

"So are you," I murmur.

At the mall, I use my old keys to get into Ned's office. We turn off the security cameras, then we carry the girl inside of the Galloway House and set her down on the living room floor.

I glance around. With the new paint, it's brighter than it's ever been, even at night.

The redhead stirs.

"What is this?" she mumbles. "Where are we?"

Rae hands the girl another bottle of water. "Here," she says. "You passed out. I took you back to my house. I hope that's all right."

"Mmm," the woman says, drinking the liquid down. Then she's back out again, lying on the floor.

We move Ned's corpse right next to her. Then I offer the knife to Rae. She wraps her hands around mine, the handle clutched between us.

"You don't need me to help you," I say.

"Of course not," she says. "I just want to kill this one together."

The knife plunges into the girl's body, mashing into her stomach. Blood splatters to the side, painting us red, and I lock eyes with Rae. My little girl's eyes grow hungry, and my dick bulges in my pants.

She's evil, just like me. And god, I want to rip her open right now.

"Let's go," Rae says feverishly. "We need to get out of here."

I squirt gasoline from the canister, dousing Ned, the redhead, and the house.

In the entryway, Rae lights a match and throws it on the ground.

Flames swallow the house, and the two of us run back into the desert night to watch it unfold. The fire burns orange and yellow, smoke lifting into the black sky. Rae clings to me, my sweet little girl's breath escaping her in short bursts. Fear. Panic. Violence. Arousal.

Sirens whistle in the distance. The fire truck pulls up, the horn blaring into the night. I wrap my arms around Rae, grasping her breasts, and she leans into me. A boulder and cacti obstruct our view, but I maneuver us so that Rae can see the chaos unfold. I want her to witness every depraved thing we've accomplished together.

I slide my hands in the front of her pants. She's soaked.

"They think you're dead," I say.

"I am," she whispers. "And you're a suspect, Officer Gaines."

"Do you like that?"

She presses herself into me, primal need oozing between her legs. A mix of pride and irritation swells in my chest, knowing that she does enjoy the fact that I'm a suspect. She likes having that power over me. She may still be planning my arrest.

It would be interesting if I finally ended up in jail because of her. I wouldn't have suspected that.

"Roderick Galloway," I mutter. She freezes, latching onto that information. "The Galloways adopted me from birth."

Her eyes drift back to the burning house. It transforms into a black carcass in front of us. Rae knows the details about the Galloway murder-suicide, but she doesn't know that the adopted son was the real killer.

I smell her neck, tasting the sourness on her skin. There's a bitter aftertaste to her, a primal rejection written into our blood so that we don't fuck each other. But I've never liked sweet things. I've always liked sour, bitter flavors. I like the way those flavors cling to my tongue.

I honestly don't care what Rae wants, as long as she's mine.

And I know Rae needs more from me too.

---

one month later

At the rental, I open the front door. Soft noises come from the bedroom closet. I expect them now.

Rae sits on the floor of the walk-in closet, watching television from a thrift store tablet on wifi stolen from one of my neighbors. A pile of comforters, old t-shirts, and blankets surround her. She holds up the device.

"Look," she says.

A news reporter stands in front of the mall.

Police have finally ruled that it was yet another murder-suicide, determining it to be another case of bad luck, the reporter says. *But some residents believe in a story far more nefarious. Some even consider it a curse.*

A short young woman with blonde hair grabs the microphone. Penny, Rae's teenage minion.

It wasn't an accident, Penny says. *Someone is out there. They didn't like that Ned and Rae got so close to the truth.*

And what truth is that? the reporter asks.

All the victims were murder victims. There was no suicide. They faked those deaths. The real killer—or killers— Penny stutters. *They're still out there.*

I raise my brow at Rae, and she points back at the screen.

The victim's brother has said that they now plan to destroy the house and expand the mall's parking lot, the reporter says. *This is Vicky, reporting from Nye County. Back to you, Steve.*

Rae clicks off the screen. "So?"

"Your friend knows too much."

She shrugs. "She's just a girl."

"You're just a girl too."

"I guess."

"We should kill her."

"Not yet. Is it time for us to move on now?"

I straighten my stance. Rae is small on the closet floor, like a doll waiting for someone to play with her. A daughter waiting for her daddy to tell her what to do.

This last month hasn't been easy, keeping her locked inside of a small house. Rae understood that it was for the best. Keeping her in the closet. Both of us sleeping in that enclosed space, hiding her from the world.

We'll get rid of Penny eventually. Right now, I have other things on my mind.

The imbalance lingers, filtering through my veins. Especially now.

In this world, I'll always be the one others trust. Men trust other men; they will believe me over Rae. And physically, I'll always be stronger than her.

It can't stay like this forever. The power dynamic is too simple. Boring. Predictable. And I like it better when things are interesting.

I grab my duffel bag from the top shelf of the closet. "Let's get the fuck out of here."

Chapter 35

Rae

We use cash to move across the country. Eventually, we end up at a motel a few miles away from the family theme parks in Kissimmee, Florida. The irony isn't lost on me—being in such a popular family vacation spot with my father—but neither of us has any interest in roller coasters or meeting cartoon characters. Our thrills lie in the darkness.

A knife rests on the nightstand next to me. It's the same one he used to kill my hookup. The same one we both held as we killed my look-alike. It's a good luck charm that helped me embrace my true self.

The television chatters through commercials. I sit cross-legged on one of the queen beds, eating a sandwich from a grocery store. Crave slouches in the motel chair. His eyes scrutinize me.

His widow's peak. His dark eyes. His lips pursed.

Since the day I showed up at his rental house asking for help with Ned's body, it's been strange. At first, I thought it was just me getting used to the idea that Officer Gaines and Crave were the same person. Now, I know it's more than that. There's something bubbling up inside of him, and with each breath, it increases in power.

He turns off the television. The room falls silent.

I wrap up the rest of my sandwich. "What?" I ask.

"You're always going to be weaker than me," he says.

His voice is low and measured, like he's waiting for me to react to his words. Another test.

I'm done with games.

I roll my eyes. "What are you talking about?"

"You're a stupid, weak little girl." He points to the knife resting on the nightstand. "Can you even use that without my help?"

I grit my teeth. "You know I can."

He shakes his head. "You poisoned Ned. You needed me to help you stab that girl. You didn't kill her yourself."

"So?"

"You can't hurt anyone, can you?"

"I did," I snap. "You watched me do it."

"You let the poison do the work with Ned. You forced me to stab that girl."

My lips pull back. "That's like saying the match burned the house when I'm the one who lit the fire."

"You're weak," he says. "Helpless. So fucking small, it's pathetic."

My vision turns red. What is he getting at?

I ball my fists. "Are you trying to piss me off?"

"You'll never make it without me."

Both of us are quiet then. I can blow off most of it, but those last words cut through me like a jagged piece of glass.

I wasn't a whole person. I wasn't my real self. Not until Crave came into my life.

"Get up," he says. He moves toward me. "It's time we end this, you little bitch."

I grab the knife, ready to defend myself. I'll kill him if I have to.

"The fuck is your problem?" I shout.

"You're so fucking easy," he laughs. "So fucking easy, it's embarrassing, baby. Watching you fall for me like that. So ready to let your daddy take care of you."

He swings his open palm forward, ready to choke me. I open myself to let him choke me.

But something tells me this isn't about sex.

Something tells me to resist him.

I raise the knife, jutting it forward. I scream.

He blocks the shot, the knife piercing his pointer and middle finger. Cutting through the flesh and bone.

One finger falls. The other hangs by the last thread of skin.

My jaw drops.

He howls.

The knife isn't supposed to be that sharp.

How is it that sharp?

How—

"Fuck!" Crave yells.

I drop the knife. Blood gushes onto the ground, spilling out of his fingers. My body buzzes.

"I'm sorry," I say. I grab the pillow next to me, holding it to his hand. "I'm sorry. I'm sorry. I—"

He nods toward the shopping bags. "Get the curling iron."

"What?"

"Get the fucking curling iron!" he shouts. "The curling iron. Turn it to the hottest setting."

I tear through the shopping bag. Find the appliance. Plug it in. A red light flashes on the black handle, the gold metal gleaming above it.

After a minute, it turns green. Four hundred and twenty-five degrees Fahrenheit.

"Bring it to me," he says.

I unplug it and carry it over. He lifts his hand, staring at me. I press it to the mound of flesh, wrapping the metal around the wound. His skin sizzles, the wound searing closed. I do the same thing to the other finger. He curses. Bones stick out of each nub.

We'll have to go to a doctor one day. For now, it works.

"I'm sorry," I say again.

"I'm not," he says.

Crave's brown eyes focus on me, irritation clouding his gaze. His upper lip twitches, daring me to defy him.

This—taunting me, getting me to hurt him—wasn't an accident. He *wanted* me to hurt him.

"Why?" I ask.

He glances at the mirror, our bodies halved in the dim reflection. Two murderers, bound together by so much more than blood.

"It was boring," he murmurs. "Always being in control."

My eyelids flutter, processing those words. "But you like power," I say.

"I still have power," he says. "I want more than that with you though."

My heart clenches in my chest. There is—and always will be—a power struggle between us. We're hot-tempered, fixated on the thrill of violence, unable to see human life as valuable. Still, we see each other. Accept each other. We fall into our rhythm, and we embrace our truest selves.

"You'll never be able to hold a weapon with your dominant hand again," I say.

Crave doesn't say a word, and his lack of an answer tells me it's exactly what he wanted. He wanted to have a disadvantage when it comes to me, so that we would have an equal fight.

I push his shoulders back until he's lying on the bed. I pull down his pants and boxers, his cock shriveled and limp against his thigh. I remove the rings and metal bars until his cock is nothing more than a calloused and scarred shaft. Bumpy. Naked. The way it was when he forced me to eat his ass.

I take all of him in my mouth, sucking him in. Biting the base. His cock pulses inside of me, excitement brewing as the pain ruminates through his body. He groans, loud and clear, transferring his power to me. I increase my movement, using one hand to hold his chest down and using the other to fondle his hairy balls. And when he comes, I pull my mouth to the tip and squeeze the base of his shaft as hard as I can, milking him of his cum.

His seed lathers my tongue. I keep it in my mouth.

I crawl over his body. He narrows his eyes, and I grab his chin, pinching him until he opens his mouth.

I let my spit and his cum drip onto his tongue. It paints his pink muscle in streaks of bubbly white. I smirk down at him. Like this—the way we are now, where I accept myself for who I am, with him by my side—I have more power than I've ever had.

He swallows it, his eyes fixed on mine. Warmth flushes my skin, arousal licking across my pussy until I can't hold back anymore.

I press my lips to his, tasting his tongue.

I'll never have what other people have. Comfort. Safety. Love. But I will have this. And this—whatever *this* is—is more than that. A connection deeper than selflessness. A relationship that isn't built on the *promises* of equality.

No—what we have is physical equality and a commitment where we both know that we'll live, breathe, and die together, because we can't stand to let the other person go. It's not about respecting each other. It's about owning each other.

I went looking for my father. To find his truth and shove it in my mother's face. To prove her wrong. To show my mother that I am good too, just like he was. We were simply misunderstood.

Instead, I found Crave, a man who forced me to acknowledge my darker side, who accepted me for who I am. A man who forced me to permanently wound him so that there would be something more than his physical strength keeping me by his side. I found a person so evil, so fucking selfish, that he'd never let me go.

And he found me.

Epilogue

Daddy

one year later

My girl stares in the mirror. Blonde hair. Black roots. A jagged nose and a scar on her eyebrow, both of which I gave to her. The same night she gave me a black eye.

I don't have a matching scar, but sometimes, my ocular nerves twitch, and it's like she's got her finger wrapped around my insides.

She squints at me, then smirks.

"Will you ever stop watching me?" she asks. This isn't the first time she's asked this question, and it won't be the last. It's a thing we say together, a routine of ours. I don't care where she is or what she's doing; if she's going to shit or eat or breathe, it'll be with me. I like fucking with her too much.

"No," I say.

She rolls her eyes, then leans over the sink, applying more eyeliner. A shadow casts over her nose, like a rock in the middle of a smooth sidewalk.

A lot can happen in a year. I told her I'd pay for her to get plastic surgery. Even doctors are susceptible to cash offers—that's how I was able to stay in Pahrump for as long as I had without anyone connecting me to Roderick Galloway—but Rae had wanted me to break her nose.

It's fucked up, but it's real, she had said. *Besides, I took your fingers.*

I lick my lips, a sense of smugness warming me as I marvel at her bumped nose. I'd honestly let her cut off a lot more than two fingers just to see what she did with my extra parts.

"Put that shit away," I say, pulling her away from the mirror. "You don't need it."

She huffs, slightly annoyed. "It's not about needing it. It's about looking like someone else."

"Little girl, you don't look a thing like you once did."

She studies her reflection. Sometimes, we don't recognize ourselves. With my shaved head, amped-up workout regime, and new tattoos, I'm not Roderick or Michael or even Crave anymore.

My normal mask doesn't matter to me, but I want to see what *she* does with this next version of ourselves. With each and every night, my girl gets a little more unpredictable. It's entertaining.

"Do you still find me attractive? Even after everything?" she asks.

My eyes glaze over her body. She's got scars now. Scars to prove where she's been and to hint at where we're going. Right now, we're Carl and Julie, and in six months, we'll have new names again. Simple names for fucked-up people.

But one thing stays the same. When we're alone, she calls me Daddy, and I call her my little girl.

A ring is placed on her wedding finger, an ugly pink stone on a silver band, an act to make strangers trust us. But there's a funny story behind it: my girl insisted on getting my fingers shipped to some artisan who put my bone fragments into a ring. She wears my ashes like jewelry every day. You would think it's a wedding ring, but my girl isn't like that. She wears my bones like a trophy, proud of what she's done to me. To her, it's a promise that I'll literally be wrapped around her finger until the day we die.

And my promise is the scar she wears on her face. She'll never be able to look in the mirror and hide from my control over her again.

A woman in a sundress opens the bathroom door, gawking at me—god forbid, a man in the woman's bathroom—and I wink at her. She scurries to a stall.

My girl pulls me out of the bathroom. "Come on," she whispers. "Let's go."

Outside, the tropical resort is bustling with people. Tan and sunburned skin. A mix of slender and thick bodies washed in a bright palette of bathing suit colors. Palm trees sway along the borders, and hibiscus flowers bloom. The scent of roasting meat floats in the air. A typical paradise for normal people; not the usual place for us.

"What are we doing here?" my little girl whispers. "This isn't like us."

"Trust me," I say.

She scans me, but something over my shoulder catches her eye.

A woman with white-blonde hair. Watery eyes. Subtle wrinkles on her skin. A cocktail in her hand.

I push my girl forward.

"Are you kidding me?" she asks, her eyes welling up with tears. "My mother?"

"She's not your mother," I say. "Not anymore."

My girl's eyes trace me. Neither of us has to say a word. Even if it doesn't make sense, my girl never liked that I didn't kill her mother. She can't help her jealousy—this idea that I was saving her mother's life.

Letting Samantha Sinclair live wasn't about loving Samantha or even being interested in her. It was about our daughter. I couldn't kill her mother without destroying our daughter's potential, and I wanted to see what would happen if our daughter grew up *away* from me. If she would still turn out like me.

Turns out nothing can stop evil from blooming inside of a fucked-up soul. All it needs is a little nudge from its creator.

My girl takes a deep breath. "Are you sure you want to do this?"

"What do you want to do?" I respond.

Her eyes flick across mine, but her decision is instant. She squeezes my hands, then she trots toward the bar. She sits beside her mother. I sit on the other side of my girl.

"What are you drinking?" my girl asks. "It looks good."

"Just a Hurricane," Samantha says. She pauses to scrutinize my girl's face. She briefly scans me too, but turns back to the woman beside her, the one she shares blood with. There must be an instinct there—a primal reaction to that shared connection, years of nurturing, betrayal, and loss.

A world has passed between them. Samantha thinks her daughter is dead, but she's looking at her. If you consider the timing—about a year since her daughter "died"—this vacation could be a way for the mother to grieve for her late daughter.

"Do I—" the mother starts. She shakes her head. "I'm sorry," she mumbles. "You just remind me of someone."

The smile fades from my girl's lips. "I get that a lot."

My girl orders the same thing as Samantha, using that as an excuse to make small talk. Warmth crawls over my skin, watching my girl in action. You would think that the woman who raised her would anticipate the tricks coming to the surface, but the mother takes shots with my girl like they're best friends.

A while later, we leave the mother at the bar. My girl and I stroll the beach, our bare feet dragging in the white sand.

"What did you see in her?" my girl finally asks.

"A warm hole," I answer.

She snickers. "Then what do you see in me?"

"An *entertaining* warm hole."

She punches me in the arm. I grin, then pull her into my embrace. I take in every part of her. The crooked nose. The scar on her brow. The bleach-blonde hair, with the roots of her natural color. Her brown eyes, so much like mine.

"I see my possession," I say. "My blood." I pull her chin up until she's staring into my eyes. "I see me."

There were twenty-five years where neither of us spoke a word to each other, where I kept my distance so that she could grow into the person she was meant to be, and yet every day feels like we've always been this way. Me and her. Daddy and his little girl. Two fucked-up people from the same bloodline.

My girl could have been good, like her mother. Instead, she chose a life like mine. Being like me—selfish, manipulative, and dark—was always her decision.

"You said you didn't want kids," my girl says. "*Didn't.*"

"Do you want kids?" I ask.

She glances back at her mother, sitting at the bar, the resort towering behind her, so much like the Galloway House. You can protect yourself from nature's destruction inside of a building, but you're never really safe. The people inside, living right next to you, are the ones you have to fear the most. You never know who you're sitting next to, who may share your blood, who may want you dead.

"No," my girl says. "But you need to explain yourself. You said that you *didn't* want kids. Did something change?"

My girl looks up at me, demanding answers. I know exactly what this is: she wants confirmation that I want *her* now.

We're not the kind of couple that says that we love each other. Love isn't what we have. But the fact that we've spared each other, that she wears my cremated flesh on her wedding finger, that she has my scar marking her face, *that's* our dedication to each other. We're selfish beyond desire. We *own* each other.

And one day, her violent hunger will reach new heights. That's when she'll finally kill me. I can't fucking wait.

"I'm never letting you go," I say. "You know that."

She nods, satisfied with my answer. Then she twirls her hair. "I still don't understand why you haven't killed her."

"You've got that poison, don't you?" I ask.

She opens her purse, showing me a small perfume bottle. It twinkles in the sunset. All it would take is going back to that beach bar and putting a few drops into her mother's drink. Her mother would never notice. It would seem like an allergic reaction.

"You want *me* to do it," she says.

"I like watching you."

"You sick little freak."

She grabs the back of my head, kissing me feverishly. I force my tongue down her throat and clutch her neck, digging my fingers into her flesh. She moans into my mouth.

Tonight, we'll bring her mother to the hotel room. If my girl wants it, we'll fuck her mother together. After that, my girl will kill her mother.

And then it'll just be us.

Also By Audrey Rush

Erotic Horror

Body Horror

Standalone

Skin

Dark Romance

Stalker

Standalone

Crawl

Dead Love

Grave Love

Hitch

Assassin

The Feldman Brothers Duet

His Brutal Game

His Twisted Game

Mafia

The Adler Brothers Series

Dangerous Deviance

Dangerous Silence

Dangerous Command

Secret Society

The Marked Blooms Syndicate Series

Broken Surrender

Broken Discipline

Broken Queen

Secret Club

The Dahlia District Series

Ruined

Shattered

Crushed

Ravaged

Devoured

The Afterglow Series

His Toy

His Pet

His Pain

Billionaire

Standalone

Dreams of Glass

Acknowledgments

Thank you to my amazing beta readers: Andrea, Ashley, Chelsea, Jackie, Jenni, Johanna and Lesli! Andrea, your pacing feedback was impeccable. Ashley, your attention to detail and tone is unmatched. Chelsea, your feedback helped me mold a better twist for other readers. Jackie, I'm always in awe of your plot hole catching and suggestions for making the story fuller. Johanna, thank you for your honesty and for letting me use your dream! And Lesli, you got what I was trying to do from the early stages, and your suggestions truly helped me shape the final story. You are all brilliant, and I am endlessly grateful for your feedback.

Thank you to my copy editor, Jackie at PR Publishing Group; your edits make the book so much easier to read, and I'm always blown away by your insight.

Thank you to my ARC readers for your honest reviews; your support tremendously helps a book's launch, and I'm so grateful for your time and enthusiasm! (And a special thank you to Caity Nicole, Charlie Parker, Deena, Emily Johnston, Katiee Comer, Kenzie, Lesli, Life.Within.Books, and Nicole for catching typos!)

Thank you to my husband, Kai, for making the perfect covers and for helping me brainstorm all of these messed-up daydreams. And thank you to my kiddo for tolerating my writing sprints during screen time and being such a good student at school.

But most of all, thank you to my readers. You are the reason I love to turn my daydreams and nightmares into books. I'm endlessly grateful for your support.

About the Author

Audrey Rush writes kinky dark romance and erotic horror. She currently lives in the South with her husband and child. She writes during school.

TikTok: @audreyrushbooks
Instagram: audreyrushbooks
Reader Group: bit.ly/rushreaders
Threads: @audreyrushbooks
Reader Newsletter: audreyrush.com/newsletter
Banned Account Info: bit.ly/bannedsupport
Amazon: amazon.com/author/audreyrush
Website: audreyrush.com
Facebook: fb.me/audreyrushbooks
Goodreads: author/show/AudreyRush
Email: audreyrushbooks@gmail.com

Printed in Great Britain
by Amazon

36005318R00148